Killed and Raised in a Barn

A Farm to Fable Paranormal Cozy Mystery

Book 5

E.L. Wilder

For my Better Half,
who has a Knack for dragging me across the finish line every time,
and should probably get coauthoring credit.

CHAPTER ONE

Harper Bennett stepped into the scar of moonlight on the library floor. She tried to steady herself, to stop her hands from shaking. She balled them up tightly and then stuffed them under her arms. When both of those things failed, she settled for chiding herself for being such a coward.

"Auntie Hazel would never be this afraid," Harper whispered. She didn't like the way her voice sounded in the library at night. Flat and dead. Despite all of the hours she'd spent in this room, browsing the collection, reading from them, or just reveling in the intoxicating aroma of old books, she'd never been in here at night. Gammy had always locked the door after sundown.

Harper had never known why until she discovered the answer in the Book of Bennett.

Gammy had been protecting them from the phone booth. To the average onlooker, it was just an oddly placed antique. Valuable but otherwise completely mundane. In truth the phone booth was a powerful knicked-knack with a very specific purpose.

The book had told Harper enough about the process that she thought she could make a call, but now that she was here, staring at it in the dead of night, her confidence all but collapsed on the floor and curled up in the fetal position.

The phonebooth looked like a cage of wood and frosted glass—like an old-fashioned elevator, if said elevator had been crafted by Tim Burton and placed directly into Halloween Town. She chided herself again for the comparison. "Not the time," she whispered, again wincing at the sound of it.

Never mind that it was the middle of the night. Never mind that it was just a few days from Halloween. She might have come from a family of witches, but that didn't mean she had to let superstition rule her. Everything had an explanation, even if sometimes that explanation was magic.

"What are you doing down here?"

The appearance of her younger brother nearly made Harper scream in surprise, but she had prided herself on never being the screaming type. Instead, she just ungraciously choked and sputtered.

Link grimaced. "That was super gross," he said at a conversational volume.

"What are you doing down here?" whispered Harper. "And why are you being so loud?"

"I asked you first."

"Go back to bed," Harper snapped.

"Can't make me."

"Oh yes I can," Harper threatened, waggling her fingers at him.

"If you use magic, I'll tell mom and dad," he said, folding his arms and smirking as if that settled everything. It most certainly did *not* settle everything. In fact, it settled absolutely nothing. She was not going to attempt her first major feat of magic under the watchful eye of an obnoxious little brother who never shut up.

She whirled on him now. "This is not about you," she snapped. "This is about finding Auntie Hazel. I'm here to use the phone booth."

Her aunt had been gone a month. A whole month.

So much had happened in that time. All of it a blur to Harper. The police reports. The searches. The media reports. Even with all that attention turned on the farm, no major magical slip-ups had been observed or caught on camera. Harper suspected that miracle was, no doubt, thanks to the tireless efforts of the farm's caretaker, Tyler, and the family's new guardian angel, Detective Gibbens. After a few days, the search had turned elsewhere. And elsewhere it had remained.

"How is the phone booth going to help?" Link asked.

Harper was silent. She didn't want to tell him the true reason she was here. She didn't think the phone would necessarily help her find her aunt's current location, but it just might be able to confirm whether her aunt was still alive.

His gotcha expression faded away, replaced with a determination and maturity she didn't know a preteen boy was capable of possessing. "Let's do this," he said. "I'll keep watch."

"Link, I don't need you to—"

"Either I help or I tell mom and dad."

"You're such a pain."

He grinned.

Harper rolled her eyes, but if she was being honest, she felt a gush of relief just knowing she wasn't alone. "Just stay over here," she said. "I'll need to concentrate."

"Good luck, idiot," he said.

Harper glowered but didn't take the bait. Instead she crossed to the phone booth, pulled the door open, and, taking a deep breath, stepped inside.

The sound was different in here. Muffled. Suffocated.

She spared the phone itself one glance. It was one of those ancient phones with no dial. Just a cone-like receiver hanging on a hook, and another cone protruding from the phone's front for the caller to speak into. The whole thing looked like an alien's skull.

Harper shivered.

She shook the thought away and dug into her pocket, pulling out three quarters. She'd retrieved them from a little dish on the vanity in her great-Gammy's bedroom—a place long empty but filled with the sort of delights only found in the former room of a witch.

Harper lined up the quarters on the wooden shelf beneath the phone, needlessly fidgeting with them until they were perfectly arranged. Three circles glowing in the moonlight. It hardly seemed like enough change to call the spirit world, but three were all that had remained, and, according to the notes she'd taken from the Book of Bennett, no ordinary quarter could be substituted for them. They had been enchanted to become more than mere quarters. They were *Obols*. The coins that the dead paid for passage into the afterlife.

Harper searched the phone for somewhere to insert the coins but found nothing. "Maybe," she whispered to herself, "they're just a focus." A magical prop that helped concentrate a witch's power.

She glanced back into the library. Through the unfrosted portions of the glass, she could see Link was no longer by the door. He had, instead, crept a little closer and was craning his neck to try to get a better look. Harper slapped her palm against the pane of glass, startling her brother and sending him scampering back to the library doors to resume his lookout.

Harper held up that hand in front of her. Her palms tingled—and not just because she'd slapped the glass. The sensation had needled her since *that* morning a week ago, the morning she'd woken up in bed. Well, not so much in bed as hovering just a few inches above it. As sure a sign as any that her birthright had come due. Her Knack had manifested.

Harper had always imagined that the moment would be filled with fanfare and drama, but it had been surprisingly . . . mundane. A tingle had rippled across her body, like static electricity kissing her skin, a sensation neither painful nor pleasant.

Harper turned her attention back to the phone. "Here goes." She could do this. She had everything she needed—a fully functioning Knack and a will to use it. There was a *process* to this. She just had to list the steps in her head and follow them to the T. This was no different than placing any other call in a phone booth she told herself. Admittedly, she'd never done *that* either, but she was no idiot.

Harper slipped the receiver from its cradle and pressed it to her ear. She'd done this a hundred times or more as a child, conducting pretend conversations with imaginary callers on a dead line. But now as she listened, she heard the faint crackle of static.

Harper leaned forward and spoke into the mouthpiece. "Hello?" she whispered.

The line popped with static.

"Hello?" she asked again. "Is anybody there? Auntie Hazel?"

The static rose and sank like ocean waves breaking on the shore. Harper fidgeted with the quarters. They were cold to the touch, and when she looked closer, she gasped. A dark mark had appeared on the first quarter and was racing to blacken the entire coin.

Something garbled broke through the line now, rising above the static like a swimmer breaking the water's surface. "Father? Father? I want to go back to the city right this instant. Call the driver!"

"Hello?" Harper whispered.

A new sound emerged, a steady beep like the blip of a heart monitor. "A most fascinating birth," said a willowy voice. "How is it possible for—" Harper jerked the receiver away from her ear as the monitor flatlined and grew into a deafening screech.

Another voice crept through the line, weak and bending like a willow in a storm. "Another Halloween, another death. The Bennett line will be snuffed out."

The glass in the booth rattled. Harper spun around, expecting to see Link trying to work the door open. Instead, she saw the door shaking without physical intervention. She turned back to the phone and pressed the receiver tighter to her ear.

"Whoever is listening," she said. "I need to know if Hazel Roisin Bennett is amongst you. Has she crossed over to the spirit world?" The phone spat and hissed even louder than before. For a moment it sounded like something was trying to break through the noise. Was that a voice?

"Hello?!" Harper called into the phone.

The phone sputtered, and then Harper heard a single word dropped out. "Harper . . ."

"Hello?!" she yelled. Desperation gripped her and she was shouting now. She didn't care if she woke everyone in the house. "Auntie Hazel? Are you there?"

She looked down at the quarters and watched as the last in the line turned black. Three black quarters in a row like frostbitten toes.

A deafening crash rang around her as the glass panes in the phone booth exploded outward and its wooden frame cracked and splintered. The force knocked her off her feet, flinging her through the air. She stopped inches away from a nearby bookcase, hovering like a leaf caught in the wind. Her magic or something else? She couldn't tell. The phone booth still demanded her attention.

The top of the booth had been blown clear off. The phone itself had remained miraculously intact. The receiver hovered in the air, weaving and bobbing like an asp as a torrent of glowing water rushed from it. No, not water. The blue deluge arced before it hit the floor, bending toward the ceiling.

No, that wasn't water, she realized.

There were *faces* in the stream. And limbs. Arms. Legs. It was a ribbon of people packed so tightly together that she had mistaken them for a single entity. But as they reached the ceiling, the entities peeled apart into individual apparitions. They only briefly considered their surroundings, looking about with the frantic enthusiasm of a dog at dinner time, before zipping off in different directions, fading through wall and ceiling and window to places unknown. In a matter of seconds, they were gone. The phone had stopped belching spirits; the spirits had left.

Only then did Harper realize she'd been holding her breath. As she let out a slow, shaky exhalation, she sank to the floor.

"Link?" she called out cautiously.

Link's head inched over the top of a couch, his eyes so huge she could see whites of them even in the dim of the library.

"Are you okay?" Harper asked.

He looked blankly around the room—at the glistening shards of glass and splinters of wood on the threadbare carpet and the shattered husk of the phone booth. He finally managed to speak. "I'm fine," he said. "But Gammy and mom are going to kill you."

CHAPTER TWO

Hazel Bennett shifted in her chair and tried to adjust the manacles binding her hands. If there was a position that would prevent the bonds from chafing her wrists, she was failing to find it. The only thing she succeeded in doing was rattling her chains yet again. Their clatter reverberated off the gymnasium ceiling, earning a reproachful look from the judge.

Though maybe *look* wasn't quite the right word. She was fairly certain the judge couldn't see her from his makeshift bench beneath the basketball net. He was, after all, a gargantuan bat wrapped in his own black leathery wings instead of the traditional black robes of a judge, a pair of round spectacles balanced on his snub nose and comically magnifying his beady eyes.

"Does the defendant have anything to say for herself on the charges?" the judge asked peevishly.

Hazel had been sitting here for nigh on eight hours. She found it difficult to believe there could possibly be anything left to say. "The charges of *allegedly* murdering Silas MacGregor? Of allegedly *attempting* to murder several others? Of *allegedly* assaulting Counselors of the city? Plenty," she said. "But I'm not sure the court has any interest in facts, so I might as well save my breath."

Her lawyer leaned in and whispered nervously, almost gagging her with his halitosis. "Remember, contrite and remorseful." Slevin Crisp was his name. He was a half-pint, green-skinned sleazeball—a goblin if she wasn't mistaken. As best she could tell, Slevin had all the legal acumen of a piece of burnt toast. Yet, he was the public defender that the Council had assigned her, which meant that he was Hazel's best shot at justice.

And freedom.

The thought was almost enough to make her want to weep.

Almost.

Hazel was pretty sure she'd cried herself dry during the first week after her arrest. No, after her *kidnapping*, she corrected herself. And even if she hadn't, she certainly wasn't going to cry here and give the audience something to enjoy.

Hazel craned her neck and looked back into the gallery, locking eyes with the older woman seated in the front row. A wicked smile spread across the woman's face.

Circe Strange.

Her skin was as pale and her features as hard as carved marble, her icy blue eyes like drowning victims trapped beneath ice. She wore a black dress-length cardigan buttoned at the waist to reveal a slash of a red blouse beneath. Hazel had no doubt the look had been chosen carefully to make Circe look vaguely like a black widow. For Hazel's benefit. A silent taunt—and a reminder of the truth of the situation. Hazel was here because of the crimes that her daughter, Cordelia, had committed. It was Circe that had used her power as the chair of the Council of Quark to cover her daughter's misdeeds and, eventually, to use Hazel as a scapegoat.

If only Circe knew that her daughter had ended up in a mundane prison. Hazel had been itching to tell her, but despite the weeks she'd languished in Quark's two-cell jailhouse, she'd yet to come face-to-face with Circe Strange.

Circe was hardly alone in the courtroom. There were others. Some she did not recognize, but there were two that drew her attention.

The first was a young man with an olive complexion and a dark wave of catalog-worthy hair. Alestranos Rosewood, an official Wand of the Council. Her interactions with him had been complicated at best so far, and she had no idea whether to call him ally or foe. He'd help make her arrest, but she tried not to hold it against him. It was his job, after all.

Hazel's eyes drifted to the back of the makeshift courtroom. An old woman, her skin like an ancient treasure map, sat watching the proceedings with a blank stare, her hot-pink lips drawn into a thin, pensive line. Her long white hair was braided into a lobster tail that draped over her shoulder and stopped just short of the Walt Disney sweatshirt she wore.

"Eyes up here, Miss Bennett," the judge gurgled.

"I see you," Hazel said. "I, unlike justice, am not blind." It was petty and stupid, but Hazel couldn't hold it in anymore. It had been clear from the outset of these proceedings that she would not get a fair trial, even if she were on her best behavior. She shifted her chains again, sending another too-loud clang echoing off the gymnasium walls. The judge flinched, though whether just from the assault on his sensitive ears or also from the assault on his sensitive ego, Hazel couldn't tell.

Slevin whimpered pathetically and then stammered, "Our apologies, Your Honor, my client—"

"Your client is impudent," said the judge. "If she cannot hold her tongue, I will hold her—in *contempt*."

"You've already held me for weeks on end without due process," said Hazel. "Are you going to hold me closer?"

"Miss Bennett, I will remind you that I am merely a circuit judge," the bat said. "You were held merely as long as was necessary. Now I am here. Now your trial may commence." She'd heard the story before. There were no full-time judges in Quark, so she'd had to rot in a cell while this one judge had traveled from town to town, at last arriving for his stint here. In the meanwhile, she'd been told that, no, she could not have one phone call, there were no phones in Quark. And, no, she could not send a messenger. Murderers and criminals did not get free use of the messaging system.

"So let's get on with it," she said.

"But for today, we will recess," growled the judge. "And the court finds you in contempt."

"Oh no," Hazel muttered. "Don't lock me up or anything."

The bailiff, a particularly dopey-looking troll, grabbed Hazel by the arm and started towing her from the gymnasium.

Slevin took up the position at her other arm, scurrying on his short legs to keep pace. He fumbled his briefcase as he tried to pull his coat on.

"If this is going to work," he said, huffing from the exertion of trying to find his coat sleeve, "you're going to have to start cooperating."

"Cooperating with a sham trial for a crime I didn't commit?"

"Well, it's getting increasingly harder to prove that."

"Maybe I need a better lawyer."

"There are no better lawyers around these parts," he said proudly.

"I'm not a murderer, Slevin."

"Then who are you?" he asked.

She stared at him, refusing to answer. "Whoever Circe Strange wants me to be," Hazel said loudly as they passed Circe Strange. It was childish, perhaps, but she wasn't feeling particularly cooperative after being locked up for a month.

"Whoever it is, you need to figure it out," Slevin said. "Then you need to consider showing it in court."

"The facts will speak for themselves."

"If that's the way you think this is going to go, then we're screwed."

Somehow, his short little legs found a burst of speed, and he hurried ahead and pushed his way out of the gymnasium.

As the troll led her from the courtroom, she locked eyes with Cass. The old woman's face was stoic, filled with wisdom. The corners of her wizened old eyes crinkled, flashing Hazel a knowing look. What was she trying to communicate? Before Hazel could consider it, the troll had yanked her from the gym.

As Hazel was dragged into the waning light of the day, somebody who had been waiting on the gymnasium steps came forward. He was tall and lanky, proportioned in a way that made Hazel think of the fisher cats that sometimes slaughtered chickens on the farm. *This* fisher cat had seen some serious action in his time. A deep angry scar like cracked earth ran the length of his face, starting at his hairline, disappearing beneath an eyepatch as it traveled south and crossed his thin, purple lips, before finally terminating at his chin.

The badge on his chest—a bird in flight, clutching a wand in its talons—marked him as a Wand of the Council of Quark, aka, one of Circe's cronies. Hazel would have known that even without the badge. This Wand had played a part in her arrest. Ryker, she was fairly certain he was called.

When he spoke, his voice tumbled out in a sharp-edged growl. "I'll take her from here."

The troll stared at him stupidly. "By order of the Council," said Ryker. "Now go lie down before you hurt yourself."

"I guard the prisoners," said the bailiff, a hint of doubt creeping into his voice.

"You can do that at the *prison*," said Ryker. "But I am to escort her when she leaves her cell from here on out. She's been deemed dangerous and a flight risk."

The troll finally relented and handed Hazel off to Ryker, plodding a few paces behind them as they made the short walk from the Quark Elementary School to the Meeting House, the upper floors of which were currently closed while, so Hazel had been told, an infestation of direrats was being exterminated.

"Why am I suddenly so dangerous?" she asked. "Surely you're not afraid of a harmless young witch wearing a pair of *these*." She held up her cuffs. The thick dark metal seemed to greedily lap up the fading daylight. A common feature of dampening magic, she'd come to realize.

Something dangerous flashed in his one good eye, and he scanned the street while they moved along as if expecting an ambush.

"Who are you looking for?" she asked.

He answered her question by digging his fingers into her arms and spurring her to move more quickly. She refused to give him the satisfaction of crying out in pain, but neither would she be herded like cattle. So she dug in her heels, making him have to work to move her along, even if she'd pay for it in bruises on her arm.

As the troll slammed the cell door and locked it, the bars shimmered, a fleeting flash of blue light letting her know the defenses had been engaged. Inside these four walls, her magic had now been rendered effectively useless.

Not that it mattered. Whenever Hazel was outside the cells, they slapped the cuffs on her—and they were laced with the same magic. Dampeners. She was pretty sure that's what they were called. But the nomenclature didn't matter. The results would have been the same regardless: Between the cell and the cuffs, she hadn't been able to cast a single spell during her imprisonment. If she could have, she would have busted out of there weeks ago and hightailed it back to the Postern.

"Until tomorrow," said Ryker dryly. Both he and the troll turned and disappeared down the hallway.

"I don't suppose I could get a few books in here?" Hazel called after them. "I'd settle for a magazine! Maybe a deck of playing cards?"

Somebody was coming back down the hall, and for a moment she thought the troll might be returning. Hazel's heart fell when instead Circe Strange appeared. "Perhaps you would settle for a copy of Quark's ordinances," Circe spat, "so that you can stop breaking all of its laws."

Circe folded her hands neatly over her stomach, like a corpse in a casket. "Hazel Bennett," Circe said, smiling grimly. "It's comforting to finally see you where you belong."

Hazel scoffed. "You must have me confused with your daughter."

Something dangerous flashed in Circe's eyes. "You are a poor misguided child from a poor misguided family that can't help but meddle where it doesn't belong. You're just reaping what the Bennetts have been sowing for years."

"You're one to speak about family failures."

Circe sneered, inspecting Hazel like a specimen beneath a microscope. "I wonder if the rumors are true," she said.

Hazel knew that Circe was fishing, that the statement was bait. She brushed it aside. "What, that your daughter is also rotting in prison?"

Circe flinched. "Lies," she snarled.

"Oh I assure you it's Gospel truth," said Hazel. "Your daughter's murderous ways finally caught up with her. So there's no sense in continuing this charade. The game is over. Cordelia is going to get what she deserves one way or another."

Circe was silent, stone-faced. When she finally spoke, she was barely audible. "Then consider this revenge." She turned on her heels and marched away.

Hazel returned to her cot and lay down. There was nothing to do but lay on her cot, wait for sleep, and hope a bit of magic might save her. When she finally drifted off, it was with thoughts of her family. Her mother, Juniper, David, Link, and Harper. Charlie.

And Tyler. Especially Tyler.

When Hazel woke, the cell was dark except for the faint glow of moonlight falling through the bars of her cell window.

Had she had heard something?

She sat up on her cot, pulling the thin blanket to her chin to ward off the fall chill.

There it was again—a low clattering and a steady squeak out in the alley. Impossible at this time of night. Soon another sound came to her ears—a scratching that made her think of a mouse caught between walls.

Hazel slipped from the cot and padded, barefoot, across the cold cement floor. Unfortunately, the window was set high in the wall and she hadn't been in the sort of shape required to do a pull-up since she'd landed the lead in a spy thriller.

As quietly as possible, she moved her cot beneath the window and climbed atop it. The cell was located in the basement of the Meeting House, which meant that standing on the cot placed her squarely at street level.

She heard the scratching again, closer this time. Something sprang out in front of the window and Hazel jumped back, landing not entirely without grace on the cell floor. A skeletal hand crept through the window bars, dragging an entire bony forearm with it. It felt around and then, seemingly satisfied, sprang into her cell, landing like a spider on her cot.

A strangled cry caught in Hazel's throat as she backed against the far wall.

The hand paid her no mind as it hopped to the floor, scuttled between the bars, and disappeared into the hallway outside her cell. What in the heck had *that* been all about?

She had only a moment to ponder before the hand returned, skittering back through the bars. It had brought something with it—a keyring looped around its wrist.

With a feat of stunning acrobatics, the hand climbed the bars of her cell, positioned itself over the lock, and deftly turned one of the keys in the lock. The bars shimmered as the dampening enchantment dissipated, and the door swung open. This felt like a trap.

"Who are you?" Hazel asked.

The hand motioned out the door.

"Hello?" she called down the hallway.

No reply.

Hazel leaned out the door, not daring to cross the threshold as she peered into the hall. Empty.

She glanced back into her cell. The hand had relocated itself, perching again in the cell window. It gave her an enthusiastic thumbs-up, then pointed out the window before leaping into the dark alley. There was another clatter and commotion in the alley, louder and closer this time. Hazel rushed back to the cot and pulled herself up to the window. A carriage stood at the mouth of the alley with somebody waiting in the driver's seat.

A prison break. But who?

Her heart sang. Had somebody from Bennett Farms finally tracked her down and come to free her? That hardly explained the skeletal hand, but there was no time to solve that mystery. She had to make her decision. Stay or go.

Hazel looked back at the cell door. "Heck, I've never been one to shut an opened door."

She stepped forward, jiggled the keys free from the lock, and padded quietly down the hall.

The prison was small, just two cells—the other of which was currently unoccupied—and the guard room at the end of the hall, which stood between her and freedom. She stepped cautiously inside. The room was furnished with a simple desk, which now supported the sleeping prison guard, and a single wardrobe-like cupboard pushed against the side wall.

The troll was slumped over the desk, his long nose quivering as he snored. Hazel crossed the room and paused at the door.

She could just make for the door and escape, but there was no way she was leaving without her possessions. Hazel moved to the cupboard and tugged one of the doors open, cringing when it groaned dramatically. The troll grunted and flopped back in his chair, his eyes fluttering open and staring at the ceiling. Hazel looked on in horror. But the troll didn't wake, and his eyes drifted shut again.

When she dared to move again, Hazel pulled at the cupboard door once more. This time it opened soundlessly enough. The shelves inside were mostly empty, except for the one that contained the belongings she'd had on her when she'd been arrested: her backpack, several odds-and-ends that she kept on hand for spellcasting, he cell phone, and the Book of Bennett.

"Entirely too easy," she whispered to herself.

But, as usual, she spoke a moment too soon. As soon as she had grabbed hold of the book, the wardrobe shuddered violently, creaking and groaning as its sides bulged. The edges of the cupboard birthed rows of toothlike splinters and suddenly it wasn't a cupboard so much as a gigantic ravenous mouth.

Hazel yanked the Book of Bennett free just moments before the cupboard chomped down where, a moment before, her hand had been. She would have to leave the rest of her belongings. She spun toward the door and slammed into a solid slab of troll.

"I don't suppose we could talk about this?" she asked.

The troll grabbed at her, but Hazel ducked. Big and strong he might be, but also slow and oafish. She had to be careful not to step back. The last thing she needed was to escape her jailer only to fall into the jaws of an enchanted wardrobe.

"I don't want to hurt you," she said.

The troll laughed at the suggestion.

Hazel scowled and raised her hand but only conjured a weak spurt of yellow sparks. The troll seemed to find her failure all the more hysterical and he filled the jail cell with a deep booming laugh. "You go back to jail now," he managed to say between chortles.

"Wasn't aware I had left yet," she muttered.

The troll lunged at her. Hazel dove to the side just in time and the oaf stumbled headlong into the waiting cupboard. Apparently the cupboard wasn't very discriminating because it clamped down on the troll. He howled and flailed, trying to pry himself free from the crafted custodian of Hazel's belongings.

Hazel hated to lose the rest of her things, but she didn't want to be here when the troll finally freed himself. Besides, she had the one irreplaceable piece: the Book of Bennett.

She darted out the door, and not bothering to close it behind her, she took the steps up to the street two at a time. She stopped only briefly enough to consider her surroundings. The houses of Quark, tightly packed together, their windows dark. Good. No witnesses.

She dashed into the alley alongside the Meeting House. The carriage was waiting. Hazel could make out the silhouette of the driver, who turned as Hazel arrived, flashing two dollops of flickering blue flame where the eyes should have been. The driver motioned her forward with a hand of bone. Another skeletal hand hung from the handle on the wagon's back door. It yanked on the handle, opening the door wide.

Hazel faltered.

Was she really about to run from one cage to another? What if this were a trap? Something Circe had designed to cinch a conviction. But what choice did Hazel have? Run back to her cell, close the door, pretend this never happened, and wait for her trial to conclude?

Hazel took a deep breath and stepped up into the back of the carriage. There were no windows. The door slammed shut behind her and she was plunged into complete darkness. The carriage jostled to life and clattered over the cobblestone as it sped through the dark streets of Quark.

CHAPTER THREE

Hazel stumbled in the darkness, barking her shin on some low and sharply angled object. She stooped and ran her hands over what felt to be a box of rough-hewn planks.

Hazel focused on her hands, trying to force the telltale tingle that accompanied her magic powers. Again, it wouldn't come. She was starting to panic when, gradually, like a waking limb, the pins-and-needles came and she was able to conjure a small ball of light. The effort was harder than it should have been for so simple a spell, and the ball was dim and flickered intermittently. But it was better than nothing.

Her breath caught in her throat as she looked upon the object she'd run into.

A coffin stretched across the floor. Hazel wasn't sure what she'd expected leaping into a vehicle driven by Jack Skellington.

That was it. She was out of here. She was turning to make her escape when the coffin jostled. Hazel yelped and jumped back.

"A little help," called a muffled voice from inside. "The latch fell shut again."

"Who is it?" she asked, her hand raised and ready to defend herself.

"Your rescuer," said the voice, "who could use a little rescuing himself."

Hazel cautiously reached out and undid the metal clasp on the edge of the coffin. A moment later, the lid creaked open, revealing the grisly occupant. A mummified corpse, its skin glistening like onyx, drawn hard and tight against its cheeks.

Hazel gasped when it sat up and smiled, revealing a row of too-white teeth.

"Well that was embarrassing," he said. "Got to be honest. I'm not sure why we even put a latch on that thing. It's not like our usual customers are trying to escape!"

Hazel threw herself back into the wall of the wagon.

"Sorry," the corpse said. "Didn't mean to startle you."

"Who are you?" she asked, hand raised and trembling as she tried to summon her powers.

"Wilhelm. We met when Clancy brought you here to investigate the murder of Silas MacGregor."

Of course. Wilhelm was the morgue driver for the city of Quark. His partner, whose name escaped her at the moment, was the animate skeleton driving the wagon. The two had hardly been menacing in their first encounter. Quite the opposite. She had pegged them as a bit of an odd couple, generally congenial and a bit skittish. Not the type to conduct a prison break.

"What are you doing in there?" Hazel asked.

"Well, I don't usually ride in the back but we have to keep up pretenses that we're on the job," he said. "Lev isn't one for chatting, so it seemed best to put him up front in case anyone stopped to question him. That and somebody had to be back here to explain to you what was going on."

"No, Wilhelm," Hazel clarified. "What are you doing *here*, breaking me out of prison?"

"Oh, right." Wilhelm climbed out of the coffin and presented her with a leather file folder. "This is for you."

"What is it?" she asked.

Wilhelm nodded toward the folder. The message was clear: Go ahead and find out.

Hazel opened the folder to reveal a thick stack of documents. A letter lay on top, penned in exquisite penmanship that flowed and looped like wind through the trees.

Dearest Hazel,

Constellations viewed up close are merely stars. Injustices viewed up close are merely unfortunate instances. But when you step back and look from a distance, everything becomes clear. I'm going to talk to Sera.

Asarum Moonwake

Who was Asarum Moonwake? And what the heck was he or she talking about? Who was Sera for that matter?

She set the letter aside and flipped through the rest of the documents. They were divided into four packets, each of them clipped together, and headed with a picture—either a photograph or drawing—of an individual. A series of names and faces she didn't recognize. Orion E. Livingston. Jonathan Northcott. Alistair and Horace Bennett. Judith Goodblood. "Look here. Horace and Alistair Bennett? Those are my great-uncles!" Gammy always talked about them. Her twin brothers had been full of mischief until one day they'd just disappeared. "They were such troublemakers a lot of people thought they had just run away."

"What are these?" Hazel asked. "Profiles?"

Wilhelm shrugged. "I didn't open it. It's from your rescuer."

"Wilhelm, *you* are my rescuer."

He shook his head. "I'm just the courier of bodies. Somebody else orchestrated this."

"Who?"

He shifted his gaze to the wagon floor.

"Wilhelm, who gave this to you?" she pressed. "Who is Asarum Moonwake?"

"Sounds like a fae name to me. But I'm not the man to ask," he said, frowning. He hesitated before pointing to the stack of papers on her lap. "Everything you need to know is in there. I'm only supposed to deliver it to you and deliver you to the Postern."

"Is there leeway in your instructions for a detour?" Hazel asked.

She wanted nothing more than to go home and reunite with her family, but she also had some lingering questions that she needed answered. The last time she'd been a freewoman in Quark, she'd left a lot of things unsaid and undone. For starters, she had left Charlie's rather-confused riven half in Cass's care.

"I need you to bring me to Silverwell Academy first."

Wilhelm fidgeted.

A bell rang out somewhere in the town, and Wilhelm looked up, his eyes widening in panic.

"That's the bell at the Meeting House," he said. "They never ring it at night. They've probably discovered your absence."

He thumped a fist against the roof of the carriage. A moment later, the reins cracked and the wagon picked up its pace.

"You should get in there," he said, gesturing to the coffin.

"What?" Hazel scoffed. "Absolutely not. There's only one time I'm going to willingly get into a coffin, and it's when I no longer have the will to complain."

He screwed up his face in puzzlement.

"When I'm dead," she clarified.

"Right." He nodded. "But it's for your own safety. If we get stopped on the road, it would be easier to keep you safe if we could pass you off as . . . cargo."

Hazel shuddered. "I'm not climbing into one of those things until I'm dead," she repeated. "No offense."

"None taken," he said. "I'm *un*dead, not dead. Though we prefer aortically challenged."

"Aortically challenged?"

He smiled. "It's partly in jest. Dying isn't all that bad. At least not what I remember of it. Which, if I'm being honest, is not much. But I do know being dead hasn't slowed me down one bit," he added with a chuckle, slapping his chest enthusiastically.

It seemed wrong to ask him what he *did* remember of his own death, so instead she said, "How long have you been . . ."

He scrunched up his face. "At least a hundred years," he said. "But everything before the Bloom is a bit hazy."

Her heart stopped. "The *Bloom*? You were around before the Bloom?!"

"Sure. A lot of ACs were."

"What was it?" she pressed. "The Bloom?"

Wilhelm scratched absently at the tip of his glossy chin. "I wish I could say having a front-row seat made me an expert, but the truth is that I don't remember much about it. Or before it. All ACs say the same thing. There was nothing, and then there was a flash of pink."

Hazel gasped. A flash of pink. Just like in her nightmares. Ever since she'd come home, she'd been plagued by that same nightmare.

They rode in silence for a while, Hazel staring at the stack of documents in her lap. She knew that she should take the time to read them. There was, doubtlessly, important information here if the person that had arranged her escape had assembled them. But she couldn't focus on it right now. Maybe once she was back in the comfort of the farm, she could take a leisurely walk to the East Barn, order up a double cappuccino, and pour over the details with Charlie. That was, of course, after she had spent a few days catching up with everyone. Farm chores with Harper and Link. Tractor-driving lessons with Juniper. Chilly evenings with Tyler on the porch of the caretaker's cottage wrapped in a wool blanket. Maybe she'd even do some morning yoga in the Cliffside Garden with her mother.

The ringing bell faded into the distance and the rumble of cobblestone beneath the wheels of the carriage gave way to the murmur of a smoother surface. A few minutes later, the carriage rolled to a halt.

"This is as far as we can take you," Wilhelm said, throwing open the back doors and revealing a darkened roadway cutting through the forest. The Yellowed Brick Road, a disused road that cut through the gnarled expanse of wilderness known as the Dimwood. "Get to the Postern."

"What about Silverwell Academy?" Hazel asked.

Wilhelm looked around nervously and shook his head. "There's no time. They're already out looking for you. They'll try to beat you to the Postern. You have to go."

Hazel begrudgingly hopped out of the back of the wagon, taking her orb of light with her. Her feet scuffed the brick of the narrow road.

"The Postern is that way," Wilhelm said, pointing through the trees.

Hazel had traveled the way several times before. The route was an exhausting hike through dense undergrowth on a path defined only by a slight thinning in the forest. She was only marginally confident she could find it now under duress and cover of night.

Hazel looked back to say something, but the carriage door was already closed. Lev flicked the reins. Even though no creatures were hooked up to the vehicle, the carriage rolled forward smoothly, disappearing around a curve in the road.

Hazel listened briefly to the chirrups of strange insects and the hoots and cries of alien birds. At least she hoped they were birds. She'd seen her fair share of skulking in the underbrush and experienced firsthand the creatures that slipped through the Postern from time to time and ended up on Bennett Farms. Clancy had reminded her those were the only creatures that could fit through a doorway.

A pang of sadness pricked her heart. She wished Clancy were here now to give her some tough love—tell her she was being a coward and a letdown, even as he pointed the way back to the Postern.

But Clancy was gone—*dead*.

Hazel hoped that was merely a temporary setback. Clancy had died once before, but a curse had resurrected him in a different form. She hoped that the act had repeated itself and Clancy was merely hunkering down with the Bennett clan, searching for her, awaiting her return. But she'd felt no tickle of her familiar pact since and she couldn't shake the feeling that she'd seen the last of her furry friend.

Hazel shook her head to banish the thought. Now was not the time to mourn. The night was not getting any younger, and she needed to beat her pursuers to the Postern.

She hugged the Book of Bennett and the folder to her chest and stepped from the road, wading into the Dimwood. The path was easier to find than she had feared it would be. The Dimwood, apparently, was subject to the same seasons as Bennett Farms. Already many of the trees had shed their leaves and much of the undergrowth had died, making it easy to spot the way.

But that did not mean the forest was dead. Things fled in the underbrush as she passed. Eyes flashed in the shine of her light. More than once she thought she felt something brush her legs, though she refused to scream. In case anyone or any *thing* was listening.

Hazel was just starting to think she might be lost when she saw a glow up ahead, a sinister red stain of light visible through the hard-cut silhouettes of the Dimwood's gnarled trees. If she recalled correctly, she had seen that glow near the Postern before—and its presence had caused the Council of Quark great concern. Enough to assign a wand—Alex, to be specific—to investigate the matter.

Fortunately or unfortunately, before she could reach the source of the light, she broke free from the woods and stepped into a weed-choked field.

Before her rose the ruins of a great tower, a jagged and rotten tusk thrusting high above the Dimwood canopy and piercing the night sky. The tower of the legendary wizard Merlin. The grand magnum opus to which the Postern was merely a footnote. Merlin must have surely been a great wizard to so casually construct a home—a summer retreat, Clancy had called it—that contained portals through time.

It was mind-boggling, really. Perhaps that sort of power helped to explain the other elements of the tower that made no sense to her. For starters, Merlin was supposed to have lived over a millennium ago. That made sense when Hazel thought about the ruins on Bennett Farms. All that stood of Merlin's tower was a scrap of stone wall that had contained the Postern. Yet here, in the future, the tower stood nearly complete.

Maybe she was trying to solve the problem with too mundane a mind. She doubted the home of a wizard that ancient would play by the rules. She made a note that once she straightened out this whole fiasco, she would return and search the tower—for clues, for secrets, for magical knowledge that she could use to improve her skills as a witch.

She turned her attention to the Postern. Not the archway of stones that had once stood there, but the beautifully carved and seriously burnt wooden archway she had used as a substitute. She stopped to ponder that briefly. She had placed the new Postern in the Tanglewood but made no such placement on the Dimwood side of things. Yet, here was the same archway, clear as day—even though it was night—a faint shimmer of pink like the skin of a bubble shimmering in the expanse. When in doubt: magic. But that answer hardly satisfied her, and a mild discomfort niggled at the back of her mind.

Hazel hesitated. A strange tingle rippled through her body. She doused her light and stepped back, crouching at the edge of the clearing and scanning the tower and the field for signs of movement. Perhaps she just had the jitters.

Just then three silhouettes dropped from the sky and landed softly in the clearing between Hazel and the Postern. If she wasn't mistaken, they'd just ridden on *brooms*. In any other situation, she might have found the mode of transportation hilarious, but right now it seemed positively horrifying. They could *fly*? What chance did she have of escaping them if they could command the skies?

You flew once too, she reminded herself. *Briefly. And without a shred of control.* Okay, maybe she had only hurtled through the air but it was pretty close. And she had done it *without* having to straddle a cleaning apparatus.

Hazel watched the trio. Two of them quickly drew wands and held them at the ready.

"How do we know she hasn't gone through yet?" said one of the three, a man. She recognized that voice. Alex.

"We don't," said another, his gravelly voice also instantly recognizable. Ryker. "Spread out."

The other two complied, fanning across the clearing and giving Hazel her first good look at them. The third figure, the one who hadn't spoken yet and who hadn't drawn a wand, was tall and lanky and feminine and moved with a sort of ethereal grace. As she stepped from the shadows, the moonlight caught on a pair of nearly translucent wings sprouting from her back, scattering in their crystalline folds like light through a prism. A fae.

The second had no wings. Ryker.

Now that Hazel thought about it, this was the same trio that had arrested her in the first place.

The fae went toward the ruins on Merlin's tower and Alex crossed the clearing. Hazel realized that he was coming her way, so she crept back into the edge of the forest as quietly as she could and pressed herself into the shadows.

Alex stopped just a few feet away from her. Had it been daylight, he would have seen her. "It's not like she's going to be staying in these woods all night," he called back over his shoulder. "Either she's already gone or she'll spend the night in Quark."

"Why's that?" growled Ryker, his voice like splintered wood.

"With the Curios Tree nearby, she'd be a fool to linger," Alex replied, turning his attention from the patch of woods where Hazel lurked and toward the red light dripping through the trees. Then, in a tone that was too low for anyone else to hear, he said, "And she's no fool."

Had that been for her, or had Alex just been talking to himself?

"We too would be fools to stay here . . ." said the fae, speaking finally. Her voice tinkled like a cool mountain stream cascading over rocks.

"We're *Wands*," said Ryker. "We do our duty without fear, Calluna."

The fae's wings flashed a deep shade of red, like dried blood. "Of course, Ryker."

Calluna. At least Hazel had names for all of her hunters now.

Ryker stepped up to the Postern and peered through the archway, then he turned back to his companions. "She must have gone through already." There was a hunger in his voice that unsettled Hazel.

Ryker continued. "One of us should go through and look for her"

Alex stepped forward. "I'll do it."

Ryker scoffed. "Why you?"

"Because I've spent time on the farm. I know it best. The places she might hide."

"Disagree," barked Ryker. "You're too familiar with this criminal."

Alex was silent for a moment. "Are you questioning my integrity?" There was a cutting edge to Alex's voice that Hazel had never heard from him before. "Take the farm if you want, but don't say you weren't warned. It has a million places to hide, and the Bennett family is tight-knit—inseparable. They'll hide her."

"Then we'll arrest them too," retorted Ryker. Hazel could hear the smile in his voice. "Circe said to bring in anyone who harbors the fugitive."

Hazel's breath caught in her throat. She would be endangering her family if she returned to the farm. But where else was she to go? She couldn't return to Quark. She'd only met a few of the town's residents, and there was nobody there that she could yet trust to aid her.

Ryker started barking commands. "Calluna, you head back to town and join the search there. Alestranos—"

"I prefer Alex."

"*Alex*," Ryker said, his disdain evident, "you will keep watch here in case our quarry has yet to arrive. I'll go through the Postern. If she's gone home, I will track her down and I will bring her to justice."

For a moment, Hazel considered waiting until the others had left and then approaching Alex, trying to appeal to his reason and his sense of decency. But she knew he took his position as a Wand with the utmost seriousness. His sense of black-and-white justice and his fealty to the laws of the city would be too strong to overcome with an emotional appeal. Besides, they barely had any history. She had, what, falsely accused him of murder and almost gotten them both killed? Then accidentally assaulted him with an overzealous spell? Yeah, those things ought to tug at his heartstrings.

Hazel didn't wait around to hear the rest. As the fae and Alex protested their assignments, Hazel snuck off into the Dimwood, heading, she hoped, in the correct direction.

CHAPTER FOUR

Harmony House was dark when Hazel crept across the cool, dew-soaked lawn toward the sunroom on the back of the building. She stopped, crouching behind a tree. She listened. The night was quiet save for the dry rattle of the dead leaves still clinging to the tree.

How was she going to get Cass's attention? Hazel had no idea what room Cass even slept in, and the last thing she needed to do was wake the entire house trying to figure it out. School would no doubt be back in session, and the dormitories full of aspiring young witches.

Hazel sat and looked at Harmony House with a new appreciation. Her niece had once pointed out to her the building's similarity to the caretaker cottage back on Bennett Farms. At the time, Hazel had just thought it a strange coincidence, but she knew now that this *was* the same building, albeit with significant additions and modifications. But the core of the cottage was still there, buried beneath new wings, additional floors, and architectural flourishes.

A light flicked on in the veranda, and a moment later a silhouette appeared before the French doors. Hazel recognized the stout woman and her slow, patient gait.

Even as Cass unlocked the doors and swung one open, Hazel remained rooted in place, watching.

"By the goddesses, kid," Cass called across the yard, "get your butt over here."

Hazel looked around to make sure there was nobody else present.

"Yes you!" Cass hissed.

Hazel hugged the Book of Bennett and the folder tighter as she sprinted across the lawn and into the warmth of the sunporch.

Cass stood in the warm glow of the light—an ornamental lantern that hovered midair—dressed in a floral-print nightgown. The older woman smiled, deepening the creases in her face into fault lines. Hazel had, thought she, never seen a more inviting sight.

"Cass," she said breathlessly, "how did you know I was out there?"

"The cards, honey," said Cass, pointing toward the card table, where rested a few decks of well-worn decks of Bicycle cards wrapped in rubber bands. "Though I have to admit the exact time of it escaped me. You're lucky you came when you did because I was about ready to pass out. I may have been a night owl in my youth, these days, I'm more of an evening owl. Don't suppose I could interest you in a cup of tea?"

After a month of prison food, just the mention of a warm cuppa made Hazel salivate. Yet, she politely declined. There was no time for that. "They're looking for me, Cass."

Cass nodded. "Circe is not one to let a fish go once she gets it on the line."

"The Wands are guarding the Postern," Hazel said. "Ryker went through to search the farm."

Cass looked grim. "That complicates things. But it doesn't make them impossible. There's *another* way to get you home."

Hazel's jaw dropped. "What?! There's another way home? Cass, how have you never told me about this before?!"

"Because I wasn't certain it existed until recently," Cass said matter-of-factly. "Necessity is the mother of exploration."

"Isn't it 'invention'?"

Cass smiled. "I meant what I said. When the Postern got axed, I pulled some serious favors and confirmed that it was more than mere legend." Cass must have seen the continued confusion on Hazel's face. "I'm not trying to be withholding, but we need to move quickly. You'll have to trust me on this. I've arranged for somebody to show you the way." Cass eyed the Book of Bennett and the folder Hazel was carrying. "You might want a waterproof bag for those."

Hazel had almost forgotten about the book and folder hugged to her chest. The Book of Bennett was enchanted to resist fire and water damage, but she doubted the folder possessed the same enchantments.

"Yes!" Hazel blurted. "Please!"

"Wait here." Cass disappeared and a moment later came back with a few bags. "We have a lot of these kicking around the place. Students leave them behind when they graduate and never return. Most of them at least have basic waterproofing enchantments on them. Who knows what else."

Hazel pawed through the selection. "A satchel!" she exclaimed, grabbing a pleasantly worn leather bag from the mix. Her old satchel had met a horrible fate and she jumped at the opportunity for a new one. This one seemed particularly well suited for her purposes— with more pockets and compartments than your average stage magician's set-piece.

Hazel slid the Book of Bennett into the main compartment of the satchel. A perfect fit. Then she picked up the document packet that Wilhelm had given her.

"Did you know who sent this?" Hazel asked, holding it out to Cass.

No look of recognition graced Cass's face. She took the folder gingerly as if she knew she was handling something of great importance.

"Do you know who sent Wilhelm to free me?"

"*Wilhelm?*" asked Cass. "I'm surprised he had the courage to do something that daring." She grinned. "Lev. Even though he's the skeleton, he's the only one with any guts between them."

Cass opened the folder and looked at the letter on top. "Asarum Moonwake." Cass arched an eyebrow. "So he got my message," she added, almost to herself. She shook her head and smiled her warm Cass smile. "Hazel, that's a very special package indeed. Do you know who Asarum Moonwake is?"

"No . . ."

"Your family knew him more affectionately as Asa," Cass explained, "a young-looking redheaded man with a unexplainable *something* about him.

Hazel's mouth went dry and her throat constricted.

"Asarum Moonwake is your father," said Cass.

Hazel felt like she'd just been socked in the stomach. *Of course. Asa.* It was one of the few things she knew about her father, other than his electric red hair and his tendency for drifting in and out of Bennett Farms throughout the years. In the excitement that fluttered through, Hazel almost missed the subtext here, but she didn't have a nose for sniffing out mystery for nothing. "What do you mean something special about him?"

Cass clucked her tongue. "There is no greater keeper of secrets sometimes than one's own family." She shook her head sadly. "For shame. Hazel, this isn't for me to tell. You need to talk to your family. Perhaps to Asa himself."

Cass didn't have to tell her. Hazel tried to solve the mystery of her father all her life, only to find every possible avenue into the topic firmly blocked by her mother. Even though they covered the Bennett family history extensively in her mother's homeschooling curriculum, there were, apparently, chapters that were closed from academic pursuit. But Hazel had always assumed that shame or heartbreak or some potent cocktail of human emotion had kept her mother from opening up about it. Hazel had never thought there might be other reasons.

"Or you could just knock back a few too many butterfly cappuccinos."

Butterfly cappuccinos? What did those have to do with anything? "They don't exactly agree with me," said Hazel.

"You don't say," said Cass knowingly, peering over the top of her glasses, a wicked twinkle flashing in her eyes.

"Cass, if there's something about my father that I should know, I'd rather have it out right now."

Cass gave her a sad smile that told Hazel all she needed to know. This was not Cass's place.

"Is *he* here?" Hazel asked, losing her patience.

"He is not," said Cass. "But you shouldn't stay here."

"So let's go," said Hazel. She knew she was being impatient—bordering on the melodramatic that she had often been accused of in the past—but she didn't care right now. She was getting awfully tired of everyone being so coy with her, especially when it came to the topic of her father.

"Oh, I'm not taking you," Cass said. "Few things are as undignified as an old woman skulking through the night in her flannel. I've got somebody younger and infinitely spryer to get you where you need to go."

Something moved in the corridor leading to the main house. Hazel jumped up from her seat.

"Settle down, honey," said Cass. "That would be your escort." Cass turned her attention to the corridor. "Are you ready, Sybil?"

A young woman stepped into the sunroom. She was gorgeous, curvaceous with smoldering dark skin, her hair shaved almost to the scalp. And something incredibly familiar about her. It took Hazel a moment to realize—it must have been the dramatic haircut that had thrown her off—but there was now no denying the girl's identity.

"Charlie!" Hazel yelped. A wave of emotion swept over her. She barely managed to hold back a torrent of tears. Now was not the time to cry.

"Hazel, this is Sibyl," said Cass, correcting her gently.

Of course. Charlie's riven half. The last time Hazel had seen her, she had been nameless and borderline catatonic, staring blankly and having to be led around by the hand. Hazel had left her with Cass for safety's sake, intending to come back and figure out a way to reconstitute Charlie. But then the Postern had broken, and Charlie's two halves were caught on separate sides of the divide. And here was the other half. Not only was she not catatonic and docile, Charlie's riven half was fully cognizant and sporting both a new hairdo and a fresh moniker.

"Does she remember me? Or know me?"

"You could ask her yourself," Cass suggested.

Hazel blushed. "Of course. I'm sorry." She took a step toward Sibyl and offered her hand. "I'm Hazel Bennett."

Sibyl nodded. "I've heard a lot about you. This must be strange for you, but no stranger than it's been for me, being my own person with bits of Charlie drifting in and out of my memory."

"We've been working on her memory," Cass said, "to see what there was of Charlie left inside."

"You can do that?" Hazel asked, astounded.

Cass chuckled warmly. "There's more to an oracle's powers than reading the cards."

"What did you find?" Hazel asked.

"That would be telling," said Cass, peering over the top of her spectacles. "And not for me to share." Cass peered over the top of her glasses, inspecting both Hazel and Sibyl. "I'll let you girls get acquainted . . . and going," said Cass, smiling. "This old maid has to get her weary bones to bed."

Cass had warned Hazel and Sibyl to speak only when necessary. The trip, she'd said, was short and Sibyl would do all the talking when the time came. Cass might have learned a lot from the cards, but she didn't know the first thing about Hazel, because as soon as Hazel and Sibyl were out of earshot of Harmony House, Hazel started in.

"You don't remember me," Hazel said in a hushed tone.

Sibyl looked around as if ensuring they were alone. "I remember you saving me," stated Sibyl. There was no emotion or gratitude in the statement. It had the feeling of an oft-repeated fact. It was just like the time that Cordelia Strange, a ravenous werespider with an appetite for all-things riven, had nearly devoured her.

"You must remember something *before* that," said Hazel hopefully. There had to be a least a little Charlie in there.

Sibyl cast a suspicious glance at Hazel. "There's nothing," she snapped.

Well, one thing was certain. Sybil possessed none of Charlie's bottomless ebullience.

But Hazel couldn't shake the idea that there had to be *something*. Sibyl was, literally, the missing piece of Charlie, the loose end that Hazel had failed to resolve before the Postern had been destroyed. Much like Hazel's own father was the missing piece of her.

"I am not Charlie," said Sybil. "I'm my own person."

Hazel opened her mouth to protest that *of course* she was Charlie. Cheese sliced from a wheel was still cheese, and Sibyl sliced from Charlie was still Charlie. But something stopped her. Maybe Hazel wasn't being fair. Fate had hardly cast Sybil a fair lot.

"We're here," said Sybil.

"Already?"

Cass hadn't been kidding. They'd gone a few hundred yards at most and arrived at the edge of the harbor. A moonlit sheen of water stretched out before them. It looked no different from the harbor at Bennett Farms. Wait, no, that wasn't exactly right. Something looked off about it that Hazel couldn't quite put her finger on.

Sibyl hopped down to the stony shore and walked to the water's edge. A rowboat had been beached there. "Let's get it to the water," said Sibyl.

"Where are we going exactly?" Hazel asked, taking one end of the rowboat and helping overturn it and carrying it into the water. Frigid water seeped into her shoes.

When they were far enough out, they both climbed into the boat.

"I'll row," said Sibyl, taking the oars. She guided the boat with an expert's skill. "I've been coming out here daily to get my head on straight. Trying to figure out who I am."

They rowed silently out into the harbor, listening to the gentle lapping of the oars.

Hazel scanned the hillside for any sign of the manor. She was insanely curious to see how her ancestral home had changed, but she could only make out the orange glow of a few lights.

Sibyl stopped rowing and let the boat coast until it bumped gently against some rocks. Turtle Rock, a crag of an island in the harbor, jutted from the darkness ahead of them. That's what had been off about the harbor. Turtle Rock was entirely too far from shore— almost entirely in the mouth of the harbor itself.

"She'll meet us here," Sibyl said.

"Who?" asked Hazel.

They only waited a few minutes. A splash of water announced the arrival of their contact, who emerged from the water just a few feet from the boat.

"Sibyl?" the still-dripping woman asked, as she bobbed in the nearby water.

"Nerissa," said Sibyl.

Hazel assumed there was a perfectly good reason why this woman had been waiting for them beneath the water. Anything was plausible on this side of the Postern.

"You're Hazel Bennett," said Nerissa. "I've seen you around."

"You have . . ."

"Sure, mostly from a distance. And mostly on the other side of the gate," she said, leaning back in the water and arching her legs up. Not legs—*fins*.

"You're a mermaid!" Hazel marveled, immediately recognizing the term might not be correct. If undead preferred to be called aortically challenged, perhaps mermaids preferred some other moniker. But when Nerissa smiled and nodded, Hazel plowed ahead. "There's a mermaid that sunbathes in the harbor at Bennett Farms!"

Hazel had seen said mermaid from time to time on the farm brazenly sunbathing as the good Lord had intended her, both her halves—fish and human—bared to the sun.

"Guilty!" Nerissa said, raising her hand and grinning cheekily.

"That was *you*?" asked Hazel. "I've wanted to meet you my whole life!"

"The feeling is mutual," Nerissa said. "The girl with the hair the color of fire—and the bloodline to match it."

"I haven't seen you for a few months. I was starting to get concerned . . ."

"I happened to be on this side of the Postern when the Watergate closed," Nerissa said.

Hazel couldn't suppress a chuckle. "The Watergate."

"Yes, the Watergate. What's so funny?"

"Oh, it's stupid. In American politics, there was a hotel that—never mind, it's not important. What's the Watergate?"

"It's the Postern's water companion," said Nerissa.

"Wait. There's a Postern beneath the harbor?"

"How do you think aquatics navigate between the two worlds?" she asked.

Hazel was floored. "I guess I hadn't really thought about it."

"Don't feel too bad. It's a fairly guarded secret amongst merfolk," Nerissa explained. "Most land-dwellers have no idea that it exists."

"Wait, wait," said Hazel. "You said the Watergate closed too?"

Nerissa nodded. "When the Postern was destroyed, it sent magical shockwaves that turned the aquatic world on its head for a while. It made the Watergate shy."

"Shy . . ."

"I hate to interrupt this riveting deep dive into magical lore," said Sibyl, clearly not hating to interrupt it at all, "but time is of the essence here."

"Right," said Nerissa. "Cass had mentioned you would be in a hurry when you showed up."

"I've made some formidable enemies."

Nerissa raised her hands, revealing a full complement of webbed fingers. "I'm working on a strictly don't-ask, don't-tell policy. Just because my father is on the Council, doesn't mean I have to follow all the rules." Nerissa's father was a Councilor? That musclebound merman that she'd briefly met at her first council meeting. "The merfolk have always had a shifty relationship with the Quarkians. Anyway, listen to me gab on about local politics when you're trying to not get arrested. Hop in. The water's great."

Hazel grabbed her new satchel, tucked it under her arm, and, hoping it was as waterproof as Cass had claimed, jumped over the side of the boat. She plunged into the water and immediately shot back up to the surface, hyperventilating reflexively because of the intense chill. "Water's great," she repeated numbly.

Nerissa reached out a hand. "Here. Hold tight."

"I hate to point out the obvious," Hazel said, treading on the surface, "but I can't exactly breath underwater."

"Aren't you a witch?"

"Guess I haven't learned that spell yet," Hazel said sheepishly. It didn't help that she'd lost an entire month when she could have been researching and practicing her new craft. "While I'm making confessions, I also can't fly on a broomstick."

"Wait here." Nerissa disappeared beneath the waves." When she reappeared, she thrust her hand out of the water, holding out something long and wriggly.

"What is that?!" Hazel asked, horrified.

"A vamprey eel."

Hazel swallowed hard, fighting the sick feeling rising in her throat. Snakes were not her favorite, and glorified water snakes, which eels qualified as, were no better. "Uh-huh . . ."

The eel seemed to sense Hazel's proximity and stretched toward her, flexing a mouth that was little more than a cavern lined with teeth. It looked almost identical to the lampreys that lived in Lake Champlain. She supposed, all things considered, maybe it had once been a lamprey. Maybe the Bloom had fundamentally changed the nature of life itself? How else to explain the differences she had seen wrought between the two worlds.

"Take it," said Nerissa.

"And do what exactly?" asked Hazel, definitively not taking it.

"Have you never used a vamprey?"

"This would be a first."

"Oh, it's super easy. You just hold it to your throat and wait for it to latch on."

Had Hazel eaten her meager prison victuals, she might have refunded them on the spot. Instead, her stomach merely twisted in knots. "Just?!" she asked in disbelief.

"Yep. Easy as spearing fish. The symbiote exchange begins and you'll be able to breathe underwater."

Hazel took a deep breath. She could do this. She *had* to do this if she wanted to get home, and there was nothing else she wanted more. The vamprey certainly seemed to know what to do. It strained and stretched toward her throat. Hazel chuckled nervously. "A little too eager, wouldn't you say?"

Nerissa smiled. "It is an exchange. You get air, the vamprey gets a meal."

"A meal of . . ."

"Blood," said Nerissa, as if she was speaking the most obvious thing. "It is called a *vamp*rey."

Hazel swallowed hard. "I don't suppose there's a magical clamshell or arcane kelp I could breathe into?"

Nerissa smiled patronizingly. "Nirp."

Hazel sighed. Well, there was no time like the here and now. Hazel took one last breath before she pressed the vamprey to her throat. The eel's kiss was cold and wet, but not entirely unpleasant as it suctioned itself to her skin.

"That wasn't so bad," Hazel said. As soon as the words had left her mouth, a brief but sharp pain pierced her throat. Hazel gasped—or tried to. She couldn't breathe.

Hazel grabbed at the eel, but Nerissa pulled her hand away.

"Give it a second," said Nerissa.

A second was all it took. A moment later, fresh air filled Hazel's lungs, even though she had taken no breath.

Nerissa smiled. "See," she said chirpily. "Nothing to it."

Hazel opened her mouth to say, "Yeah, nothing except getting stabbed in the throat," but no words came out.

"Oh, I should have mentioned," said Nerissa. "You won't be able to speak while the vamprey is attached."

Hazel slumped her shoulders and settled for flashing a subdued thumbs-up.

"Great!" exclaimed Nerissa. "Just hold on!"

Hazel conjured a small light and took hold of Nerissa's outstretched hand. It was scaley and impossible to interlock fingers with on account of the webbing, so Hazel settled for a firm middle school–worthy hand-holding.

Nerissa winked and dove beneath the surface, dragging Hazel with her. Instinctively, she tried to hold her breath, but the vamprey had other ideas. It *forced* her next breath. Perhaps wearing this thing was a necessity, but Hazel couldn't wait to get it off.

Nerissa pulled her along the contours of Turtle Rock down into the depths. They reached a dramatically recessed shelf in the island. As they neared, Hazel's light revealed a massive stone sculpture hiding just beneath the shelf. The sculpture was so encrusted with zebra mussels that it took Hazel a moment to recognize its shape. The rock had been carved into a colossal turtle's head—mouth closed, eyes shut, and withdrawn just inside its shell.

Nerissa let go of Hazel's hand and swam to the turtle. She reached between the head and the shoulder, in a fold of rock carved to look like the skin around the turtle's head. If Hazel wasn't mistaken, Nerissa was tickling it.

The rock shuddered.

Hazel watched in amazement as the rock beak of the turtle parted in an exaggerated yawn, revealing a tongue that was very much not carved of stone but crafted of flesh and blood. But that's not what drew Hazel's attention. Deep in the turtle's throat swirled a blinding vortex of pink light.

Hazel only had a moment to marvel at it before the water around her started twisting. Suddenly Hazel was being dragged toward the open mouth on a violent current. She tried to swim against it, but the effort was futile. Nerissa's hand found her wrist and closed around it, holding on tight. At least, Hazel thought, as they were both sucked into the turtle's open beak, she wouldn't be devoured alone. It served as a small comfort when she bounced off the creature's gigantic tongue and torpedoed down its throat into the pink light.

CHAPTER FIVE

Hazel dragged herself onto a slab of stone on the edge of Turtle Rock and collapsed, shivering from exhaustion and cold.

"And here we are," said Nerissa from somewhere behind her. "Home sweet home."

Hazel felt at the vamprey eel on her throat and gave a gentle tug. She was dismayed to find that it was firmly implanted. It even seemed to reject the attempted extraction, repaying her efforts with a stabbing pain.

Nerissa slid up on the rock next to Hazel. "Here, there's a trick to it." Nerissa reached forward and grabbed hold of the vamprey. "You just have to do something the vamprey doesn't see coming. And . . . voila!" After delivering one last parting stab of pain, the vamprey detached.

"What *was* that?" Hazel asked, her voice a raspy cry.

"Vamprey," said Nerissa matter-of-factly, holding up the eel, which now hung limply in her hands.

"No, the *turtle*," sputtered Hazel. To think that this whole time Turtle Rock had not been merely a cute name. It was actually a turtle, albeit one carved from or covered with rock. Honestly, this raised more questions than her weary brain could handle at the moment.

"No idea," Nerissa respond. "My people call it Varav. Our ancestors used to think it was a Supernal. That idea has fallen out of favor with some of my people."

"Supernal?" Hazel asked.

"A god or goddess," said Nerissa casually. She paused and tossed the vamprey in her hand as if judging its weight. "Oh this sucker is *full*. It'll be comatose for hours. I'll make sure it ends up back on the other side of the Watergate. *You* on the other hand might want to lie down for a bit."

"I don't have time to lie down. I need to get to shore." Hazel rubbed her throat and winced. It was tender to the touch.

"The vamprey is at least polite enough to close up shop when it leaves," Nerissa said. "No holes or anything. Just a little mark. Should clear up in a few days."

Hazel nodded. All in all, it was a small price to pay to get back to the farm. "Would you mind giving me a lift to the shore?" she asked.

"Sure thing. Merfolk Express coming right up."

Hazel slipped back into the water and again took hold of Nerissa's hand. They skimmed along the surface with a stealth and speed that were surprising. In a few minutes, they were gliding into the open entrance of the boathouse, a dilapidated hut with a sagging roof. The building held little more than a rowboat, a clutter of beach toys, and other odds-and-ends. The Bennetts hadn't bothered closing the boathouse for as long as Hazel had been alive. If somebody were to come along and steal some of the junk that cluttered the Boathouse, they would only be performing an act of public service.

Hazel pulled herself up onto the stone dock. "I can't thank you enough," she whispered.

Nerissa smiled. "Don't mention it. It was good to finally meet you, Hazel Bennett. Maybe someday you can give me a full tour of Bennett Manor. If we can figure out the logistics." She flitted her tail above the surface to punctuate the point. "I should get this glutton back home," she added, waggling the vamprey in the air, "before he gets free and turns into an invasive species."

Hazel looked at the engorged eel in Nerissa's hand and shuddered. "Good thinking."

"Hey, be careful out there," Nerissa said. "I'm not certain what you're walking into, but I've seen some strange things on shore the last twenty-four hours that are enough to unsettle the bravest of hearts."

"Like what?" Hazel asked.

"Like I was skimming along the cliffs to the south last night just soaking up the midnight and I . . ." Nerissa trailed off and then shrugged. "I'm sure it was nothing. Weird stuff must happen here all the time." With that, Nerissa slipped beneath the water and was gone.

Strange things? What had she meant by that? She was already on full alert, so if there was something else to worry about, she would be ready for it. She only hoped the effects of the dampener had fully worn off.

Hazel checked the bag to see if the Book of Bennett and the mysterious packet had stayed dry. Satisfied that both were unmarred, she crept to the door of the boathouse. The boathouse sat just down the hill from Bennett Manor, making it an ideal place for her to stake out the house and, if the coast was clear, make a run for it.

Hazel peered out into the night. Bennett Manor cut a sharp shape against the night sky—the countless peaks and roofs and towers. What a glorious sight!

The way looked clear. She was about to make a break for it, sprint up the hill, and hope for the best when she saw something drop from the sky—a rider mounted on a broom—and hover just above the lawn.

Ryker.

She cursed under her breath. There was no way she could get to the manor with him lurking nearby. Especially considering what she'd overheard him saying. Circe wanted to arrest and prosecute anyone willing to harbor Hazel. Going home would mean endangering everyone she loved, and she just couldn't risk that. Though it pained her, she would have to bide her time.

Hazel snuck out of the boathouse and slipped down the stone retaining wall onto the stony beach edging the harbor. She crouched below the wall and started the slow and laborious process of sneaking away.

Hazel was shivering violently by the time she reached the caretaker's cottage. It turned out that following up a late-October swim fully clothed with a late-night stroll was a horrible idea. Who knew?

The cottage was dark. No doubt Tyler was still in bed.

She pushed the gate open, slipped into the yard, and crept around to the back. Tyler still had a propensity for locking his doors, but he had started hiding a key around back, tucked inside a flower pot. She let herself in.

The house was silent, cold. A fire in the woodstove had dwindled down to mere embers.

"Tyler?" she called out. The last thing she needed was to finally return home only to get immediately brained by a boyfriend who mistook her for an intruder. She called out a few more times as she approached the bedroom, but her efforts had been in vain. The bedroom was empty.

Where was he? She didn't like this at all.

Hazel knelt down and peered under the bed and found the little suitcase she kept there packed with some extra clothes. The sight of it brought a tear to her eye. He'd left it there, even after she'd disappeared. Part of her thought he would misinterpret her disappearance and assume she'd once again pulled a runner from the farm like she had ten years prior.

She peeled off her wet clothes and changed into a fresh pair of jeans and a long-sleeve shirt. Then she helped herself to one of Tyler's fleece-lined flannels. It still smelled like him and she relished the scent of it, a combination of Old Spice and pencil shavings. *Just how an aspiring writer should smell*, she thought.

Hazel moved on to the rest of the cottage, though she knew she wouldn't find him anywhere. Mostly she was hoping for a clue to his whereabouts. She went to the den, a mostly empty room except for the writing desk he'd pushed up against the back window. There, she found a perfectly collated stack of papers that looked suspiciously like a manuscript. Had Tyler finished a book in her absence? She approached the desk but stopped short of looking at the papers. It felt wrong to intrude, even if it was Tyler. He was guarded about his writing—and always had been. Hazel closed the den door and headed toward the kitchen.

She grabbed a piece of paper and a pen from the counter and scrawled a note for him. *I'm back. Come and find me where the HRBs reside.* She trusted he would understand the message, but she wanted to be obtuse, in case somebody else picked it up before him. She had to be careful. She couldn't just spell it all out, and she certainly couldn't leave the note in the open. Would Ryker let himself in here to search for her? She wouldn't put it past him.

Hazel went outside and crossed the backyard to Tyler's chicken coop. She opened the egg-collecting door on the back of the coop and ignored the mild uproar of clucks and shuffles from the dark interior. A few eggs huddled in the nests, meaning he hadn't collected before the end of the day. Again, concern gripped her.

Hazel reached into the coop and tucked her note between two eggs. This felt safe from prying eyes. When Tyler returned, he would come collect for his routine breakfast of eggs, sunny-side up, with a few slices of Charlie's signature sourdough slathered with Bennett Farms butter and honey. She only wished she could be here when he returned so she could cook that breakfast with him. But it was too risky.

Satisfied, Hazel was about to close the coop door when her senses were wrestled away from her. Suddenly it was like she was no longer gazing *into* the coop but *out* of it. The sensation was disorienting but not entirely unfamiliar. It only lasted a moment before her consciousness snapped back into her own body.

A moment later, something fluttered into her head like autumn leaves raining from a tree, a string of words that she didn't hear so much as perceived. *Oh goddesses in a chicken basket, this is all I need. An intruder. Maybe it's a raccoon. Come and kill me. Put me out of my misery.*

Hazel's heart stopped in her throat. It couldn't be!

"Clancy?" she practically shouted. "Clancy, is that you?!" She didn't dare hope it was possible. She had buried his fragile rodent body on the top of Split Tree Hill. And yet . . .

Hazel?! HAZEL ROISIN BENNET?!!

"Clancy, what are you doing in there?! You're dead! And won't chickens *eat* mice?!"

A commotion kicked up inside the coop, followed by unsettled chicken chatter. What stepped to the edge of the nesting boxes was no mouse, but a bona fide chicken. Hazel burst into laughter even as tears welled in her eyes.

"Is that *you?*"

Well, it isn't the tooth fairy.

"You're alive!" she shouted.

If you can call this living.

"And you're a chicken!"

A rooster, if we're trying to be as precise as possible. Clancy seemed to think better of what he said and course-corrected. *Wait, no, I'm not a rooster. Though if I spend another night in here, I might start believing otherwise. You have to get me out of here.*

"What *are* you doing in there?" Hazel asked.

Courting hens, he growled sarcastically. *It's not like I had a choice in the matter. One minute I'm waking up in the woods and stumbling around just trying to get my farm legs. The next thing I know, your sister mistakes me for an escaped farm fowl and wrangles me without so much as a how-are-you.*

"I kind of like you as a chicken," she said. "It seems fitting, somehow."

If I could glare at you right now, I would. But I have just one look. One stupid, blank look. Now, how about you answer questions? Where the hell have YOU been?

"Rotting in the basement of the Quark City Hall."

Oh no . . .

"Oh, yes. Circe Strange is intent on seeing me punished for crimes I didn't commit. And sent to someplace called the Squeeze."

Clancy's psychic gasp hit like a blast of arctic air.

"I take it you've heard of it," she said.

Heard of it?! I've had nightmares about it. It's a maximum-security prison for the vilest and most dangerous casters and creatures. It's a black hole, Hazel. Nobody who goes there ever returns.

"Well, it's a good thing somebody busted me out."

Say again . . .

"My father—with the help of Wilhelm and Lev."

Wilhelm? That coward?

"Yeah, maybe he's got facets to him you don't even know about."

Somehow I doubt it.

"Well, *he* came to save me. Not that Circe isn't already trying to haul me back in. She's got a group of Wands hunting me down. Ryker is surveilling the manor, so we're going to need to find somewhere else to hunker down."

Something crashed through the tree line nearby. She raised her hands in defense, pleased to find her palm crackled and popped with energy. The residual effects of the dampener must finally have worn off.

"What was that?" she asked in hushed tones.

Probably a raccoon. I swear they come sniffing around the coop every night. It's terrifying.

Something in the trees let out a low unearthly moan that made every hair on Hazel's neck stand on end. She thought of what Nerissa had said about seeing strange things on land.

"Speaking of terrifying. Have you seen anything weird going on around here?"

From the inside of a coop? Just your boyfriend's weird chicken talk.

Hazel cracked a smile. Keeping chickens had, in just a few short months, become something of an obsession for him. He talked to them the way she imagined most men spoke to their dogs. She found it endearing in a quirky sort of way.

"How about we get out of here and find a safe place to hold over until morning," she said, reaching out to pick up Clancy, but, as if on cue, Clancy opened his beak wide and started crowing.

"What are you *doing*?!"

I don't know. This happens every day.

"Well, stop it!"

I can't!

"You always said you were not a cat and not a mouse. How about you try being not a rooster for a few minutes?"

She looked around in a panic. She doubted Ryker or anyone would come running to investigate a rooster crowing at the coming dawn, but it still felt like she was marked. And the thing in the bushes . . .

"Clancy, I can't sneak around the farm with you like this."

Can't we just hang out here until I stop?

"I-I-I'm sorry," she stammered. She couldn't think straight. She was too tired and trying to process too much. "I need to hunker down before the sun comes up and make a battle plan."

How about inside? Tyler should be back soon. Clancy crowed again, louder than before, but this time he moved to jump from the coop.

She shook her head. "I'm sorry, Clancy," she said, pushing the door shut before he could make his escape. "I'll come back for you later."

Hazel, do not put me back in here!

"You're safe in there," she said.

That's distinctly a matter of opinion.

"I'll come back for you," she said, tapping the door for good measure as if to finalize the deal.

With Clancy's angry psychic chatter in her ear, she hurried away.

CHAPTER SIX

Hazel cut across the center of the farm, forgoing roads and paths in favor of sneaking through forests and traipsing across fields as she raced the coming dawn. She crossed the North Track and pushed toward the boundaries of the farm, bringing herself perilously close to Cassius's Folly, the marsh along the northern edge of the farm. She'd always steered clear of it—mostly because of the terrifying stories her Gammy had told her about it.

Her ancestor, the eponymous Cassius W. Bennett, had gotten drunk one fateful night and stumbled into the marsh, never to return. Ever since, generations of Bennetts had claimed to hear tearful wails drifting through the fog in the middle of the night. Hazel had been a brazen child, but never quite bold enough to investigate a haunted marsh in the middle of the night.

So when Hazel sank a foot into the cold, sodden edge of the Folly, she immediately changed course. Instead, she skirted as close to the North Track as she dared while she made her way, at last, to the chapel.

The small stone building, surrounded by a small cemetery, was tucked in the wooded northwestern corner of the farm, off the beaten path. Hazel liked it there. It was peaceful being amongst the headstones of her ancestors.

Hazel had funneled some of her own money—despite Juniper's protests—to fund much-needed renovations for the Chapel. It had seemed wrong for the final resting place of all Bennetts to be left in decay and ruin. As she broke from the tree line, she was pleased to see that the renovations were still underway and the entire building was encased in scaffolding.

She wasn't entirely certain what day of the week it was and whether workers would show up on the job site. Still, she hoped she could steal a few hours of sleep without being disturbed and endangering her loved ones. At the very least, she felt confident no Wands would think to come here.

She was crossing the cemetery when her foot slipped into a hole. She pitched forward, sprawling onto the ground and only narrowly missing an intimate face-to-face with a rather sizable gravestone. She got to her feet and inspected the hole that had tripped her up. Somebody had dug down into the grave. *Or burrowed its way out*, she said to herself. She conjured a dim light and held it up to the stone.

Orion E. Livingston
Mar 8, 1772 – Oct 31, 1847
Custodian

Custodian? Like a janitor?

Somewhere in the distance, she heard a deep tormented moan. Hazel doused her light and looked warily around the cemetery. Nothing stirred.

Undead couldn't breach holy ground, right? she asked herself. *Doesn't a chapel graveyard count as holy ground?*

She hurried to the chapel door. As she wove a path between the stones, she saw that Orion's wasn't the only grave that had been disturbed. More than once, she nearly stumbled in another oversized gopher hole.

She finally reached the chapel and, much to her chagrin, found it locked. She cursed. Historically, the chapel was kept unlocked, but she had given the restoration company a set of keys to lock up their equipment at night.

"Having trouble, Lady Bennett?" inquired a voice.

Hazel stepped back just as a faintly glowing hand passed through the door. Then followed a man dressed like a chorus member in a production of *Hamilton*.

Hazel recognized him instantly. "Theo?" she gasped. Theophilus Cincinnatus Bennett, her distant ancestor. A veteran—and casualty—of the American Revolution. And her assistant in solving the murder of Eric Moore, until a bit of black magic had destroyed him.

Theo bowed deeply. "Lady Bennett, it is a pleasure to once again be at your service. I'm sorry to have been away for so long. I was . . . well, I was indisposed for a time."

"Theo, you were *destroyed*," she said.

"Ah, yes," he said, embarrassed. "I do seem to recall a flash of the most wretched shade of purple before everything went murky for a while. Then when I woke up, I was in the manor library. I'm afraid that's about all I remember of my . . . holiday."

"The library?" Hazel asked. "Why there?"

"If you want a full account of the scene, I fear I will be of no help. It was pure chaos. Elbows in eye sockets. Clawing. Hair-pulling. It was horrid. Perhaps we should conduct this reunion inside."

"I would love to, but the door is locked," Hazel said.

Theo cleared his throat delicately. "Perhaps this is a bit presumptuous of me," he began, adjusting his spectral spectacles, "but as the resident Bennett witch perhaps you could . . . ahem, well . . ." He motioned toward the door and mimed turning a key.

"Can't say I know that spell yet," she said sourly.

"Perhaps you could, ahem, improvise one?" he asked, before again looking around nervously.

"Why are you so on edge, Theo?" she asked.

"I'm afraid there are spirits afoot, Lady Bennett."

"Theo . . ." she said.

"The dead are walking. And these are not your garden variety spirits, my dear. They are . . . *problematic*. Specters, poltergeists, shades. And I dare not mention the *corporeal* undead that are afoot. Ghouls, zombies, wights." He shivered. "It's ghastly." He seemed to have reminded himself of something. "And ghasts!"

Hazel thought of the chilling groan she'd heard from the Tanglewood. "Why is this happening, Theo?"

"I really think explanations would be best deferred until we are inside," said Theo.

"Right."

She could do this. For months now, she'd been improvising spells far more complicated than this. Oftentimes she had used props to help get herself into character, but her captors had taken every last trinket and token she'd had on her. No matter. A good actor could set the scene even without props. Surely, she could tickle a lock open.

Hazel stuck out her pinkie finger and jabbed it at the lock like a key. She closed her eyes, focused her energy until the tip of her finger tingled, and then turned it. The lock clicked.

"That was surprisingly easy," she said.

"A witch worth her salt!" Theo beamed. "I daresay you've improved since our first meeting."

Hazel slipped inside and shut the door tightly behind her, again securing the lock. Only then did she dare to conjure up a little light. The chapel's interior was also in a state of triage—the pews were covered with drop cloths, the massive wooden relief that covered the altar wall was hidden behind plastic sheeting, and power tools littered the floor near the door.

This had been her base of operations during her first investigation. It seemed as good a place as any to get some shuteye—and to get some answers.

She spun about on Theo. "So what's the deal, Theo?" she asked. "How bad is this undead problem?"

"They're *everywhere*, dear," he said.

"That explains why it looks like the set of the 'Thriller' video out there," Hazel said. "Well, at least they're already dead. I've had my share of the recently deceased and murdered."

Theo flinched. "You'd best be careful about saying that word too loudly," he whispered hoarsely.

"What, murder?" asked Hazel.

Theo flinched again, and then suddenly he stopped, his eyes going wide and his head tilting to the side as he listened intently. "Oh, now you've done it . . ."

Hazel had only a moment to ponder the significance of that statement before a violent clattering and rattling came to her ears, followed by an obnoxious high-pitch beep.

A moment later, another apparition passed through the door of the chapel. It was a woman, though she looked haggard, her face gaunt and her eyes wreathed in dark circles. As she advanced, Hazel saw why. She was attached to a series of wires and tubes which trailed to a team of spectral medical machines—an IV stand, a heart monitor that squealed in a constant flatline, and a stalled ventilator.

Hazel backed away as the woman advanced, but she realized there was nowhere to run. The spirit was between her and the door.

"Did somebody mention *murder?*" she asked, her voice thin and papery, like a wasp's nest.

"No!" interjected Theo. "No, no, no, Judith. Nobody mentioned murder. You must have misheard the young lady. She said the farm really must hire a new *herder.* For the sheep, my dear. But not a stitch about *murder.* That's what you get for eavesdropping."

Still the woman came closer, dismissing Theo with a snide lip curl as she dragged her cadre of medical equipment ever closer to Hazel.

"I'm Judith," the spirit said. "Judith Goodblood."

Judith Goodblood. Why did that name sound familiar? "I've heard your name before," she said.

"You bloody well should," Judith said. "I've delivered more Bennetts into this world and onto this farm than any other single family."

Hazel shook her head. Even if that were true, it would have been before her time. Hazel, in fact, had been the first Bennett *not* born on the farm in generations. All on account of how the doctor that had come to deliver Juniper had up and gone missing . . .

"Are you the youngest Bennett?" Judith asked curiously, drawing closer and inspecting Hazel like this were a yearly physical.

"I have a niece and a nephew," said Hazel.

Judith stopped and looked at her curiously. "Hmm. Who's your mother?"

"Amy Bennett," said Hazel wearily. She didn't entirely trust this spirit, but neither did she want to anger her. Something about the woman was unsettling. Dangerous.

"Amy," Judith repeated as if testing the word. "Of course." She tried to take Hazel's face in her hands, like a doctor checking her vitals. The effect was disconcerting—a cold and clammy sensation snaking up and down Hazel's face. "What was it she named you? Juniper? I was there the night you were born. I *delivered* you." She passed her hands up to Hazel's hair, and it was like a cool breeze lifted her bangs. "Interesting. Very interesting."

"Madam," said Theo, offended. "Unhand that young lady."

"I'm okay, Theo," said Hazel pulling away from Judith. "But I'm not Juniper. She's my sister. I'm Hazel."

Judith stopped, her hands still poised like she might dive back in and frisk Hazel's face.

"Another one," Judith said. "Interesting. I delivered your sister. And your mother. I would have very much liked to have attended to you as well."

It dawned on Hazel where she had heard the name before. "That's it!" Hazel dropped her satchel to the floor and pulled out the folder. She flipped through them until she found what she was looking for. "Here!" she practically shouted, springing up and showing Theo and Judith the sheet of paper. "Date of death, October Thirty-First," she said. "Halloween. You died the night you delivered my sister . . ."

"Died makes it sound so incidental," Judith said, the pitch and volume of her heart monitor suddenly creeping up into pain-inducing territory. "I was murdered."

"I was shot by a British regular just ten yards from my own front step and you don't hear me complaining about it," mumbled Theo.

Judith glared at him. "I was not a wartime casualty. I was cut down in cold blood. This is why I need your help."

"I will help you," said Hazel. "But I just can't right now. I *can't*. I can't even walk across the farm out in the open—how could I possibly investigate a murder, never mind four different murders."

The monitor's pitch crept higher.

"Listen. I—I just need some sleep," Hazel said, almost begging.

"You hardly picked the ideal place for that . . ." said Theo, eyeing the heart monitor.

"I can't make any sense of this until I've slept," Hazel continued.

"You *have* waited nearly forty years," Theo pointed out. "What's a few more days?"

"Do you think I'm here on vacation?" Judith scoffed. "Somebody left the door to the spirit world open long enough for me to escape. Don't think our absence has gone unnoticed. No doubt they'll come to round us up."

"I'm not doing anything until I get a few hours of sleep." Hazel slammed the Book of Bennett and the folder down on a nearby pew and stalked off into the chapel, collecting drop cloths from the pews with which to assemble a bed.

Somehow Judith didn't lose her cool. The heart monitor continued to report an absence of heart rate in a reasonable monotone. Judith called after her. "Maybe whoever assembled the packet wanted you to investigate the murders."

Hazel paused. Her father? Obviously he had wanted her to investigate these murders. Had that been the reason he'd broken her out of prison? Not out of paternal affection and obligation, but to solve some cold cases lingering around the farm?

"You see," Judith pressed, "there are others! They came through the doorway with me. Their justice is my justice! This isn't just about me."

"What does that mean exactly?" Hazel asked, annoyed.

"Look at the dates."

Hazel sighed. She shuffled back to where she'd set the folder down and thumbed through the packets. She had no idea what Judith was talking about; the dates spanned centuries, going all the way back to Orion E. Livingston, who died in 1781. "Wait a minute," said Hazel. "Orion E. Livingston. That was the grave I tripped on outside. It looked like somebody had busted out of the grave."

"Perhaps because somebody *did*," said Theo nervously. "A most terrifying ghoul, that one."

"You saw it, Theo?"

Theo gulped dramatically. "When his spirit finally found the place of his interment, he immediately set to work reuniting with his, uh, *self*."

Judith was becoming impatient. "The *day* of death, though. Look!" She jabbed a ghostly finger at the listed date of death for Orion: October 31, 1781.

"Halloween," said Hazel. She flipped through the other documents. All of them were the same. Though they had all died years apart, their lives had all ended on the same calendar day: Halloween. "That's a strange coincidence."

"There are no coincidences," spat Judith. "You have to help me."

"My dear," said Theo. "I would say you're a bit beyond help, and I should know."

"I want *justice*, fool," spat Judith. Her monitor pitch and volume found new heights and Hazel had to clap her hands over her ears until the squalling died down. "These other people want justice too, whether they know it or not."

"What do you remember about that night?" Hazel asked, turning to Judith.

A triumphant smile flicked at the corners of the spirit's mouth. Judith furrowed her brow and scowled, her eyes darkening—literally—until they were pits burrowing into her head. "Why are you questioning *me*? I'm the one who was murdered here."

"And how do you know you were murdered?" Theo asked.

"Because I was a fit and healthy septuagenarian," Judith said. "I was taking the scenic way home and I had just passed that ridiculously oversized barn—" Her heart monitor squeezed out a low mournful tone. "Everything gets a bit fuzzy after that . . ."

Judith had to be referring to the East Barn.

"So you must have lived nearby," said Hazel, "if you were walking home?"

"In town, yes," she said.

"But where is the *evidence*, my dear?" asked Theo.

"Evidence?" Judith asked, seemingly offended by the insinuation that she needed to present any.

Theo cleared his throat. "The *body*. There can't be murder without the body."

Her face seemed to go slack for a moment, the drone of the monitor suddenly beeped the steady rhythm of a heartbeat. "I don't know," she said. "I feel it calling to me but there's a disconnect. I close my eyes and I see"—she closed her eyes—"a pasture and open sky. The smell of old hay and manure and fresh sawdust."

Again the monitored flatlined and Judith opened her eyes.

There *was* still a little time before the sun came up. Perhaps Hazel could make the most of it. She stuffed the documents back into the satchel and shouldered the bag.

Judith opened her eyes and her face lit up as much as its gaunt, tormented features allowed. "You'll do it?" she asked.

"I'll look into it," she said. "But I'm going alone."

"I can show you to the barn!" Judith protested.

"I grew up here," said Hazel, as she turned on her heel and headed for the door. It was clear she was going to get no rest—at least not here. "I think I can find my way around."

CHAPTER SEVEN

Even though it was cold enough for Hazel to see her breath, the windows of the Cup and Crumb were cracked open, spilling warm light and the smell of fresh bread into the East Barn's courtyard. Only now did Hazel realize how hungry she was. If she didn't get up those steps fast, she was liable to start drooling on the ground.

Besides, she needed to hurry. In another hour, Charlie would unlock the doors to serve the farmhands and the East Barn artisans as they showed up for work. But even as she pondered that, one of the corner tower doors opened, spilling an orange light into the courtyard. Hazel looked over in time to see a feminine silhouette disappear inside before the door once again shut. *Another early riser*, she thought. *No worries.*

As Hazel crossed the courtyard and started climbing the steps to the café, she was a tangle of excitement and nerves. She only hoped this wasn't a mistake—that she wasn't endangering Charlie by coming to see her. Yet Hazel knew she couldn't do this alone.

She was surprised to find Charlie's vintage yellow VW Beetle parked right at the bottom of the café steps. Maybe Charlie had brought in new supplies, or else was preparing a big order of baked goods for delivery.

"Almost there, Lady Bennett." Theo apparated from thin air, nearly sending Hazel into cardiac arrest.

"Theo, I thought I told you to stay put," she scolded. "I need to talk to Charlie alone."

"I can be discreet as a cat," he said. "Besides, I needed to put some leagues between me and that dreadful midwife."

"You can stay," Hazel conceded, "but you need to keep out of sight. Charlie doesn't handle this whole spirit thing well. Seeing me again is probably enough of a shock to the system."

"Of course, Lady Bennett," said Theo, bowing. "Out of sight, out of mind." He faded until he had disappeared entirely.

Hazel climbed the stairs and peered in the cafe window. Charlie stood at the worktable, dancing, hips swaying as she boxed trays of fresh-baked donuts.

Hazel grinned. Should she call out to Charlie? Try to surprise her? What was the proper protocol for returning after an extended disappearance? No. She settled on the obvious answer: No fanfare. The proper way was just to appear as demurely as possible.

Hazel knocked.

"We're not open yet!" Charlie called in her faux-pleasant voice, though Hazel could hear the restrained annoyance. Charlie muttered something, eliciting laughter from somebody just out of Hazel's line of sight.

A moment later, that somebody hopped up from behind one of the barn beams next to the worktable, a fancy camera in hand, and padded toward the door. Hazel gawked. She immediately recognized the woman's black-licorice bob and red cat-eye glasses.

Aashvi Dhawan?! The videographer and techie for the Odd Lot was just about the last person Hazel had expected here, never mind the *first* person. Though, now that Hazel thought about it, Charlie had shown an intense romantic interest in Aashvi. What else had changed in Hazel's absence?!

When Aashvi saw who was standing at the door, she stopped.

"Uh, Charlie," called Aashvi over her shoulder.

"Tell her to come back in thirty," shouted Charlie. "I won't open the door until then. Not even for coffee."

"No, it's not *her*," Aashvi replied.

Exasperated, Charlie punched the wad of dough once more and turned to see what the trouble was, wiping her hands on her apron, and marched across the café floor. She looked ready to deliver a piece of her mind—which for Charlie was really saying something. The woman was so ebullient she was practically a human cinnamon bun.

But when she got close enough to see through the window in the café door, she stopped in her tracks. Immediately, as if by reflex, she started bawling.

Charlie practically tore the door off its hinges and yanked Hazel's arm out of its socket as she pulled her inside and into a crushing bearhug. "Oh, thank the heavens," she blubbered. "I knew you weren't dead. I *knew* it."

"Charlie, I might be if you don't ease up."

Charlie only squeezed that much harder. "I haven't slept at home a single night since you went missing."

"You haven't?"

"And leave Mama Bennett alone in her hour of need? Hell no."

"Charlie, you're the best friend a woman could ask for."

"My twin from another kin," said Charlie, finally letting go of Hazel and holding her at arm's length. "I can't believe you're—oh my god, is that a hickey?"

Hazel put a hand over the mark on her neck. "No, it's not a hickey! Try to focus here, Charlie."

"Sure looks like one. Never mind that. I have so many questions!"

"*You* have questions? When I left, the farm was on the verge of being discovered by the real world and I'd left Cordelia in Tyler's hands to be delivered to Detective Gibbens."

"And delivered she was," said Aashvi.

Charlie grabbed a newspaper off the rack on the counter and tossed it to Hazel. It was that day's edition of the *Larkhaven Scryer*. The headline "Black Widow Appears in Court" ran over a chilling photo of Cordelia Strange clad in an orange jumpsuit. Cordelia stared straight into the camera, hair swept back, revealing the patches of waxy spider flesh on her face.

Hazel unfolded the paper to read the article, but her attention was drawn to the headline below the fold. "Police Continue Search for Local Celeb."

Hazel scanned the article. " 'We're continuing to consider the circumstances suspicious'?"

"We had no idea what had happened to you," said Charlie. "But you're back! This calls for a celebration!" Charlie said. "Wait here one second. Don't go disappearing again or anything." She stopped for a moment, gripped either side of Hazel's head as if she might try to pop her cranium. "You're back!" she marveled.

Charlie rushed toward the back hall that ran behind the café, leaving Hazel and Aashvi alone.

"Welcome home," said Aashvi, smiling.

"Thanks. If I had known I was going to get womanhandled when I got back, I might have stayed away."

Aashvi chuckled. "She's been worried sick about you. Everyone has."

Hazel nodded. She'd spent all that time so concerned about her own fate that she hadn't considered everyone else's suffering. Hadn't that always been her problem though? A little too concerned with her own goals and her own plans?

"I didn't expect to see you here," said Hazel.

Aashvi laughed. "Let's just say another witch knocked some sense into me—or out of me. I did what she said and it might have saved my immortal soul, but I definitely did not save my job. Not that there was much of a job to save."

"What do you mean?"

"I sent that footage to Detective Gibbens like you asked . . . then I deleted it from the Odd Lot's computers. All of it. Angus was *not* pleased. He had been teasing some huge drops and major reveals to his followers. And then he had nothing. He threatened to sue me, but I had enough dirt on him and his shady practices to keep him off my back. It seemed like a good time to part ways."

"Since then, they've focused on posting videos complaining of magical malfeasance, huge conspiracies, and coverups. It's astounding that in five short weeks they've managed to destroy what it took five long years to build."

"Won't they come back?" Hazel asked. "They've spent years looking for a place like Bennett Farms. I can't imagine they'll give up so easily."

Aashvi tapped her lips as she pondered the possibility. "They might. But it wouldn't matter if they did. Even if they got new footage, nobody would pay them any mind. They're desperate now, and that desperation will cast everything into doubt. People will say it's a fake now."

"Would Callie seek revenge?"

Aashvi shook her head. "I don't think so. All of her skills were limited to petty hexes."

"It didn't feel petty . . ." said Hazel, recalling the way Callie's text-message hex had caused her to lose control of her powers.

"Now that Callie knows what you're capable of—and that I'm on your side—I don't think she'd have the guts."

Hazel smiled. "I'm glad you're here. You did the right thing." Still, she couldn't help but feel a little bad for having cost Aashvi a gig that any twenty-something techie and videographer would have killed for.

"I'm getting back on my feet," Aashvi said. "I'm starting my own business. Charlie is helping me get a start. I'm creating content for her. Photos for her Insta. We're working on a commercial." She shrugged. "I'm just going freelance. Hopefully I can stick around for a while."

Hazel smiled. "That would be nice. Listen, I need to talk to Charlie."

Aashvi nodded. "Yes, of course."

Hazel hurried into the back hall, where she found Charlie rifling through her desk, muttering to herself. "Come on. I know it's around here somewhere." Hazel took in the scene. The back hall looked like a college apartment the night after an epic party. There were cups, saucers, and bowls on just about every available surface. The desk, which was usually a catchall for bills and papers and odds-and-ends, had been swept clean of paperwork and was instead covered with countless cups and bowls and sauces. Hazel approached, looked cautiously at the contents of the cups, and grimaced. Water, tea, coffee, hardened butter, oil. Some of the cups harbored flotillas of mold. One cup contained a gelatinous mass of curdled milk.

Charlie looked up and smiled. "I've got a bottle of bubbly around here somewhere," she said. "And we're going to toast your return."

"Charlie," said Hazel. "This looks like a health-code violation." But as horrified as she was, she was touched by the scene. Charlie was a fledgling Oracle—a soothsayer whose powers of divination dovetailed perfectly into her professional leanings. Charlie was able to far-see by gazing into the reflective surfaces of drinks and cooking liquids.

Charlie frowned. "There were *so* many theories. You were dead. Kidnapped for ransom. You'd had another crisis of faith and run away from the farm. I spent most of my time staring into every consumable liquid I could get my hands on." She gestured lamely to the horde of vessels and shook her head sadly. "But I failed."

"Charlie, I'm back. It doesn't matter."

"Ah!" Charlie exclaimed, brightening. "There it is!" She reached into a cluster of bottles next to the desk and withdrew an unopened bottle of champagne. "This is a moment worthy of celebration!"

"Charlie, it's not even seven o'clock . . ."

"That's why God invented the mimosa." She led the way back to the café floor, produced three glasses and some orange juice, and started pouring. "There. Now we can just sit down and you can explain what the hell happened to you."

"Charlie, it's not that easy," said Hazel. "I'm being *hunted*. You're in danger just by my being here," she said. "I need to find a way to clear my name."

Charlie stopped pouring and turned her attention to Hazel, eyebrow cocked. "They're going to have to go through me first. You know that, right? Now tell me what you did that made you the target of a womanhunt."

Hazel smiled. Between sips of mimosa, she explained the situation, from the moment she'd been arrested to the month she'd spent inside a jail cell in Quark as she awaited her trial. "I thought if I just made it home, I would be safe, but . . ."

"Are we talking about the cast of the *Walking Dead*?" Charlie asked.

"So you know," Hazel said.

"*Know*?" Charlie scoffed. "As soon as the sun goes down, this place turns into the set of a George Romero flick. It's not safe to go it alone out there. Why do you think Aashvi has woken up at the butt-crack of dawn to accompany me to work?"

"I'm here for professional reasons too," countered Aashvi, grinning.

"There's more, Charlie," said Hazel. She slipped the folder from her bag and slid it across the table. "When I was busted out of prison, I was given this."

Charlie flipped the folder open and eyed the letter that topped the stack of papers. "Asarum Moonwake? Sounds like a Burning Man alter ego."

"It's my father."

"Ooooooh—sorry." Charlie stopped as the full impact of Hazel's statement hit her. "Oh! Did you see him?"

Hazel shook her head. "It would seem he's waiting in the wings for now. But this must be important. I didn't understand it at first, but I think they're all murder victims." She fanned out the separate files on the tabletop. "Five of them. I've already talked to one of the victims and—"

Charlie raised a hand, halting Hazel midsentence. "Let me stop you there." Charlie shuddered. "All of this undead business is too much for me. Dark wizards? Okay. Giant moths? Sure. Evil scarecrows? Why not. But I can't handle all of these ghosts and ghouls."

"They might be the key to this," Hazel said. "According to Judith."

"Judith?"

"Judith Goodblood, belated midwife and current wandering spirit," Hazel repeated, tapping the file with Judith's name and evoking another shudder from Charlie. "According to her, the other victims are all roving around the farm. We just need to find them and question them."

"So we have to investigate five separate murders?" Charlie asked. "That seems like a tall order, even for you."

"Unless they're all connected," Hazel said. "Look. They all died on Halloween night."

Charlie looked at the files and frowned. "Hazel, some of these people died more than a hundred years ago. How could they possibly be connected? Please tell me this isn't another time-travel caper . . ."

"I'm not ruling out anything at this point," said Hazel. "Open mind, open eyes. I will not be caught off guard this time."

Aashvi leaned in close and eyed the files. "Jonathan Northcott?" she asked. "Like *the* Northcotts?"

"Color me ignorant," said Hazel, "but who are the Northcotts?"

"A formerly wealthy family from the Gilded Age," she said. "They were railroad tycoons and coal magnates. They had more money than the Rockefellers . . . until they squandered it."

"Sounds like another wealthy family I know," Hazel noted grimly.

"Look," Aashvi said. "There's a pattern here. These murders are all exactly thirty-four years apart. 1985, 1951, 1917 . . . but then it jumps to 1847. There's one missing. There should have been a murder in 1883."

"She's sharp like that," said Charlie. "That's why I kept her around. Plus, she's got a great butt."

"Charlie," admonished Aashvi.

"Just calling them like I see them."

Hazel shuffled through the papers. Aashvi was right. "But that means . . ." She did her best quick mental math. "This year would be the thirty-fourth year since Judith's murder."

Aashvi nodded.

"What's the date?" Hazel asked. "What's today?"

"The twenty-ninth," said Aashvi.

"Two days," said Hazel. "We have two days to figure this out so we can stop it from happening again."

"But how?" Charlie asked.

Hazel drained the rest of her mimosa and slammed her glass down. "We need to talk to the victims," she said.

"Well, that's going to be tough, considering the sun is up and those things go into hiding," Charlie said.

"Then I have something in common with the dead. I'll need to make myself scarce when the sun comes up."

"Hazey," said Charlie, peering toward the front windows, "the sun is already up."

"Then we'd better get moving," said Hazel. "Let's start with the crime scene. Judith said her bones were in the barn. Have you seen strange activity around here lately?" Hazel wracked her brain for somewhere in the barn that might have been hiding bones for thirty-four years.

"Besides your sudden disappearance? And the wandering undead?"

"And Mrs. Prim and Proper?" Aashvi asked.

"Who?"

"This lady is more uptight than a British royal," said Charlie. "*Definitely* an out-of-stater."

A sharp knock sounded at the door. Hazel pushed back her chair and sprang up, ready to start flinging spells if a Wand busted down the door.

"You don't have anything to fear," said Aashvi to Hazel. "That would just be Mrs. Prim and Proper."

"Speak of the devil," said Charlie. "Right on time."

"This lady is an unapologetic pain in the butt," Aashvi said, "but she's about as dangerous as unbuttered toast, which, by the way, is exactly what she'll order."

"I've got this," said Aashvi, springing up and padding to the door.

"She's shown up a half hour before opening for the last few mornings," muttered Charlie, pouring herself another mimosa. "Doesn't take no for an answer. She'll stand out there and stare through the window until we open. It's super creepy in its own right, but, again, I don't think she's here for you, Hazey. Aashvi will tell her to cool her jets."

But as soon as Aashvi unlocked the door, somebody brushed past her. A woman strode into the café, her high heels like polite applause on the barnboard. She was dressed in a slate-gray, business-smart skirt and jacket like her next stop was a board meeting. Officious, maybe. But as far as Hazel could tell, nobody attached to the Quark or the Council, which meant she could relax at least a little.

The woman set her leather briefcase on the table near the window, sat down, and fixed her gaze on some indeterminate point ahead of her.

"I've got this," said Aashvi. "You two sit." She jumped up and went behind the counter.

Charlie watched her go, her eyes wide and dazzling as Aashvi sliced some sourdough and grabbed a decanter of hot tea water. "She's pretty great, huh?"

"I feel better about being gone for a month knowing she was here for you. I can tell she really cares about you."

"Stop it," said Charlie, blushing. "Speaking of which, your man has been struggling."

"I stopped at the cottage and he wasn't there . . ."

"That's because the boy has been busy playing Van Helsing," Charlie said. "He's been patrolling the farm from dusk till dawn making sure nobody gets in . . . and nothing gets out."

"Tyler?" Hazel asked. He was an exceptional caretaker of the farm, but he was hardly the picture of action hero brawn and debonair.

"Oh heck yes," said Charlie. "He's all decked out with wooden stakes and axes and shotguns," said Charlie. "If I swung that way, it would be hot as Hell."

Aashvi returned to the table and slid back into her seat. "So how are we going to get started finding dem bones?" she asked.

"She said her bones were at the East Barn?" Charlie asked, looking around edgily like she expected a skeleton to tumble from the ceiling at any minute.

"Judith said she could sense her body but she wasn't able to find it. Something about open skies and the smell of old manure and fresh sawdust."

"Maybe she meant the new barn," Aashvi suggested.

"New barn?"

"Oh yeah!" Charlie crowed. "The new sheep barn! Your sister and David are having a barn raising on the site of the old barn." The old sheep barn had collapsed in June after a bit of black magic had accelerated its decay and precipitated its collapse. "I'm supposed to head over there in a few hours—hence the feast of scones and coffee."

"Wouldn't they have discovered a body when they cleared the debris and prepped the site?"

"Maybe not," said Charlie. "They just cleared the old rotten timbers. They're keeping the original foundation in place."

"So they never set a shovel in soil . . ." said Hazel. Hazel put the papers back into the folder and stuffed it back into her satchel. "We have to get there before everyone shows up."

"We . . ."

"I was hoping you could assist."

"I'm a weak digger," Charlie deflected. "Physical labor isn't really my thing."

"That makes two of us," said Hazel. "Which means it would be helpful if I knew exactly where to search. If only I had a means of seeing beyond my senses . . ."

"It's not a party trick," Charlie protested. "I can't just do it at will. Hell, I couldn't even do it *at all* while you were gone. I tried to track you down and never got so much as a vision . . ."

"It doesn't matter," said Hazel. "Do you think my powers always work how and when I want them to?"

Charlie nodded. "I know. But you've been preparing for this your whole life. There's no Book of Campbell to help me through this . . ."

Hazel sighed. She thought of Charlie's riven half, Sybil. It was unfair that she could benefit from Cass's tutelage right now when Charlie herself was left to figure it out on her own. "You're right, Charlie," Hazel said. "It's not fair of me to keep asking this of you. You didn't ask for any of this."

"None of us did," said Aashvi, shrugging. "I didn't ask for magical aptitude any more than you did. Our circumstances have robbed us of a shot at a normal life. But who wants one of those? If I'd have lived a normal life, I'd never have met you and sure as heck wouldn't be sitting here."

Charlie grimaced. "Just what I needed. Not one but two women in my life who keep talking me into the craziest stuff." She knocked back the last of her mimosa. "Fine. I guess I could use some help schlepping donuts and coffee over to the site. And I suppose it wouldn't kill me to give it one more try."

"Charlie, you're the best."

"I know, girl," Charlie said, "but it wouldn't kill you to say it more often." She shook her head.

"You two go," Aashvi said. "I'll watch the shop."

"Aashvi, are you sure?" Hazel asked, feeling a pang of guilt.

"You go," insisted Aashvi. "I think I can manage to refresh a tea and slice some bread."

"Aashvi, I couldn't—"

"You could," said Aashvi. "And you should. Partly because you two need to catch up, and partly because I need at least a few minutes to shoot some footage without you stepping in my shot." She brandished her camera and flashed a winning smile.

"Only back a few minutes and here we go again . . ." muttered Charlie.

CHAPTER EIGHT

Charlie's yellow VW Beetle bounced across the Skylark Meadow, with Charlie wincing as they rolled over another bump. "There go another dozen doughnuts. I just know it," she said, finally pulling up in front of the old sheep barn and cutting the engine.

The wreckage of the barn had been cleared, leaving behind only the old stone foundation. Already-assembled frames lay in position and countless beams and boards were stacked nearby.

Hazel and Charlie started unloading the folding table and the goodies.

"It's good that we have a few minutes," said Hazel. She'd been pondering how to tell Charlie about Sibyl and whether she even should, but in the end she'd decided that being open and honest was the best policy. "I have something I need to talk to you about."

"Other than the hordes of undead and the string of cold cases?" asked Charlie, setting up the table.

Hazel didn't know how to broach the topic delicately, so she just blurted it out. "I saw her."

"Judith?"

"No, not *her* her—*you* her. Your riven half. That her."

Charlie did the most uncharacteristic thing. She walked on in silence.

"She was—" Hazel started to say, but Charlie cut her off by merely raising her hand.

"I never thought I'd say this to you, Hazel, but this one feels too close to home. I need time to think about it. With everything that's going on right now, it's just one too many things."

The air next to Hazel shimmered, and Theo appeared, his hands folded solemnly in front of him. In the golden morning light, he appeared dimmer, merely a hint of a man in outdated wartime regalia. Charlie nearly jettisoned the box of donuts she was carrying.

"We need to work on your timing, Theo," said Hazel.

"My apologies, Lady Bennett," Theo said. "I merely wanted to make my services available. It is not my aim to frighten Miss Campbell with my countenance."

"Not unless you can convince all of your graveyard buddies to go back home," Charlie said.

Theo frowned. "I assure you these ruffians are no friends of mine."

"You're nothing if not a gentleman, Theo," Hazel said, trying to defuse the tension. "Though perhaps you could help by figuring out which venues these victims are currently haunting."

Charlie shuddered.

"I wouldn't know where to start," Theo said. "The farm has changed so much since my time. There are so many dark, dank, and cobweb choked places for monsters to hide . . ." He shivered. "I hadn't ventured beyond the chapel grounds before your return. I really should get out of the chapel more."

"How about a game of Halloween hide-and-seek to get you started," Charlie suggested.

"Of course," said Theo. "If the lady so wishes it." Theo faded from view.

"You were a little harsh with him," said Hazel. "He is family, technically."

"I'm trying," Charlie said, sighing, "but there are some things I will never get used to. Overalls, ghosts, and wine in a box. In that order." Charlie muttered as she set the coffee urn down on a bit of foundation nearby. She grabbed a paper cup and pumped out a few steaming spurts of hot coffee.

"Is that your crystal ball?" Hazel asked, cracking a smile.

"Nope." Charlie handed it to Hazel. "This one's for you."

"You're a goddess," Hazel marveled. Not so much as a single drop of caffeine had passed her lips since she'd been arrested. She inhaled deeply from the cup before taking a cautious sip. Hot, bitter, and perfect. She rolled her eyes and moaned in ecstasy.

Charlie grabbed another cup, filling it from the apple cider urn. She took a careful sip and groaned. "That's the stuff. But it could use a little cinnamon." She reached into her coat pocket and pulled out a curled bit of cinnamon bark.

"You carry a cinnamon stick in your pocket?"

"In the fall? Absolutely," Charlie scoffed as if Hazel had been crazy to even ask.

Charlie stirred the cup with the cinnamon as she thoughtfully looked at the scene. "Well, here goes nothing," she said. "And I do mean nothing." Charlie walked into the footprint of the barn and sat on the ground. She took a sip from her cup and then started swirling the contents, creating an amber whirlpool inside. She stopped and looked up. "I can't do this if you're hovering."

Hazel retreated to the edge of the foundation and pretended to busy herself with the investigation documents.

Charlie resumed staring into the cup, stopping periodically to take a sip or to mutter to herself. "This is stupid," Charlie grumbled. "Maybe it's gone. My power just—poof—leaked like jelly from a doughnut."

Hazel just stayed quiet and let Charlie complain. And complain she did—in a steady stream of increasingly offensive curses. Just when Hazel thought Charlie would gain velocity and break the swear barrier, her friend fell silent.

Hazel glanced up.

Charlie remained seated on the ground and she had stopped swirling the cup. Instead, she herself was swirling, rocking back and forth.

"Charlie?" Hazel called out cautiously.

Hazel ventured closer and came around to a place where she could finally see Charlie's face. Hazel gasped. Charlie seemed to still be staring into the cup, but it was hard to say exactly where her eyes were fixed. They had gone completely white as if they were stricken with cataracts.

"Charlie?" Hazel called out, cautiously again. She'd always been told you should never wake a sleepwalker. She was never sure if that were true, but the adage came to her now, and the wisdom it offered seemed prudent in this situation too.

"The hidden shall be revealed," Charlie said, her voice shouldering its way out in a low growl. "Those that are two have become one. Those divided, whole."

A moment later, Charlie startled, gasping suddenly like a free diver surfacing. The milky haze in her eyes dissipated. Without skipping a beat, she peeked into the cup and, satisfied, took a deep sip. She looked up and, seeing Hazel, smirked. "I thought I said I can't do this if you stand so close."

"Charlie," Hazel breathed. "What *was* that?"

Charlie glanced at the cup. "Just some Bennett Farms cider."

"No, Charlie, you were in some kind of trance!"

Charlie frowned. "I was? That's embarrassing. Did I at least say anything useful?"

Hazel shook her head. "Something, yes. Useful? I'm not so sure."

"Dang."

"So how do we find this body?"

"Oh that's easy," said Charlie, casually pointing toward the corner of the barn's footprint. "It's over there." Her eyes went wide with realization and she pointed again, this time with greater force. "It's over there!" And, without skipping a beat, added, "How do I know that?!"

"Lucky guess," said Hazel, winking. "Now we just need to put our backs into it." She scanned the scene, finally spotting a couple of tools somebody had left leaning against a pile of lumber, including a shovel.

Hazel retrieved it and returned to the spot that Charlie had indicated. "You down there, Judith?" Hazel asked.

"Talking to ghosts is one thing," said Charlie, "but I'm going to have to draw the line at talking to skeletons."

"Fair enough," said Hazel, driving the nose of the shovel blade into the earth.

"I hope you have a plan B, Hazey, because people are going to start showing up soon."

Hazel chewed at her lower lip, nodding. "Though, you might want to back up a few feet."

She rubbed her hands together, wringing them together until she had summoned the telltale magical tingle to surface. Then she gripped the shovel with both hands, took a deep breath, and pushed all the energy pooling in her hand through the shovel. The earth in front of her exploded upward.

Hazel flinched and closed her eyes. When she dared to pry them back open, she saw a large island of dirt hung overhead like an impenetrable cloud.

"That is some serious Matrix-level trickery right there," said Charlie, her eyes wide as she inspected an earthworm wriggling free from the underside of the island.

"Yeah, well sometimes I get a little carried away and"—she gestured—"*this* happens."

Hazel turned her focus groundward. Her spell had gouged a deep furrow into the ground, uncovering a skeleton in tattered clothes.

Hazel sank the shovel into the earth and started down the side of the pit, but Charlie grabbed her arm. "Is that going to hold?" she asked, eyeing the hovering dirt mound.

Hazel could feel the spell tugging at her like a leash trying to slip away. "One way to find out." She shuffled down the side of the depression and crouched beside the skeleton.

Judith's skeleton.

The bones were shrouded in a cracked and dirt-caked leather bomber jacket and a pair of threadbare blue jeans. A midwife dressed like Tom Cruise in *Top Gun*? This Judith must have been a heck of a character in life. Nearby, half-buried and caked in dirt, lay a black medical bag.

Charlie called to her from the edge of the pit. "Now what?"

"I haven't the foggiest idea," said Hazel.

"You're the sleuth here," said Charlie. "How many murders have you solved now?"

"I'm not sure you could say I've solved any of them. Show me one case where I actually figured it out."

"Ronnie!"

"I believe he got the jump on me in the end."

"Cordelia! You got her *twice*!"

"She caught me off guard twice," Hazel corrected.

Charlie faltered now. "Chet?"

"He's the world's biggest jerk and I didn't even see it coming."

Charlie gnawed at her lower lip. "Well, you know what they say. Fifth time's a charm?"

Hazel chuckled. She grabbed the bag and pulled it free from its earthen cradle. "Judith was murdered the same night Juniper was born," said Hazel, trying to pry open its dirt-crusted hasp.

"Is that a big clue?" Charlie asked.

"You got me."

The hasp finally gave way. The bag's contents had held up surprisingly well, considering it had spent thirty-four years buried under a sheep barn. Hazel found a collection of medical instruments, most of which Hazel vaguely recognized from TV medical dramas, but none of which she could have named, except for the stethoscope and syringe. There were vials of assorted medicines and painkillers. And then . . .

"What the heck is this?" asked Hazel, pulling out a small plastic baggie.

"Oh hey now," said Charlie, frowning. "This is supposed to be a family-friendly establishment."

"They're . . . *feathers*?" asked Hazel, unsure if her eyes were playing tricks on her. Yet the baggie seemed to contain a handful of down.

"As in birds of?"

Hazel had never seen plumage like this before. Even as she looked at the fluff, it seemed to be shifting color from a bleached white to a powder blue. "It's hard to see," Hazel said. She held the baggie higher so it caught in the sidelong morning light. The bag erupted in a supernova of pink light. Hazel flinched instinctively and dropped the baggie.

"If these are birds feathers, then it is *rara avis* indeed."

"Come again?"

"*Rara avis*. It's Latin for 'rare bird'," said Hazel. Latin had always been a regular part of the Bennett family curriculum. While Hazel's brain had scrubbed most of her declensions and conjugations free from her brain, a few handy phrases remained.

Charlie just frowned.

"Well," said Hazel. "My mother would have appreciated the reference."

Cautiously, she opened the baggie, keeping her head back as if a live snake might spring out at any moment.

"Are you sure that's a good idea?" Charlie asked.

"No. But when has that ever stopped me?" Hazel removed a pinch of feathers and held them on her open palm. Though the morning air was still, the feathers danced and swirled about.

"Well that's just freaky," said Charlie. "Are they haunted?"

"Only one way to find out," said Hazel. "It's time to trot out a classic." She set to work casting her next spell—a simple detect magic incantation. She'd become so proficient at this one, there was little thought and effort that went into the casting. It was more muscle memory than anything, and she almost felt smug about the act. Until she saw the result. Her detect magic spell typically resulted in a range of colors, from a pure white light to indicate the general presence of magic to a deep purple for black magic. But neither color was present now. The feathers glowed a brilliant pink.

"What does *that* mean?" asked Charlie.

"I have no idea . . ."

She would need to sit down and see if the Book of Bennett had anything to say on this. But for now she needed to get going. She had a feeling she'd discovered everything she needed from here. She turned and scrambled up the side of the pit.

"Don't we need to put the dirt back?" asked Charlie.

Hazel shook her head. Instead of replacing the island of dirt, she swept her hand through the air like she was opening an invisible curtain. The dirt responded, gliding sideways so that when, a moment later, Hazel severed the tie to her spell, the earth collapsed, hitting the ground an earth-shaking thump.

"Dude, your sister is going to be ripped about that," said Charlie.

Hazel nodded. "Probably. But Judith deserves justice and a proper burial more than Bennett Farms deserves a new barn. Now when the crew gets here, they can call Detective Gibbens."

Hazel grabbed her coffee cup from the foundation and drained the already chilled liquid. Her hands were trembling, she didn't know whether from nerves or exhaustion—though it was probably a combination of the two.

"What's that?" asked Charlie. She was no longer looking at the crime scene, but toward Split Tree Hill, the top of which rose just over distant trees. A silhouette too large to be a bird but too small to be any aircraft was circling the hilltop. Hazel didn't need to see it clearly to know that it was a rider on a broom. Had they no tact? Any minute, farmhands and East Barn artisans would start arriving, and the last thing she needed was to have to explain accounts of a broomstick-riding wizard.

Hazel sucked air through her teeth. "You need to get out of here *now*."

"No way I'm abandoning you," Charlie said. "I told you we're ride-and-die kind of friends."

"Charlie—"

"To the Beetle!"

They sprinted to the VW, and Charlie flung the front of the vehicle open, where the trunk was located. "Quick, get in!" she snapped.

Hazel didn't argue. She dove headlong into the space, banging elbows and knees as she curled up small enough for Charlie to get the trunk shut. "Take me to the chapel!" Hazel called from the cramped darkness.

"That hardly seems—"

"The chapel, Charlie!"

Charlie didn't argue this time. A moment later, the driver's door slammed shut. Charlie started the car and took off, bouncing the old Beetle across the Skylark Meadow.

CHAPTER NINE

Hazel was awoken by the sound of somebody trying to get into the chapel. Judging by the dim light inside the chapel, she knew that she had slept longer than she'd intended. When Charlie had dropped her off, Hazel had locked the door, laid down on one of the pews, and despite its hard, unforgiving surface, had almost instantly fallen asleep. Now as she bolted upright, she saw that it was nearly dark again.

Had she really slept through the entire day? She'd meant to spend some time with the Book of Bennett and see if she could find any information about the strange pink light she'd detected at the crime scene. She had hoped to find Judith still here, but there'd been no signs of the spirit. Disappointed and worn down, Hazel had slumped onto a pew and slipped into a dreamless sleep.

The door rattled again.

Hazel slipped onto the floor and crawled to the end of the row. If Ryker was coming for her, she would be ready to fire the first shot. A voice in the back of her head reproached her. *Sure, and give them a real reason to lock you up. I'm sure that's just what Circe wants you to do.*

The jangling of metal sounded from the other side of the door. Were those keys? Then that meant . . .

The chapel door lurched open, spilling light into the chapel. In with it stepped somebody she'd been longing to see.

"Tyler!" Hazel shouted, jumping up from behind the pew.

Well, it isn't Merlin.

Tyler had a rooster tucked under his arm as if he was a running back cradling a football.

"And Clancy," Hazel said, a bit more subdued.

Excited to see you too.

Hazel ignored Clancy and turned her attention to Tyler. "You found my note!" she whispered.

Tyler closed the chapel door. He had changed in the month she'd been gone. His hair was longer, unshaped, like he hadn't bothered to maintain it, and he'd grown a bit of a beard, also unkempt. A series of jagged cuts ran horizontally across his face, starting at his ear and stopping just short of his eye and the corner of his mouth.

She couldn't help but gasp when she saw him. He winced and closed his eyes, turning his face to hide the wound.

"I didn't leave this time," she said.

"I knew," he said. "I know." His voice was ragged, primal in a way she'd never heard from him before.

She reached out, tucking a finger beside his chin and turning his face back to her. "You look rugged." She refused to strain the emotion from her voice.

"Beastly," he said.

She smirked.

She reached out and touched the flesh just below his cut. "You came for me."

"I failed you," he said, shaking his head.

"You never have, never will." She leaned in to kiss him. He flinched. "I'm not leaving again. Not while I still breathe. But they'll have to drag me back in a body bag next time."

If it's not too inconvenient, could you set me down? Or just kill me? I'll take my chances on getting resurrected again.

Hazel cleared her throat and couldn't help but laugh.

"What?" asked Tyler. "Is there something in my teeth?"

"Clancy would like to be unburdened."

"Oh, right." Tyler set Clancy on the floor. Her familiar strutted away indignantly.

Hazel looked at Tyler again, and without hesitating, she broke the invisible wall between them, throwing herself into him so hard he barely kept his footing. He wrapped his arms around her. She didn't cry. There was too much to notice to waste the effort on tears—the feel of him, the smell of him. Oh god, the smell of him.

"Tyler," she said delicately. "Have you showered?"

He pulled back, a guilty look flashing across his face. "I got back to the cottage and went to collect the eggs from the coop. That's when I found your note."

He fished it out of his pocket and held it up.

It wasn't much for subtly or artistry, and had Ryker found it, it would have been a serious problem. But her gamble had paid off. He was here with Clancy.

"What time is it?" she asked.

"Six forty-five," he said.

"And you *just* got home?"

He exhaled shakily. "I've been up since yesterday around this time," he said. "I was tracking some zombies through the Tanglewood. They're shockingly spry for something that moves at a shamble."

There was another gentle knock at the door, and a moment later Charlie popped her head in. "Can I come in yet or are you two still . . . reuniting?"

"Charlie!" said Hazel. "Aren't you supposed to be at the barn raising?"

"Supposed to, sure," said Charlie. "But if you will recall, you left a skeleton at centerfield and now the place is crawling with Staties. So there's been a delay of game. I went to Tyler's house and woke his lazy butt up. Told him to collect his eggs already."

Tyler blushed and looked anywhere except at Hazel. Had he lied? Hazel tried to ignore the sting she felt. She turned her attention back to Charlie.

"Juniper must be thrilled," Hazel said.

"She says this just means everything has to get done tomorrow."

Hazel smiled. "That's Juniper—always thinking in terms of solutions."

"Don't get me wrong. She was angry. I swear when she gets mad, her eyes change colors."

Hazel laughed. Charlie was dead on to make the observation. When Juniper got angry—which was a rare occurrence—her eyes seemed to brighten just a tad, like somebody had stoked a literal fire just behind her irises. "Evil Juniper," she said. It was the name she'd given Juniper when, as kids, Hazel had done something to tick off her much bigger sister. Which was often.

"So we've got ourselves another murder," said Tyler slowly.

"Five, actually," said Hazel. "Dating back to the early eighteen hundreds."

"Does this mean we have to time travel again?" he asked.

"That's what I said!" crowed Charlie.

"No need," Hazel said. "The past has come to us this time. All these undead lurking around the farm—apparently, some of them are our victims. We just need to track them down and question them. How hard can it be? They must want justice. It's almost convenient."

Tyler arched an eyebrow. "I'm not sure if convenient is the optimal word."

"Well, considering we have absolutely zero suspects and even fewer leads, we're going to call a gift."

"Maybe some things are better left buried," he said slowly, his eyes shifting again. Why was he acting so strange?

"Tyler, you can't mean that!" Hazel snapped. "If these people were murdered, they deserve justice."

"What about justice for you?" he asked. "Charlie says you spent last month in a Quark jail cell."

"I'll have to worry about that later," Hazel said. "As the Bennett witch, I have an obligation to figure this out and get the farm back into shape."

Tyler nodded. "I've spent the last few nights trying to wrangle a horde of unruly undead with Bart's help."

"Bart?" she asked. As the farm's resident vampire, Bart seemed like the least likely candidate to participate in an undead roundup.

"Juniper has shut down all farm activities past sundown, which is really cutting into Bart's bottom line. He's eager to get things back on track."

"Just seems a bit Benedict Arnold of him," she said. "Capturing other non-lifers."

Tyler shook his head. "These things aren't like Bart. Forget your mild-mannered, tax-paying, contributing members of society. Half of them are mindless and nonsensical—the other half are diabolical and vindictive. There are a pair of poltergeists that I swear are going to get me killed. They cut the brake lines on Yota and I nearly drove into the lake."

"What?! After all the money I spent getting him restored?!"

"I was fine too," he muttered. "Anyway, I've managed to wrangle a few of the slower ones. I'm keeping them in the sugarhouse until I can figure out how to deal with them. I have absolutely no clue how to deal with the spirits. Know any good exorcists?" He flashed her a goofy grin. "Though I suppose my fortunes might have changed now that my witchy sidekick is back. Impeccable timing, by the way."

"I do know how to make a stage entrance," Hazel beamed. "I've already talked to one of the victims—Judith Goodblood. She said all the other victims wanted justice too."

"Well it would be nice if they'd come looking for it so we don't have to play hide-and-seek with them," said Tyler.

There was a shimmer in the air and Theo appeared, hands folded neatly in front of him. "Good evening, young gentlewomen and gentleman. You said to work on my timing, and this seemed like a good moment to, ah, interrupt as it were."

Charlie grimaced, but held her tongue as she edged further away from Theo.

"Much better, Theo," said Hazel.

Theo smiled. "Very good, Lady Bennett. You asked me to perform some reconnaissance regarding the little problem pestering the farm. I have had some success as it were. I believe one of the spirits you seek is occupying the Carriage Barn—though I admit I was not able to get too close on account of the troubling miasma of . . . *despair* that suffocated."

"Miasma?"

"A *bad air*," he said.

"We're on a farm, Casper," Charlie pointed out. "There's bad air everywhere."

"Maybe *now* would be the best time to go investigate it," said Hazel. "If these aortically challenged things simmer down during the day and go into hiding, maybe that's the best time for a little Q and A."

"We're going to the Carriage House?" asked Charlie, her enthusiasm piqued. "Fun! We haven't played hide-and-seek there for years."

"Something tells me it won't be quite so carefree, Charlie," Hazel said.

"Suit yourself, but as soon as I see a ghost, I'm heading for my favorite hiding spot," Charlie said.

Hazel laughed. "Okay, I call shotgun." She grabbed her bag and headed for the door.

"Hazel, you can't just go traipsing around the farm," said Tyler, "even if it is for the right reasons."

"I'm not *traipsing* anywhere," she countered. "I've spent the last month contained in a jail cell. I didn't escape one jail cell just to end up in another."

"Mon amie," said Charlie, leveling an unimpressed gaze at Hazel. "Don't be melodramatic. Ty has a serious point. You came out in the daylight and nearly got your sorry butt arrested again. If you don't think your fan club is on high alert now, then you're kidding yourself."

Hazel glowered. "I suppose you're right. Sorry, Tyler."

"It's all good," he said. "We're just not interested in losing you as soon as we've gotten you back."

"So we'll wait until dark," said Hazel. She slung her satchel onto one of the pews. "Let's review the files while we wait." She conjured a ball of light and pulled out the folder.

"What's that on your neck?" asked Tyler, the pitch in his voice rising ever higher.

"Why is everyone so concerned with my neck?"

Charlie guffawed. "I *told* you it looks like a hickey!"

Hazel set the folder aside. "Okay, change of plans. Let me tell you about the time I needed to get a hickey to breathe underwater . . ."

CHAPTER TEN

Even by day, the Carriage Barn had a seriously creepy vibe. By night it was downright terrifying. It hadn't always been that way, but the Tanglewood had slowly claimed the structure over the years, and now it had been all but swallowed by the trees. Yet, something kept the forest from tearing it to pieces. It surrounded the barn but it didn't invade. All things considering, the Carriage Barn had held up pretty well against the ravages of time.

Maybe that's what made it so unsettling. It looked almost live-in ready, like at any moment the doors might open and a carriage might emerge, pulled by a full team. But no horses had been housed here in Hazel's lifetime, and the vehicles had been all but forgotten.

But tonight, as the last of the day drained from the sky and a leaden cloud cover moved in, blotting out the rising full moon, the building seemed particularly foreboding. Hazel, Charlie, and Tyler made their way down the overgrown footpath that led to the barn.

Theo had been right. There was something about the air here that was heavy, almost suffocating. Clancy, who was tucked under Hazel's arm, squirmed and shifted.

Do you feel that? he asked.

"We'd have to be dead inside not to," said Charlie, wincing at her own choice of words. Ever since her rivening accident and the emergence of her powers, Charlie had earned the unfortunate ability to hear Clancy's psychic missives.

"Let's just get this done and get out of here," said Hazel.

"No complaints there," said Charlie.

Tyler sorted through his prodigious ring of keys. Bennett Farms had no shortage of locked doors. "Figure out what all of the keys go to while I was gone?" Hazel teased.

"Not even close," he said without a shred of humor. He frantically sorted through the keys, stopping to glance nervously at the sky, wiping sweat from his forehead despite the deep chill in the air.

"Are you okay?" she asked.

He smiled grimly. "Just exhausted," he said, not a shred of conviction in his voice.

At last, Tyler found the correct key and he threw the doors open wide. Hazel conjured a light for each of them before they stepped inside.

"Is it just me or is it hard to breathe in here?" Charlie asked.

She was right. The air outside was effervescent compared to the thick, cloying miasma.

They searched the Carriage Barn, checking every nook and cranny, in every empty stall, arriving at the carriage and wagon garage. The restored carriage that had headed the farm's public grand-opening parade had found its way back here. Hazel had no doubt it would sit here again and slowly slip into decay.

"Perhaps we should check out the interior of the carriage," Tyler suggested to Hazel.

"Like the good-ol' days, I suppose," said Hazel, eyebrow arched. When they'd been teenagers, the carriage interior had been their favorite make-out pad.

"See, you're a brilliant detective," said Tyler. "You really nailed that one. Speaking of—"

"Ooookay, okay, okay," interrupted Charlie, who stood a few feet away, peering into the back of an ancient wagon. "I know we're in a carriage museum, but I'm not interested in third-wheeling *this* hard. Super happy that you two have been reunited, but if you could keep your clothes on and your minds out of the gutter for just a few more minutes, then we can remain friends."

"Message received," said Hazel.

"What exactly are we looking for?" Charlie asked.

"Something that moans in the night," said Hazel.

Tyler smirked.

"Seriously," said Charlie. "I will gladly end up in a jail cell for a month or more if that's what it takes to make you stop."

"I'm not sure what we're looking for, but I'm sure we'll know it when we find it," said Tyler. "Or hear it."

They moved on, passing through the long halls and into an open space housing canvas-covered vehicles. Hazel approached one and flipped back the canvas to reveal a classic car—a cranberry-colored Duesenberg Model J. The Duesenberg was a Prohibition Era car fit to take Al Capone for a cruise. "Tyler, it's your car."

Tyler shifted uncomfortably. "I told you—not my car."

"Oh contraire, sir," retorted Hazel. "I believe this was part of your sign-on bonus." When she and Tyler had first discovered the Duesenberg in the barn, Tyler had seriously geeked out over it. When he agreed to sign on as the farm's newest caretaker, Hazel had convinced her mother to throw in the car as a perk. Her mother had only too gladly complied. "What do I care for cars?" she'd asked.

Charlie whistled. "That is one helluva sign-on bonus, Ty."

"A sign-on bonus I roundly rejected and continue to reject," he pointed out,

"Didn't your mother ever teach you it's rude to refuse a gift?" Hazel asked.

"Hey, if neither of you want it, I could take it off your hands."

"What about your Beetle?" Tyler asked.

"That thing is a hazard on wheels," Charlie said.

"A *classic* hazard," he corrected.

"More like a classic money trap."

"Well, I'll have you know I'm more loyal than that," Tyler said. "I could never turn my back on Yota."

"Dude, it's a miracle that thing hasn't turned its back on you," muttered Charlie. "So does that mean you'll sign it over to me? I would look like a boss in this thing."

"As far as I'm concerned, it's all yours," said Tyler.

Charlie barely had time to celebrate. A deafening moan like screeching metal filled the air, so loud it felt to Hazel like she was standing in front of the speakers at a rock concert. Her bones and her organs thrummed with the vibrations. Clancy squawked.

"I'll have you know that's *mine!*" shrieked somebody. The orb of light in Hazel's hand dimmed. A choking gloom settled around them like a fog. A moment later, something shimmered in the driver's seat of the car, an ethereal wisp that thickened until at least it congealed into an entity. The apparition was of a young man dressed in an old-fashioned tuxedo, his hair slicked back like a Prohibition Era mobster, and his face fixed with dangerous arrogance.

"How did you get here?" Hazel asked.

"Some silly little girl opened the window and forgot to close it," he said, sneering. "It would seem that dealing with silly little girls is my *curse* in life. As a Northcott, I deserve better."

Northcott. This must have been the Jonathan Northcott mentioned in the file.

"I hate to break it to you, dude," said Charlie, "but you're post-life now."

"Don't you think I know that," he spat. "And how do you think I ended up like this?"

"Educated guess . . . you died?" Charlie asked.

"Of course I died!" he snarled. "All on account of two infernal women!"

"Whoa now," said Charlie.

Hazel was fuming. She'd dealt with her fair share of alpha males in her time in Hollywood, and it was hard enough to bear when the jerks were coworkers or, worse, bosses. But she was hardly going to put up with that from somebody that had both feet in the grave. Under the best of circumstances, she wouldn't tolerate this kind of crap, never mind when she was putting friends and herself in harm's way to provide said blockhead a service. "We didn't come to deal with your toxic masculinity," said Hazel.

"*Toxic what?!*" scoffed the spirit, as if he'd just heard the most absurd combination of words in the English language. The pitch of his voice had shifted, slowly climbing high until he was on the verge of shrieking.

Careful now . . . said Clancy, the warning tiptoeing into Hazel's head.

"Careful my butt," said Charlie.

"Let's settle down," said Tyler.

Jonathan shot him a look, the tough-guy persona quickly evaporating. "Don't tell me to settle down!" he shouted. The act of speaking seemed to cause him great discomfort. He put a hand on his stomach, and a moment later belched, blowing a black cloud out of his mouth. "I've been waiting years for a chance to return and avenge my murder. I'm not going anywhere again until I see some justice."

"And that's why I'm here," said Hazel. "I'm here to investigate your murder. But you're not alone. There were five others, and I have reason to believe your murders were all connected."

Jonathan looked offended at the suggestion—that his fate might in any way commingle with the plebs. "A *woman* detective?" This was more than the spirit could take. He sputtered and coughed so violently that he launched another black cloud into the air.

Charlie had to clap her hand over her mouth.

"What is her problem?" Jonathan snapped. Was he not aware that he seemed to be belching smoke? It seemed best not to put the question to the emotionally volatile spirit.

"So it's really yours," said Hazel, putting her hand on the hood of the car.

"Don't touch," Jonathan snapped. "Of course it's mine!" He sniffed with contempt. "My father had it shipped here from the city for the wedding. I was to rescue my betrothed from this meaningless existence and drive her back to New York in proper style."

Ah-ha, an opening, Hazel thought. Like all narcissists, the only window into a proper conversation was by focusing on the vain one's favorite topic of themselves. Hazel motioned to the others to back off as she reached into her satchel and pulled out the file. "You aren't Jonathan Northcott, by any chance, are you?"

"The *fourth*," he spat.

"And who was the lucky Mrs. Northcott?" she asked.

She seemed to have struck a nerve, because he stiffened and looked like *she'd* been the one belching up black clouds. "There *was* no Mrs. Northcott because the woman wouldn't take my family name. And"—he started sputtering on his own words, and the sounds that leaked out were creeping up in pitch—"can you believe she wanted *me* to take *her* name? A *Northcott man* taking the name of a . . . of a *Bennett woman*?!" He was just shy of shattering stemware at this point, so Hazel did her best to hide her smile. This sounded like the MO of a Bennett-family witch.

Oh I think I remember this guy, said Clancy. It was a rare moment for Clancy, being able to remember something that long ago. His memory was unreliable at best—a possible side effect of the curse that had doomed him to a life of seemingly endless resurrection in various animal forms. *He was betrothed to one of your ancestors. Henley Roisin Bennett, if I'm not mistaken.*

Henley. Hazel's great grandmother.

"My father had insisted we come all the way from New York City to this backwater estate so that I might do my part to 'help the family.' It was a marriage of *convenience*. Though there is nothing *convenient* about dying outside of the city."

Hazel gritted her teeth but managed to hold her tongue.

"So why'd you lower yourself enough to come? Surely there were other eligible heiresses you could have wed back in *the city*."

Jonathan glowered. "A few bad investments had put an unfortunate kink in the Northcott coffers," Jonathan explained. "The Northcotts put all of their money into *railroads*. It made us one of the wealthiest families in the country. But when the Northcott Lines were undercut and sabotaged by competitors, everything changed."

"And you came here hoping to restore your family's wealth."

"Oh please," he scowled. "I can sense your disdain and I'm here to alleviate your sense of moral outrage. Families do it all the time."

Bennett Farms had suffered many interlopers, but this Jonathan Northcott was the worst variety. The unscrupulous leech. The Bennett family had a long, proud tradition of driving away people who came to these lands for all the wrong reasons, so it made little sense that this creep had weaseled his way into marrying into the family.

Still, she would get nowhere right now by treating him like the scum he so clearly was. Hazel took a deep breath and assumed her best neutral face. She hoped she got an Oscar nomination for this performance.

"The only moral outrage is that you were murdered," said Hazel, again stroking his ego. She didn't even mention the other four. She doubted he would care, and it only stood to cloud the issue.

"Even if you had it coming," Charlie muttered just loud enough for Hazel to hear. Hazel elbowed her.

"That's . . . that's right!" Jonathan said,

"Why don't you start by telling us what you do remember?" Hazel asked.

"I have a mind like a steel trap," Jonathan huffed. "It might be easier to ask me what I *don't* remember."

"We'd settle for what you *do*."

Jonathan considered this, his lips parted and leaked another black cloud as he seemed to decide whether to take offense.

"I'd taken her for an evening stroll and we came here," he said, gesturing to the barn around her. "She suggested we hook the *buckboard* and go for a moonlit ride. *Imagine*, me steering a wagon like an inbred farmer, especially when my father had *this* shipped all the way from the city for me to impress the lady."

"Hey now," snapped Charlie. "Those inbred farmers are my friends."

"Thanks, Charlie . . ."

"Got your back, Hazey."

Jonathan sneered. "You should be more careful about the friends you keep."

Hazel bit her tongue. "Did it work?" Hazel glowered. "Did it *impress the lady*?"

"It most certainly did not! She still insisted on a carriage ride!"

"Did you go?"

"Do I look like an inbred farmer to you? And certainly *not* for the future wife of one. I demanded she heed me."

"And did she? . . ." asked Tyler, dully.

Good boy, thought Hazel. She would have to reward him for that later.

"She went without me!" he shouted incredulously, exhaling yet another horrific cloud.

"She didn't even bother hooking up the carriage. She just said something incredibly rude, climbed up on the horse in her evening gown—can you imagine?!—and rode off into the night on her own!"

Hazel grinned. Now *that* sounded like a Bennett through and through.

"I waited here for her," he said. "That's when the other woman showed up . . ."

"This just got racy," said Charlie, leaning in closer. "Go on."

Jonathan positively glowed, his chest puffing, his head held high like a rooster ready to strut.

"She asked me to follow her to the stables," he said. "And then . . . everything is difficult to recall from there. The lady asked about my betrothed. She seemed particularly upset that the Bennett woman was not with me . . ."

Something tells me he's not just trying to play the role of the gentleman, Clancy said.

"That's when my betrothed returned . . ."

"Busted," said Charlie.

"A dealbreaker for your engagement," said Hazel, "but it doesn't explain how you ended up murdered."

"When the stranger spotted my betrothed, a transformation came over her," he said.

"What kind of transformation?" Hazel asked.

"I . . . I can't recall," he said. "The memory of it is . . . unclear. When I try to think of her, I can't picture her face."

Hazel wondered if the spirits of all ghosts suffered from this sort of amnesia surrounding their demise. Judith had said the same thing regarding the circumstances of her death.

Jonathan shook his head and continued. "But what happened next I remember with perfect clarity. She grabbed a pitchfork and made to stab the young Lady Bennett with it. I . . . intervened," he said. "Say what you will of my indiscretions, but I am still a man of honor. The young lady was in peril, and I threw myself in front of her."

"I guess even the biggest jerks aren't all bad," Charlie said.

"The ladies were no doubt fighting for my love," Jonathan explained. "I have always had this effect on women."

"I take that back . . ." Charlie said.

"And then . . . then I was in a strange place," he said, shaking his head in confusion. "I tried to find my way back, but there was no *way*. How do you find your way from one nowhere to another?!" He was getting worked up again, his face turning a shade of red now like the belly of a furnace.

"I begged them but they try to keep me stuffed in a box!" he shouted. He was growing livid, the flesh around his eyes sinking until there was nothing but two black pits filled with glowing coals.

"They?" Hazel asked.

"The doormen!" he shouted indignantly, spewing puffs of black cloud. "They think they can tell me where I can and cannot go! I'm a Northcott! A *NORTH*—" Jonathan's shout was cut short as a train of black smoke, huge and billowing, poured from his mouth. Hazel slapped a hand over her mouth and nose as the smoke quickly filled the room. "Stay low!" she shouted to the others.

Tyler was the closest and his proximity seemed to have made all the difference. The cloud drove him to his knees.

"Calm down!" Hazel shouted between coughing fits. "We're here to help you."

"HELP ME?!" Jonathan shouted. "Another Bennett Farms bumpkin is the last thing I need! Now if you'll excuse me, I think I'll be taking my car and returning to the city, thank you very much!"

"Hold on a second—" Hazel started, raising her hands to try to calm him, but the spirit must have taken it as a sign of aggression. He reeled back, his mouth opening wide, stretching like a snake preparing to swallow its prey. For a moment Hazel thought that's what he intended to do, but instead he disgorged an endless black cloud that twisted and swirled around them until they were gasping for air.

"Stop it," Hazel wheezed. "Jonathan, you'll kill us . . ."

He took no notice.

Somebody finally spoke, but not Jonathan. The voice cut clear through the chaos. "If this is a bad time, I can come back."

At first, Hazel assumed another aortically challenged player had entered the stage, but that assessment quickly fell apart. The smoke parted for a moment, giving her a clear view of a man sauntering into the car storage. He was dressed oddly for a cold Vermont night— what with a bright Hawaiian shirt, a pair of wrinkled Bermuda shorts, and flipflops. But he appeared to be flesh-and-blood, and not a bit of it rotten. If anything, he was put together better than the average living human—surfer blonde hair pulled back in a high pony, cheekbones for days. When he flashed a smile, as he was most certainly doing at that moment, he showed a set of teeth so straight and white, they had to be veneers.

"Ah-ha," he said, looking at Jonathan, "here you are!" From the breast pocket of his Hawaiian shirt, he drew a pen dangling a delicate chain as if he'd stolen it from a bank. He lifted the pen over his head, swung it around once, and whipped the chain toward Jonathan. The chain erupted with fire and grew until a flaming whip stretched out and reached Jonathan. The spirit made a weak attempt to escape, but the inferno-ed chain sought him out, wrapping around him tightly. He opened his mouth to scream, but he spewed a cloud of hot embers.

With a loud crack, like thunder, the chain retracted, dragging Jonathan with it. The embers dissipated, along with the black cloud. Hazel gasp, sucking in a lungful of cold night air tinged with the scent of motor oil and old hay. She lay on the floor, panting as the man approached and looked down at her.

"Talk about your heavy smoke," he said, tucking the pen back into his pocket and flashing her a winsome smile. "Thanks for doing my work for me. Most of it, anyway."

CHAPTER ELEVEN

What do you think you're doing?" Hazel demanded, stepping toward the newcomer.

Both Charlie and Tyler reached for her, attempting to hold her back, but Hazel pulled away. She wasn't going to sit idly by and watch this guy interfere with the investigation.

The man patted his pocket and stepped forward, offering his hand. "The name's Ignatius Baker. But just call me Baker. Ignatius is too stuffy."

"We were talking to him!" Hazel exclaimed.

"And it seemed like it was going very well for you," said Baker. "Or perhaps choking on a cloud of death was part of your plan?"

"Who do you think you are?" she sputtered.

"I believe we've already covered my introduction. But you have me at a disadvantage."

"Hazel Bennett," she said. "And maybe I should have asked *what* you are."

He stopped and looked at her, his lips curling into what could have been a smirk or a sneer. Hazel couldn't say which. "Ah, a Bennett," he said, completely ignoring her question. "I should have guessed, what with that outrageous hair."

"Excuse you," she sputtered.

"And *what* I am is really not your business. Not even in the slightest."

You're a Transcendent, interjected Clancy. It was impossible to mistake the look on Baker's face now.

"That voice is so *familiar*," Baker said. "But what are you doing looking like *that*?" He chortled. "Didn't you use to be a *cat*?"

"Wait a minute," interjected Hazel. "You know each other?" Why was it every time they met an unsavory character, Clancy went way back with them?

"Forgive me for interrupting, Clancy," said Charlie, finally speaking up. "But what's a Transcendent?"

"Interesting," said Baker, stepping toward Charlie now and scrutinizing her. "This one isn't a witch and she can hear the familiar? What's her quirk?"

"I'm a black lesbian living in the middle of one of the whitest states in the Union," said Charlie. "Is that quirky enough for you?"

Baker chuckled, seemingly satisfied by the answer.

"A better question," said Hazel pointedly, "is what are *you* exactly? A Transcendent. Help a poor uneducated girl understand."

Baker sighed and shook his head in a patronizing manner. "We are the agents of the Supernals."

"Supernals?" asked Charlie.

"Relax," scoffed Baker. "You introduce two new vocabulary words and people freak out. Supernals, or as you mortals like to call them, gods.

"Supernals are gods?" asked Hazel.

"Like angels and demons?" said Tyler.

Baker laughed. "That is one popular interpretation of our race. But humans could never appreciate the subtle nuances of Transcendents. We are the mediators between the world of the living and the world of the dead. We are messengers for the Supernals, guardians, and all-around gofers. Humans have made amusing attempts over the years to understand us—most of which have failed miserably. We've been labeled as angels and demons, protectors and tempters, beings of light and beauty and monsters of darkness and horror."

Darkness and horror aren't much of a stretch of the imagination, are they?

"Would you prefer I call all familiars bird brains?"

Hey, I am not a bird.

"He's just playing the part temporarily," said Hazel.

Baker smiled, his eyes flashing gleefully. "Oh I know," he said.

Are you here solely to make fun of me or are you here to fulfill some other purpose?

"Somehow spirits like Johnny-boy here always manage to find a way to slip back out of the spirit world, and when they do, it's our job to track them back down and bring them home."

"Sounds like somebody screwed up big," Hazel pointed out.

Baker's wisecracking exterior hardened. "I don't make mistakes. *Somebody* opened a side door. Which is why *I'm* here *working*. On a holiday, no less! Can you believe that?"

"A holiday?" scoffed Charlie.

Transcendents earn days off?

"What you humans call All Hallow's Eve, we call Fall Recess. It's the one time of year when we get to kick back and relax."

"Why would you take time off during the time of year when spirits are most active?" asked Tyler.

"Oh, it can talk," Baker condescended, eyeing Tyler contemptuously. "You have it all wrong though. It's not that we have our official holiday when spirits are more likely to escape. That would be silly. It's *because* we're short-staffed that so many spirits are able to make their escape back to the world of the living. Fewer guards equals greater opportunity to escape. And, of course, which guy gets called back to clean up? Is it the other Transcendent on my rotation? Of course not! Just Ignatius Baker. After two millennia of service, you think I'd be the one to rest—that they'd send the junior agent, but *nooo*. It's not bad enough that I've rotated back to this awful backwater station, but here I am, doomed to work the holiday without so much as an extra cent. The joys of salaried employment . . ."

An idea popped into Hazel's head and she voiced it before the opportunity passed. "Is there any way I could do it for you?"

Baker snorted with laughter. "What?"

What?! echoed Clancy forcefully enough to make Hazel wince.

"You don't want to work, and I need to talk to your escapees before they return with you."

Baker scoffed. "You could hardly interview one escapee, let alone handle the lot."

"I *need* to," she said.

"I hate to point out the one problem with this plan," said Tyler. "You can't exactly walk freely around the farm at the moment. Or perhaps we've forgotten that you yourself are being hunted."

"It takes a fugitive to bring in a fugitive," Baker said.

"That sounds made up," said Tyler.

"It is," said Baker. "By me." He paused and ruminated over the complication. "I suppose if you're going to be doing my job, you can borrow my gear. Like my mask. You seem like the kind of person that could benefit from a mask on a regular day."

"Hey there," grunted Tyler.

"What is *that* supposed to mean?" Hazel gasped.

I'm starting to like this guy.

Baker grinned, glowing over the offense he'd caused. "One second," he said.

He reached up to his face and started feeling around the edges of his jaw. Hazel looked on in horror as his fingertips sank into the folds of his flesh and in one fluid motion, he peeled his face away like the rind of an orange.

The shucked layer instantly changed, any features of Baker melting away from its surface and leaving in its place a mask of carved wood. What he revealed was just as unsettling. The face hidden beneath the mask was indistinguishable. The more Hazel tried to focus on it, the less she was able to discern any features. It was like a thumb smudge on a pencil drawing or a blurry photograph.

"I know it's probably not polite to ask," said Charlie, "but exactly how many mouths do you have?!"

"You can see me?" Baker asked. "My face?"

"Can't everyone?" Charlie screwed up her face in confusion, then glanced at her companions, first to Tyler, then to Hazel.

"Interesting," Baker said slowly. "What is it you said your quirk was again?"

"She didn't," said Hazel.

Charlie gave her a quick I-got-this look and stepped forward. "I'm an oracle," said Charlie.

Baker nodded. "That makes sense. Oracles have traditionally kept the channels of communication open with the spiritual world. The Oracle at Delphi, for starters. I'd love to stand around here and talk the mechanics of the afterlife with you all day, but I've got a book to get back to and some food to eat. Did you know they sell ice cream and coffee at the barn now?"

"It's the East Barn Village," Hazel said.

Baker shook his head in disbelief. "Things change so quickly in the human world."

Without warning, he tossed the mask to her. Instinctively she caught it to keep it from hitting her in the face, but the result was the same. It was in her hands now.

"I don't want it," she said, offering it back to him.

"Take it," he said. "Use it. Don't use it. What does it matter to me? It's my holiday."

"I never said I agreed to this arrangement."

He cocked his head. "Aren't you?"

She hated to give him the satisfaction of being right and she cursed herself for raising the protest in the first place. Of course she was agreeing to it. She had to get to the bottom of these murders, and this looked like her best ticket.

"So do we have a deal?" Baker asked again.

"Hazel . . ." said Tyler cautiously.

Hazel, I don't normally agree with lover boy's judgment, but you might want to listen to him on this one. Never trust a Transcendent.

"You're going to hurt my feelings," said Baker, showing absolutely zero signs of damaged feelings as he straightened the collar of his Hawaiian shirt.

You have about as many feelings as you do morals.

"That's rich, coming from you," said Baker, positively purring at the provocation.

"I'll do the job," Hazel said. "But I'm not interested in putting on the mask."

"Putting it on is the easy part," he said, the place where his mouth might have been blurring more fiercely than the rest of his face. "Hiding behind a mask can become habit-forming. Taking them off is always the hard part."

Very deep, Socrates.

"You should know what I'm talking about," said Baker, again delighting in this. "Maybe if you do a good job," said Baker, turning his attention to Hazel once again. "I can reward you with some insight about identities."

"I've already agreed to help you," she said. "Why are you being so withholding?"

"Because some truths should have to be earned," he said, then turned his gaze upon Clancy. "And some sins should be sufficiently punished." He flashed a flippant smile, fished the pen out of his pocket, and tossed it to Hazel. "You'll probably need this, too. Good luck finding your murderer. If you need me, you know how to call."

"No," said Hazel. "I don't."

Baker considered it for a moment and then shrugged. "It's just as well," he said. "I hate being bothered." With an arrogant "tata," he nodded and stepped back into the shadows.

"Wait!" Hazel called. She ran after him, but when she stepped through the doorway into one of the long corridors of the Carriage Barn, Baker had already vanished.

Well, this is quite the mess you've gotten yourself into now.

"If you had a better way out of that, I would have loved to have heard it," said Hazel, turning the mask over in her hands. The design was plain, a wooden mask with no special markings. "What is this thing made of?" she asked aloud, tapping it with her nail.

No idea. And I'm probably better for not knowing, Clancy said. *You'd best be careful with that. No doubt it's infused with Transcendent magic.*

"How does that differ from the magic I've been messing with until now?"

Transcendent magic is right up there with fae magic as the only true forms of magic in the world, Clancy explained. *Or in the future world. You don't see that kind of magic around these parts. Witches and warlocks—even the best of them—are working on borrowed magic. That's one of the reasons Transcendents and fae are always at odds with each other.*

"At odds how?" she asked.

They've been waging a cold—and sometimes not-so-cold—war for millennia.

Hazel turned the mask over in her hand. It was warm to the touch, and yet it made her shiver. She couldn't deny that such an item would be beyond useful at the moment. Yet instead of putting it on, something made her slip it into her satchel instead. Maybe later. When she needed it.

Tyler's radio squawked and a moment later the most blessed sound came lilting through the airwaves. Never had a younger sister been so happy to hear her older sister's voice. "You there, Ty?" she asked.

"Present and ready, boss," he said.

"You need to stop calling me that."

"Then you need to stop employing me."

"Don't tempt me," came her sister's wry reply. Hazel could hear the sarcastic smirk coming through the staticky airwaves.

"Whatcha got for me?" Tyler asked.

"We've got another potential resident for the sugar shack," said Juniper.

Hazel hurried forward now and grabbed at the radio, but Tyler pulled it away and gave her a what-are-you-doing look. "I thought we were leaving family out of this for now."

He was, of course, right. She pointed at the radio.

"You still there?" Juniper asked. "Or did the undead hordes claim you?"

"I'm here," said Tyler, depressing the radio call button. "Thought I just saw a gigantic rat." Hazel punched him in the shoulder. He winced and dramatically rubbed the spot.

"Lovely," said Juniper. "Once you've got that taken care of, rumor has it there's something lurking in the woods near Petrichor House."

Petrichor House. The former farmhand lodging turned Summer of Love hippie commune turned rotten pile of lumber. Hazel hadn't been there since she'd gone gallivanting through time to rescue her nephew, solve a murder, and regain the Book of Bennett. The idea of going back after she'd seen it in its heyday had seemed wrong. She feared the place might seem . . . *dead*.

"Could we be so lucky as to bag two in one night?" asked Tyler.

CHAPTER TWELVE

I signed on for one ghost hunt tonight," said Charlie. "*One.*"

She brought up the back of the line as the three of them, Hazel and Tyler in the lead, walked a barely defined path that snaked its way along a wooded cliff's edge. To one side lay the Tanglewood, to the other, a sheer drop-off to a rocky shore and the frigid waters of Lake Champlain.

"That means I've fulfilled my contractual obligations," said Charlie. "I really should have stayed back at my car."

"We really should have brought more flashlights," said Charlie, swatting at a low-hanging branch and trying to disentangle it from her hair. "Or maybe turn on the *one* we did bring."

"We can't risk being seen," said Tyler as he picked his way through the underbrush. The path to Petrichor House was challenging even by day. At night it was positively treacherous. At this point, Hazel had lost track of the number of times she'd stumbled.

"I think we can risk a little light," said Hazel.

Tyler stopped abruptly and Hazel almost ran into him. "No way," he said. "We're not doing anything that risks losing you again."

"We get it," groaned Charlie. "You're the super dedicated boyfriend. But if I roll my ankle on another rotten log, I'm turning on the flashlight, a few tiki torches, and a pack of glowsticks."

The three pressed on in heavy silence until, at last, they crept into the overgrown clearing that was once the epicenter of Amy's coven in the summer of love.

"Did you know 'petrichor' means the smell of rain falling on dry earth?" Tyler asked.

"That's very . . . specific," said Charlie.

Hazel smiled. She had no doubt her mother had chosen that moniker for the little building.

Just for the record, said Clancy, squirming in his spot under Hazel's arm. *I'm feeling more than a little vulnerable out here.*

"Are you scared, Clancy?" asked Hazel.

"That's adorable," said Charlie, reaching over to tickle Clancy's comb for the dozenth time since they'd left the Carriage House.

If you do that again, I'll peck your fingers clean off.

"Hostile much?" Hazel asked.

Meeting a Transcendent does that to me, I guess.

"What was he talking about, Clancy?"

Honestly, I have no idea.

"Your spotty memory is getting increasingly irritating."

You think it's irksome to you? Maybe if I could remember more, I could figure a way out of this curse.

They came at last to the clearing where Petrichor House stood—or had once stood would be more accurate. The small cabin was little more than a pile of rotten timber and shingles now, the clearing little more than a lot slowly being reclaimed by the forest. On the far side of the clearing, a door was set in the side of a hillock—the entrance to a root cellar. Except that door stood wide open, barely hanging on by a single hinge.

"Do you smell that?" asked Charlie. A rancid stench filled the air. "Is it too much to ask to encounter a ghost that burps cotton candy and pukes rainbows?" she asked.

Something rustled in the brush.

"The only thing I smell is a Bennett," bubbled a voice, wet and roiling from the darkness.

"Okay," Charlie said, putting up her hands in exasperation. "I don't care if that's Godzilla hiding in the bushes. That's just plain wrong. Come on out, creeper."

The bushes shook once more before disgorging one person, then another, until a small crowd stumbled into the clearing and lurched toward Hazel and her friends.

"Charlie!" shouted Tyler, grabbing her by the wrist and pulling her back just as one person broke free from the crowd and lunged at her. Hazel rushed to meet the challenger, her palms bursting with fire.

"One step farther and I'll roast you!" she warned.

The crowd failed to heed the advice as they pressed forward, arms outstretched.

"Stop!" shouted the same gurgling voice Hazel had heard initially. The horde halted so suddenly that they swayed on the wind coming off the lake. A moment later, the cloud cover blew off, dousing the clearing in moonlight, and illuminating the horde long enough for her to get the gist of it. They were the walking dead in varying stages of decomposition. Hazel looked to Tyler. His eyes were wide and a thin sheen of sweat dripped down his brow.

Zombies.

A moment later, they shuffled aside, creating a path for a lone figure standing behind them. The newcomer was bent and twisted, its posture somewhere between a sanctuary-seeking hunchback and a gnarled apple tree. Its eyes glowed an insidious shade of red.

Hazel held her breath . . . and her ground. Just because the horde was behaving at the moment didn't mean they always would and she didn't trust it one bit. She would be ready to barbecue the lot of them if they so much as twitched the wrong way.

The figure shuffled forward now. The creature turned its face to the sky and took a deep quivering breath, revealing a grisly visage—a lipless mouth flashing a gruesome grin.

"Yes," it said. "I do *smell* Bennett." He fixed his gaze on Hazel. "It's been a long time."

"Who are you?" she asked.

He chortled, a sound that bubbled up from his throat. "I would expect nothin' less from a Bennett," he said, "than to not recognize those *beneath* them."

"Does that mean you're not going to answer the question?" asked Charlie.

The creature noticed her for the first time and snarled at the intrusion. "Even with friends, you're still outnumbered. I should have my companions turn you into a feast. What is it they say now? Eat the rich?"

Charlie cleared her throat. "Just for the record, my butt is broke and I eat a lot of baked goods, so you're not exactly going to get the choicest cut, if you catch my meaning."

Hazel gritted her teeth. "Listen," she said. "I don't know what Bennetts you had to deal with in the past, but the farm isn't what it used to be. We've tried—my *sister* has tried—to turn this into a place for the people. The community."

Suddenly, it dawned on Hazel, who she was talking to. She grabbed at her satchel, perhaps a little too quickly. The horde of zombies seemed to interpret it as an act of aggression, moaning uneasily and taking a step forward. Hazel put her hands up in a show of innocence. "You're Orion Livingston," she said.

The creature started to slow-clap, but the impact proved catastrophic and a finger or two fell into the underbrush. "You deign to learn the help's name."

"You were the first caretaker of Bennett Farms."

"*Caretaker?* I was the Bennett Farm's first *custodian*. I was its guardian and I paid the heavy price the Bennett family required to enter their world. To protect their secrets. But I learned it was a prison. That's what the wealthy always want you to think, isn't it? That they're gracing you with privilege when really they're grinding you under their bootheel?"

Hazel tried to carry forward the lesson she had learned with Jonathan. "You're right," she said, biting her tongue. "You were wronged, but I'm here to deliver you justice."

"Oh?" Orion laughed, gurgling again. "Can you give me back the life the Bennetts stole from me?" He stepped forward, and his zombies followed in lockstep, shrinking the circle that Hazel and her friends stood in.

"No," she said. "I can't. But I can catch the person that ended it. I'm here to find your murderer." Whatever monstrous form Orion was in now, he'd once been a human. And his life had been mercilessly and nefariously cut short. "I'm here to solve your murder."

Orion was quiet, his dead eyes examining Hazel and her companions. His horde of zombies continued to sway behind him.

"We're just here to ask questions," Hazel said. But that wasn't entirely true, was it? She had made a deal with Baker, and as soon as she was done questioning Orion, she had an obligation to catch him.

"What year is it?" Orion suddenly demanded.

"Two thousand nineteen," said Hazel slowly.

The answer hit Orion like a punch in the face. The pinpoints of light in his eyes flickered. "Has it been that long?" He seemed unable to square away that reality.

"That's a long time to go without justice," Hazel said. "Why don't you start by telling me what you remember?"

"How far back should I go?" he asked.

"Oh god," muttered Charlie. "I sense a flashback coming on . . ."

"The Bennetts appeared here as if overnight," he said. "Where they came from was just as mysterious as how they gobbled up all of this land so easily. They had no roots and yet overnight they had their fingers in everything. It was like they came here on a mission. Like they *knew*."

"What does this have to do with how you got offed?" Charlie began, but Orion silenced her with an aggressive step forward and a flaring of his eyes.

"Everything," he snarled.

"The Bennetts didn't just come here to Vermont and take up residence on the land," said Orion. "They were *invited*."

"By whom?" Hazel asked. "And why?"

"That's the crux of the whole thing," he said. "It's the first secret the Bennetts kept. And it's Bennett secrets that have brought nothing but misery to those around them."

"Who?" Hazel asked again.

"The man who built the maze," Orion said, grinning a horrible grin.

Hazel's blood ran cold. The maze. Surely he meant the hedge maze that had once stood at the farm's center. It appeared on old maps and had even stood, in some form or another, until the mid-1900s. By that point, it had long passed its prime—overgrown in some places and dead and withered in others. The farm's last caretaker, Ronnie Skilton, had razed most of it to the ground. Now only a few scant pieces of shrubbery were all that was left, their skeletal remains scattered in the woods that hemmed the base of Split Tree Hill. Hazel had never seen the maze, but that hadn't stopped it from regularly starring in her nightmares since she'd returned home.

"You know who built it?!" Hazel asked, unable to maintain her composure.

Orion stopped and grinned, the flame in his eyes burning brighter than ever. The source of his mirth was clear: He enjoyed having something that Hazel desired so badly.

"The man of the Postern," Orion said.

"*Merlin?!*" she shouted so loudly that it set the zombies to shuffling like a flock of chickens.

"That's the one," he said, smirking. "He was a constant presence in the early years."

"Merlin invited the Bennetts to live here?" she asked. "But why?"

"Come now," said Orion. "Think about it."

"Because we have the Knack?" she asked.

He chortled, a violent, full-bodied action that brought with it another round of spasming and another dousing of whatever liquids churned inside Orion. "No, the *other* thing."

Hazel didn't like this dynamic at all. Orion had something over her, over the Bennetts, and Hazel was completely in the dark.

"What other thing?" she asked, an awful feeling growing in the pit of her stomach. She thought of her conversation with Cass. What secret had the Bennetts buried so deep that even the Bennetts didn't know about it anymore?

"Are we sure we want to solve this guy's murder?" asked Charlie.

"Charlie!" Hazel reprimanded.

"Just saying . . ."

"Orion," snapped Hazel. She was done stepping gingerly around him for reverence of the service he'd once done her family. It was clear Bennett Farm's first caretaker had a huge chip on his shoulder. If her time in Hollywood had taught her one thing—it was that somebody with a grudge was usually looking for revenge. "I'm here to help you, but if you just want to play games, maybe we're done here."

She slipped her hand into her jacket pocket and closed it around Baker's pen.

Orion sniffed the air again. "I can smell that secret on you," he said. "Why don't you ask mother about it?" He sniffed again. "Because she's been keeping it."

Hazel pulled the pen out and brandished it overhead, wishing she'd asked Baker for a quick tutorial. But the pen knew what to do.

"You tricked me!" Orion growled. "I should have known not to trust a Bennett!"

"This is your last chance!" she shouted. "Either you let me help you, or I'm sending you back to where you came from."

"Just like a Bennett," he hissed.

Whatever invisible bond had been holding back the horde of zombies broke, and a gnashing, groaning, pile of rotten flesh pressed forward. There was no time for Hazel to think. "Get down!" she shouted to the others.

She didn't have time to think about how it might work. She whipped the pen around her head like she'd seen Baker do. The chain roared to life with a burst of ethereal flame and stretched, lashing each of the zombies in turn. As it struck each of the shambling entities, the chain came away with a ghostly veil of material attached to it.

Once it had made a full revolution, the chain immediately retracted toward the pen, dragging the bouquet of souls with it. Hazel flinched as the glowing mass hurtled toward her.

She closed her eyes, awaiting an impact that never came. When she opened her eyes again, she saw that the corpses hovered in place, teetering precariously until a gentle breeze sifted through the clearing, and they all dropped to the ground.

Charlie climbed to her feet. "I always knew the pen was mightier than the sword, but that's ridiculous." She saw the zombies stacked like cordwood and grimaced. "Ugh. Cleanup on aisle seven."

Hazel held up the pen and looked at it, but it just looked like a regular cheap plastic pen. "Are they in there?" she asked. "Their . . . essence?"

I have no idea how the mechanics of it work, Clancy said.

"Doesn't that unnerve you?" Charlie asked.

Hazel didn't have time to be unnerved. Between her fleeing from the Wands, the undead outbreak on the farm, and the quintuplet of murders, she had a growing sense that she was decidedly not in control of any of these events. Hazel frowned as she looked towards the vanquished pile of undead.

"Why are you so miffed?" Charlie asked.

"Because I needed to ask him more questions!" said Hazel. "That wasn't nearly enough information."

"That dude had a bad attitude," said Charlie. "He needed to go."

You did what you set out to do, what Baker should have done.

"Wait," said Hazel, turning circles. "Where is Tyler?"

CHAPTER THIRTEEN

Charlie popped her Beetle into neutral, cut the engine and the lights, and rolled to a stop along the edge of the North Track. "We need to find Tyler," Hazel said. "We . . . we have to go back."

How are you going to do that in the middle of the night? Clancy asked.

"I . . . I don't know," Hazel sputtered. "Maybe the Book of Bennett has something to say about tracking spells. Or maybe I can figure it out myself. I've improvised spells before, right? Maybe I just need an article of clothing Tyler's worn recently. That's how bloodhounds do it, right?" She could sense that she was spinning out now, losing control, but she didn't have the mechanism to stop herself.

Charlie reached out and put a hand on her shoulder. It was the anchor Hazel needed. For the moment, the world stopped free falling. "You did what you could," Charlie said. "We looked for three hours. He wasn't there."

"Then *where* did he go, Charlie?" Hazel demanded.

"I don't know," Charlie answered softly. "But we have to let it go for tonight. Maybe there was a stray zombie on the run and he went after it."

Hazel nodded slowly. It sounded plausible. And seeing as how neither of them had a way to call him at the moment—on account of Charlie being staunchly anti-cellphone and Hazel's having been devoured by a cupboard—there was no way to check on him for now.

"But what if he's the next target?" Hazel asked.

Charlie was quiet. "Then we need to figure this out," she said, her tone soft but resolute.

"So what do we know?" Hazel asked. "Five murders spread over a hundred and fifty years and repeating every thirty-four years to the day. We need to assess our suspect list."

"I hate to ask a stupid question . . ." started Charlie.

History would suggest otherwise, said Clancy.

Charlie gritted her teeth and ignored the jab. "Do we even have any suspects at this point?"

Sure we do, said Clancy. *Everyone that is old enough to have committed the murders.*

"Come again," Charlie said.

We have a killer that is particularly long in the tooth. Which is good news. Few things can live that long, so it really narrows down our list of potential suspects. We're most likely looking for an undead, a Transcendent, or a fae. They're the only things that could possibly live that long.

"You forgot cursed familiars," said Charlie.

Wait, what?

"I'm not saying you did it, KFC," she said, "I'm just saying if we're putting together a list of possible suspects based on longevity . . ."

You can question me all you want, but even if I am the murderer—and I'm not saying it isn't possible—I'm going to prove to be an extremely unreliable interviewee considering the significant gaps in my memory. Besides, didn't both the spirits say that they were murdered by a woman? Wouldn't that count both me and Bart out?

"Perhaps," Hazel said, rejoining the conversation. "But I've been thinking about it. I think there are ways around your memory lapses. And I think we both agree there could be huge benefits to dredging up some of the sludge in that skull of yours."

You put it so warmly.

"Maybe there's something in there about the murders that would be of use," she said, reaching out to pat him on his comb. Clancy nervously ducked.

And how do you propose we do that?

"Cass mentioned that an oracle's powers include—"

A memory dredge?! Absolutely not!

"You've heard of it before."

Heard of it? Yes. Witnessed it? No. Want to be the recipient of it? Never.

"Care to let the oracle in on this?"

"I saw Cass on the night of my escape and she mentioned she was helping . . . somebody with memory retrieval using her oracular powers. She mentioned it was something that came as part of the oracle package."

"So, in theory, I could do it?" asked Charlie.

"Reason would stand."

No, reason does not stand. Reason sits. Reason should maybe lie down and take a nap. Cass may seem like a harmless gramma, but she's one of the most powerful oracles of her time. What's more, she's experienced and has received training. Even then, performing a memory dredge is incredibly risky. One misstep could, best-case scenario, leave the subject a catatonic vegetable for life.

Charlie grimaced. "Yeesh. What's the worst-case scenario?"

Their head implodes.

Charlie frowned. "We need to work on your understanding of best- and worst-case scenarios." She turned to Hazel. "Hazey, it's possible this would be a good solution, but this doesn't sound like something I'm ready for. I can't even look into a glass of water these days without feeling a little uneasy. I'm not ready to perform some sort of psychic surgery."

"Then it seems we're at an impasse," she said.

We still have two more spirits to wrangle. The poltergeists. Perhaps they'll yield more answers.

"Yes, the mischievous ghosts should be more helpful," said Hazel sarcastically. "Our victims have given us nothing but more questions. I liked these investigations better when we had a true list of suspects."

We really shouldn't be sitting at the side of the road this long, said Clancy. *The Wands are still searching for you.*

"You should just come home with me," Charlie said. "The Wands sure as heck aren't going to look for you in a one-bedroom apartment."

"I couldn't, Charlie," Hazel said. "I've already endangered you enough. And . . . I need to be here if Tyler comes back."

Charlie stared at her long and hard. Finally she sighed. "At least let me carry your groceries."

Hazel eyed her. "What are you talking about?"

"You didn't think I was going to let my main squeeze go hungry, did you?" Charlie twisted around and retrieved a brown paper grocery bag from the back seat.

"Charlie, you didn't—"

"I did. You've got yourself a fresh loaf of sourdough in there, a jar of peanut butter, and some of Mama Campbell's homemade raspberry jelly. That's your dinner, and maybe your breakfast. You're a grown woman, you can figure out what to eat and when. Also, I put a few Snickers, and a bottle of wine—a Lambrusco, which everyone knows pairs best with PB and J."

Hazel burst out laughing. "Thank you, Charlie. I needed a good meal and a good laugh."

Charlie leaned in and pressed her forehead to Hazel's. "We'll find him," she said.

They got out of the car and headed down the nearby footpath, quiet except for the soft scuff of their shoes. On the inside, Hazel was a cacophony of clashing thoughts and ideas as her mind flitted from one thing to another. Her father. These murders. Tyler. Clancy. Halloween. She sensed strings were connecting all of them—a spiderweb in the dark—but she couldn't see how.

They came to the chapel yard and Charlie stopped in her tracks.

"I can take it from here, Char," said Hazel.

"I'm good," Charlie said, "scanning the cemetery. I just wanna make sure I know where any ghosts are at."

Sure enough, Hazel spotted a few glowing apparitions wandering around the far side of the cemetery near the mausoleum.

"You can go back if you want," Hazel said.

"Nope. I'm seeing my best girl to her doorstep."

Hazel smiled and set out for the chapel. She eyed the graves that had been disturbed by the rising dead—no doubt the additional holes had been burrowed by Orion's horde. "We're going to need to find a way to reinter those bodies," Hazel said thoughtfully.

"That sounds like a job for your man, Tyler," said Charlie. "Maybe that's why he ran away into the night."

"Oh, you will be doing hard labor," said a voice from above. "It just won't be on *this* side of the Postern." A dark shape dropped from the chapel roof and landed deftly in front of them. Tall and lanky, like a skeleton, broom in one hand and wand in the other. The moonlight was enough to make out his distinguishing features.

Ryker.

"I have to hand it to you," Ryker said. "You've given us a run for our money so far. But the road ends here. You will—*both* of you—be coming with me."

"Who's this dude?" Charlie asked.

"I am Ryker Flint, Wand of the Council of Quark, and I have been charged with arresting Hazel Bennett and everyone aiding her flight from the law. I demand that you identify yourselves."

Ah-ha, so he didn't know who Charlie was. If Hazel could just keep it that way . . .

"Ryker, there is something bigger at play here than just my guilt or innocence," said Hazel, stepping forward now to draw his attention.

"That is *exactly* what is at stake, my dear," retorted Ryker. "I will return you and see justice done."

You're calling that justice, Ryker? Or is it just Circe Strange's version of it?

"It's not my job to question," said Ryker. "I'm just here to carry out the order of the council."

So you're a puppet.

"I am loyal," he said.

Blind loyalty goes hand in hand with puppetry.

"Keep your *chicken* quiet," sneered Ryker. Before Hazel could reply, Ryker made his move, falling sideways onto his broom. It lifted him from the ground and pulled him skyward. He arced back downward, bringing himself on a collision course with Hazel. She barely jumped aside in time, leaving Ryker to grasp at empty air as he zipped by.

Run, Hazel. You don't want to mess with Ryker. I've seen him at work over the years.

"You can remember *that* but you can't anything about this case?" Hazel shouted as she whirled around to face Ryker.

An epiphany struck her. "That's it, Clancy! Your memory is only shoddy when it comes to intimate details of your own life! Maybe that's part of your curse!"

Now is hardly the time!

Ryker swooped back around again. This time he had his wand drawn.

Hazel's hand closed around the pen. She had no idea what effect this would have on a living person, but she was about to find out. She withdrew the pen from her pocket and with one swift motion, whipped the chain through the air. It caught the tip of the broom handle and quickly snaked around it. Before Ryker could react, Hazel yanked hard on the pen, snapping the broom in two and sending Ryker hurtling through the air. He slammed into the scaffolding that surrounded the chapel and then fell to the ground in a heap.

This might not do wonders for proving your innocence.

"Is he dead?" Charlie asked.

Clancy strutted across the grass and hopped atop Ryker's body. *Alas, no. Just knocked senseless.*

Hazel let out a long shaky breath. She had reacted instinctively, defending herself, but the results had nearly been catastrophic.

Might I recommend you find a new hiding place? Something tells me they're going to call in the cavalry after this one.

"Great," muttered Hazel. She hurried over to Ryker and searched around until she found his wand resting in the grass. She picked it up and tucked it inside her satchel.

"Let's go, Foghorn," she said.

"Where are you going?" Charlie asked.

"I don't know. Somewhere that's *not* here. You should do the same. You heard Ryker. If he figures out who you are, he'll arrest you too."

"So what is your plan?" Charlie asked. "Just keep running?"

Hazel faltered. Honestly, she didn't know. Even if she wasn't guilty of the trumped-up charges that Circe had pinned on her, she was undoubtedly guilty, as Clancy had pointed out, of assaulting a Wand of the Council. "I'll figure something out," Hazel finally said.

"That's it," said Charlie. "You're coming with me. Get in the Beetle—we're going to my place."

CHAPTER FOURTEEN

Welcome to mi casa," said Charlie, hip-checking the door open.

"I still think this is a bad idea," said Hazel. "This is needlessly endangering you, Char."

"Endangering? Maybe. Needless? Not a chance."

Charlie fumbled the lights on. Somehow this was the first time that Hazel had been to Charlie's apartment, an old carriage house just outside the center of Larkhaven that had been converted into an apartment. The older couple that rented it to her lived in the main house next door, a Victorian mansion that had seen better days.

"It's adorable, Charlie," said Hazel.

"Oh knock it off," said Charlie. "It's claustrophobic and you know it. Let's just say making the dough isn't the same thing as bringing the dough home, if you know what I mean."

"Charlie, I always know what you mean."

But the apartment *was* adorable, even if it was a bit cramped. Hazel recognized Charlie's touch in every facet of the apartment, from the vibrant choices in paint to the decor that gave off a sort of Arabian Nights vibe.

A moment later, Aashvi shuffled in from the bedroom, dressed in a pair of flannel pajama pants and an oversized T-shirt and rubbing sleep from her eyes. "I was just getting ready to call Gibbens," she mumbled. "Did you two have any luck?"

"It was a mixed bag . . ." said Charlie, carefully.

"Is it something we can hash out?" she asked. "I can get my laptop. I've got this program that would be great for sketching out details."

"That's very kind of you, Aashvi," said Hazel, "but I'm more of a pen-and-paper kind of gal."

Aashvi nodded. "Of course," she said. She hurried back into the bedroom and for a moment, Hazel thought she had offended her, but Aashvi returned a moment later with a pad of paper and a pen. "Use the medium that works best for you. It works pretty well for witchcraft and writing. If you need me, I'll be unconscious. Good luck." Aashvi disappeared back into the bedroom.

"What should I do with the rooster?" Hazel asked, nodding at the bird under her arm. Clancy, as best she could tell, was sound asleep, head tucked under his wing.

"Put him somewhere he won't poop on my furniture."

"How about the bathroom?"

Charlie frowned. "Fine."

Hazel set him on the shower curtain.

What's going on? he asked sleepily.

"Nothing," she said. "Just go back to sleep."

He dutifully complied and Hazel rejoined Charlie.

"I'll take the couch," said Hazel.

"Let me get you some pillows and sheets."

"No need," said Hazel. "I slept all day, remember? Even if I wasn't buzzing from everything that happened today, I don't think I would be able to fall asleep. Besides, I've got some serious reading to do." She patted her satchel.

"You need anything?" Charlie asked.

Hazel shook her head. "I'll be fine, Char. Thank you for everything."

"Help yourself to anything. What's mine is yours dans la maison, and all that."

Charlie said goodnight, and within minutes gentle snores emanated from Charlie's room. Hazel checked in on Clancy once more and found him roosting on the curtain rod just as she left him.

"Time to get to work," Hazel said to herself. She put on a kettle, and once she had a hot cup of green tea, she placed her satchel on the coffee table in the living room, got comfy on the floor, and set to work.

Hazel emptied the satchel and arranged its contents on the coffee table. The Book of Bennett, the folder her father had given her, the mask, and the plastic baggie she'd discovered in Judith's medical bag. She pushed both the mask and the baggie to the corners of the table and placed the book, folder, and her notebook front and center. She reached into her pocket and fished out Baker's pen and set that next to her notebook.

There were so many details to keep straight, so she started writing. But as she jotted down the details, only one consistent piece of evidence came to the forefront. It was clear there was going to be a murder on Halloween, and the most likely victim would be a Bennett—or somebody close to the Bennetts. The evidence seemed to be pointing toward the same truth: people were dying because of a Bennett-family secret. This didn't sit well with Hazel. She took a nervous sip of her tea and faltered again when it came to considering her suspects. Clancy had mentioned the most likely suspects could be divvied into three categories, so she jotted that down now. Undead? Bart. Transcendent? Baker. Fae? She stopped. Did she really know anyone that was fae? She'd only had a handful of encounters with the butterfly-winged creatures. One that had sat on the Quark Council, and the other was Calluna, one part of the trio of Wands currently hunting her down. She wrote it just in case, though she knew right off the bat that it felt wrong.

In fact, none of them felt right.

She tapped the pad with her pen and then wrote one more thing—"Clancy?"—and underlined it three times. Somehow he was enmeshed in this. "I will not be blindsided again," she whispered to herself.

She set the notebook aside and opened the Book of Bennett. It was good that she had a long night ahead of her. While most books were designed to facilitate easy reading, the Book of Bennett seemed to have been custom crafted to confound, confuse, and conceal. If it wasn't the near-impossible-to-read handwriting, then it was the liberal use of foreign language—everything from French to Latin to Ancient Greek—and the unapologetic employment of codes and ciphers. The overall message was clear: Idiots need not apply.

She had some familiarity with the book already. Yet despite her efforts, she found no mention of a pink light—or any light for that matter. The book seemed shockingly sparse on detect magic details. Hazel would have to fix that once she'd gathered more field data. It would be her first contribution to the Book of Bennett—a reference chart for magical light. The feng shui of detect magic.

There was no time like the present to take notes for her contributions. She'd need to cast the spell again on the feathers and get some details on the exact shade. Hazel bounced into the kitchen, looking for a bag of flour or sugar to steal a pinch from and was dismayed to find Charlie's cupboards were barren of essential baking ingredients. It was plentiful in Ramen, minute rice, and sleeves of Oreo cookies. Hazel was horrified.

She at last found a canister of Folgers Instant Coffee Crystals. "Ew, Charlie, say it ain't so," Hazel bemoaned. She scooped enough to create a small pile in her palm and returned to the living room, cast her detect magic spell, and blew the coffee crystals over the table. Folgers might not work wonders for properly perking her up in the morning, but it did the trick for waking up the magic inside the feathers again.

They pulsed with the same pink light they had the first time Hazel had cast the spell. But this time it wasn't the pink light that got her attention. Her eyes were drawn to the brilliant, almost-blinding golden light shining from the mask on the opposite corner of the coffee table.

Clancy had said the mask was filled with Transcendent magic. Hazel made a note. "Gold = Transcendent." Below it, she wrote, "Pink =" and paused.

Equals what?

She took the feathers from the baggie and placed them in her open palm. Why had Judith kept these in her bag? She still needed to find her spirit again. She'd made a deal with Baker to capture her, but Hazel refused to do so until she got the information she needed.

She slapped her notebook down on the table in frustration. She needed to take a walk.

Outside, the air was cold and crisp and mercifully devoid of Wands. The moon was full, and somewhere in the distance, something howled a long mournful lament.

Hazel paced the driveway in front of the carriage house, growing more frustrated with each passing moment. She shouldn't be here right now. She should be back on the farm working to solve this mystery. No book would give her the answers she needed, and no pen would solve the mystery for her.

Maybe she could take Charlie's car and come back for her in a few hours when she'd need to get to work. Hazel hurried back inside, intent on swiping Charlie's keys from the kitchen counter, but she got no farther than the living room.

The glow from the feathers and the mask were still going strong, and they acted like twin spotlights on the ghostly performance now playing out on the coffee table. Baker's pen hovered over her notebook, tip pressed to the page as it slowly scratched out a message in a continuous line of golden ink.

Hazel looked on incredulously as the pen completed its message, drifted aimlessly for a moment, and then plopped down on the table exactly where she had left it. She waited a moment to make sure it didn't move again and then snatched up the notebook.

A single word was written on the page.

SERA.

CHAPTER FIFTEEN

Hazel dreamed.

A familiar dream that was somehow new and urgent every time. It was the only dream where she was distinctly aware she was dreaming and yet completely unable to wake herself.

It was nighttime and she was lost. As usual, thick hedges towered above her, wrapped around her, snaking away in all directions. She was once again lost inside the giant hedge maze. Some part of her brain snarled in protest. "No," she said, and then repeated herself, louder, shouting into the void, "No! I'm not going to do it this time. I'm not running your maze!" She didn't know who she was yelling it to, but it didn't matter. She felt confident that she was heard.

She crossed her arms and sat on the ground, and though she was vaguely aware that she looked like a pouting toddler, she didn't care. She wasn't going to play this game again. No more endless wandering in the maze while being stalked by the terror du jour. She was just going to sit here and wait for the inevitable tsunami of pink light that would carry her back to the waking world.

But the dream had other plans.

The ground beneath her feet suddenly shifted. She looked on in horror as the earth seemed to bubble and boil, pitch and heave, as if Mother Earth had eaten something that did not agree with her. She wanted to jump clear but she couldn't find firm enough footing.

The ground erupted, and a half dozen skeletal hands sprouted upwards, each one grasping at Hazel's leg. She gritted her teeth and kicked them away.

"Fine," she muttered, and started running. She rounded a bend in the maze and nearly tripped over a rooster who was scratching at the ground. Clancy was here? Clancy *never* appeared in these dreams.

"Clancy!" she shouted. But if it was Clancy, he wouldn't say. Mostly he seemed annoyed that his scratching had been disturbed. Sensing a threat, he responded accordingly, puffing up his chest and strutting aggressively.

Hazel looked back over her shoulder. Somebody else was strutting toward her too. A flock of skeletons clattered forward, stretching their brittle arms out to grasp her.

She didn't have time for this baloney. She scooped up the nonverbal Clancy and again started running.

We need to find it, Clancy said, suddenly finding his psychic voice.

"Find *what?!*" she asked.

Find . . . he paused, his presence lingering in her brain like a sustained exhale. *I don't know . . . I can't remember . . .*

She gritted her teeth again. "Not the time for your selective amnesia," she said.

Clancy failed to reply.

Hazel looked down and realized she was no longer carrying a rooster, but a mouse. The rodent squirmed and tried to escape her hands, but she held on and planted him firmly on her shoulder, where he seemed content to gnaw on the threads of her sweater.

Hazel was off and running, ducking through archways and turning blindly around bends and twists in the labyrinth.

Where are you going? Clancy asked.

Hazel looked to her shoulder, displeased that Clancy was asking a question to which he should have known the answer. Clancy the mouse was gone, replaced with Clancy the cat, the two-tailed, two-eared version of Clancy that had served her family for generations.

"Maybe if you could figure out what you actually *are*, you could figure out what you *know*," she snapped.

She took another turn in the maze, crossing a small stone footbridge.

Up ahead stood an archway out of which spilled a dazzling pink light. Her breath caught in her throat. At last—she had found it. Somehow she knew she had found the center of the maze. The prize around which the entire maze had been constructed.

Hazel approached the archway, stopping just in front of it, and letting the warm tingle of the light wash over her.

Careful, Clancy said. *I'm not sure this is a good idea.*

Of course this was a good idea! She'd been searching for the center of this maze for . . . *forever* it seemed. Hazel looked over at him if only to better chastise him. Clancy the cat was no longer perched there. In his place squirmed a majestic bird of prey. Was that a hawk? An eagle? Falcon? She had no idea.

"I know it's Halloween but you might need to slow down on the costume changes."

Clancy didn't reply again. He simply shifted his weight, digging his talons into her flesh as he tried to find a comfortable purchase. Hazel sensed that he had somehow become lost in the transformations—that with each progressive transformation, he was drifting farther from whoever or whatever he had once been. Not a cat, not a mouse, not a rooster. Not Clancy.

"Easy there," she said, stroking the gray feathers on his back.

Something shifted in the passage behind her and she turned back. A shadowy mob of zombies rounded the corner behind her, filling the passage from hedge to hedge.

Hazel stepped into the center of the maze.

She was awash in blinding pink light. She held her breath and waited for the dream to end, as it always did when the tsunami of light washed over her. But the ending didn't come. The light, though painfully intense, didn't shove her back into the waking world. Here at its source, it was more than just a light though. It was an energy. A sound. A sensation. A humming vibration that set her teeth, her bones, her organs to humming.

She was safe here. She could sense that. The undead that had chased her could not enter this place. Though it was uncomfortable, she walked deeper into the light. The sensation grew, like putting her hand closer to a fire: simultaneously pleasant and painful.

She stepped forward and something soft caressed her face. She waved her hand through the air and caught it. A downy feather. She squinted into the light and saw that the air was filled with them—feathers all adrift like dust motes. She moved deeper into the light.

There was something there, in the center of the light. She could sense that. There was something there. An underlying throb of sound, like a subsonic tone. A television with the sound muted. Rhythmic. Like a drumbeat. A *heart*beat.

"Clancy, what is that?" she asked.

She looked to Clancy again, but he was gone. No rooster, no cat, no mouse, no bird. He had disappeared entirely, leaving behind a dark smudge in the air.

"Clancy?"

The smudge shifted, stretched its boundaries—seemed almost to be yearning to take some other shape—but it failed each time.

She took another step and instead of finding steady ground, her foot found nothing but empty air. She pitched forward and suddenly she was falling. She plummeted, the light and the rhythmic beating growing louder until they had swallowed her entirely.

CHAPTER SIXTEEN

Hazel woke with a start . . . and a serious backache to boot. It turned out Charlie's couch, a cute little mint-green sectional, was a lot better for sitting on than sleeping. The apartment was still dark, but Charlie now stood over Hazel, shaking her awake.

"Dude, are you okay?" Charlie asked.

"Maybe," said Hazel, rubbing the sleep from her eyes. "I don't know."

"It was that dream again, wasn't it?"

Hazel just nodded. How could she explain that the dream had somehow raised the stakes?

Clancy squawked and fluttered through the bathroom doorway, tumbling across the hardwood floor in a clatter of talons.

"Rough landing, Clancy," said Charlie.

These wings are rubbish, Clancy grumbled.

"I'll have to work on upgrading my digs to be more poultry friendly," said Charlie dryly. "But today we have a barn raising to attend. Speaking of, I need to be on the road in fifteen to get refreshments going. Hazey, feel free to kick around here today if you want—just don't eat my entire stash of chocolate."

"I'm coming with you," said Hazel.

"Come again," said Charlie, her jaw dropping.

What?! echoed Clancy.

"You didn't think I was just going to wait in the wings, did you?" Hazel asked. "Tomorrow somebody is going to get murdered unless I can figure this out. I have to go, even if it puts me in danger."

"You don't know that for sure," said Aashvi as she shuffled out of the bedroom and into the kitchen.

"Coffee before you go?" Aashvi asked, pulling a can of Folger's crystals out of the cupboard and giving it a shake.

Hazel cringed. As a member of a family with a history of wealth and a celebrity who'd made her own small fortune in just a few years, Hazel had spent a lot of time and energy ensuring she did not slide into a morass of snobbery and elitism. She liked to think she did a pretty good job. She shopped at Old Navy. She mended her clothes when they needed fixing. She even clipped coupons on occasion. But she drew the line at coffee. This was the one domain where she refused to bend. Give her organic fair trade or give her death.

She kept those thoughts to herself right now. Instead she offered Aashvi a polite smile. "No thanks. I'm going to see if I can score a cappuccino at the Cup and Crumb. But while we're on topic, what's with the barren cupboards? I would have thought a professional baker would have a fully stocked larder."

Charlie leaned back into the room. "No way, no how!" she interjected. "I bake all day, every day. No way I'm coming home to do more of the same. Mama always told me never do what you're good at for free." Her message delivered, she again disappeared into the other room.

An uncomfortable quiet settled in the living room.

"Are you guys suggesting I take the chance?" Hazel asked. "What if we're wrong? Somebody dies and—what—we have to wait another thirty-four years to catch this killer? Could you live with yourselves if we could have prevented it?"

They remained quiet.

So what's your plan? Just skulk around the farm like a burglar?

"Nope. I'm going to waltz right out in the open." She pulled the mask out of her satchel and held it up. "It is almost Halloween, after all."

Hazel, no.

"Why not?"

Because it's incredibly dangerous! Transcendents can't be trusted. Humans don't call them demons for nothing, you know.

"Yes, but they also call them angels, no? Heaven forbid anyone judge humanity by the worst of us.

Maybe they should . . .

"Well, I'm not going to be a pessimist," Hazel said, "and I'm not at the liberty to pass up the best tool I have for getting back to solving this case. I can't be seen on Bennett Farms and I can't stay away. So let's hope it works, dangerously or otherwise." Without waiting for Clancy's retort, she pressed the mask to her face.

For a moment nothing happened. "See?" Hazel said. "Nothing to worry about."

But she spoke too soon. It felt like somebody had slapped her in the face, and she reeled back, dropping to her knees.

"Hazel!" Aashvi cried out.

Hazel tried to pull the mask away, but it was stuck firmly in place as if somebody had glued it. It felt like the mask was bending, squeezing her face. Oh god, would it suffocate her? Her thoughts flitted not to her own wellbeing, but, for a moment, to her family's. Would they find out she had finally come so close to returning only to meet a grisly and foolish end here in Charlie's apartment? Her mother would never get over it.

Suddenly the pain stopped.

Hazel blinked away the tears that blurred her vision. Charlie, wrapped in a bath towel, and Aashvi both stood over her, aghast as they looked on. Hazel reached up and touched her face but felt only flesh. Had the mask fallen off? Thank the universe for small miracles. Note to self: Don't accept gifts from strange otherworldly beings.

She scanned the floor for the artifact but didn't see it anywhere.

"Where'd it go?" Hazel asked.

"Hazel. Mirror. Now," barked Charlie, grabbing Hazel by the hand and hoisting her to her feet. She practically shoved Hazel the entire way to the bathroom.

"Okay, okay, Charlie," Hazel said. "I'm going."

She slipped into the bathroom and looked at herself in the mirror. Except it wasn't her own face that stared back.

"My *mother*?!" Hazel practically shouted.

"I know we're all doomed to become our mothers, but you went a little too early and a little too hard, mon amie."

In the name of all that's holy. Panic saturated Clancy's voice that she'd never heard before. His usual cool, almost caustic, aloofness had been cast aside and here was honest-to-goodness *concern*.

"That's hardly helpful," Hazel said. "I can't exactly go to the barn-raising looking like my mother, who, need I point out, is also going to be at the barn raising!"

"Take it off," said Charlie.

"Right." Hazel felt along her jawline, trying to find the seam like Baker had done. The task proved more difficult than he'd made it look. "No worries," she said, noticing the unmistakable tinge of worry creeping into her own voice. "It's just a little trickier than it looks."

Uh-huh . . .

After a few more seconds of trying, she was most definitely panicking. She jabbed at her face like a kid eating cake without a fork. "Clancy, it's not coming off!"

I told you not to do it.

"Now is not the time for gloating," Hazel snapped.

Maybe if you pull at it from the nostrils.

She did that, wrenching her nose was like lifting a six-pack by the plastic rings. Tears welled in her eyes, but there was certainly no improvement in her situation. The mask remained fixed in place.

Clancy's laughter tiptoed into her head like a museum thief.

"Do you think this is funny?"

Only if you look at it from the right angle.

She took the advice to heart, leaning in close to Charlie's bathroom mirror and scouring her face for any seams. She found none, but she did gain a new appreciation for the thoroughness of the mask's disguise. She looked every bit like her mother, from the emerald eyes and the gentle crow's feet that framed them. But the transformation didn't stop at her face. Her molten-red hair had turned black, marbled with veins of white. She held her hands up and inspected them; her mother had always seemed to defy age (a fortunate Bennett-family trait), but these were not the hands of a young woman who had crested her mid-twenties and could see thirties just on the horizon.

"Maybe you're looking at this the wrong way," said Charlie. "Your mom has complete access to every part of the farm. She even ignores that family rule that says only Bennett witches and caretakers can go into the Tanglewood. If you can't be *you*, I'm not sure there's a better person you could be at this moment."

Hazel nodded grudgingly. Charlie was, of course, correct. While this transformation was disconcerting, perhaps it was a useful tool.

Hazel leaped to her feet and grabbed her bag. "In that case," she said. "Let's get you to the farm, Charlie. I've got work to do."

CHAPTER SEVENTEEN

The East Barn was still sleeping soundly when Charlie pulled her VW into the courtyard.

"So where do we start?" asked Charlie.

"We?"

"Oh puh-lease," scoffed Charlie. "Have you been gone so long you've forgotten I'm your partner in crime? Or in solving crime. However that works out." Charlie waved her hands dismissively. "You know what I mean."

Hazel smiled. "I do. I appreciate the help," she said, "but I've already put you in enough danger. We should probably part ways at this point."

"Have you forgotten you look like your mom?" Charlie asked. "And not in that inevitable we-all-turn-into-our-mothers sort of way."

"Won't it look suspicious if we're together?" Hazel asked.

"Look, I worship Mama B," said Charlie. "So it's not that outside the realm of possibility that we might be seen together."

"But if the Wands can see through the disguise, the consequences could be serious. I can't put you at risk."

"Hazey. Girl. Mon Amie. Would that be more or less dangerous than sneaking into a crime scene with you and getting into a tangle with a dark wizard?"

Hazel shifted uncomfortably in her seat.

Charlie went on. "Or more or less dangerous than joyriding with you through the halls of time? Or how about the time I got split in half and was never put back together?"

Hazel cleared her throat and nodded. "Point taken."

"Excellent. So we can agree to stop treating me like I don't know what I'm getting myself into and assume I've signed all the waivers, crossed all my t's, dotted all my i's, and given away all my f's and get down to solving this mystery before somebody else ends up dead?"

Hazel smiled. "I do love you, Charlie."

Charlie beamed. "Ain't I the luckiest the gal in the world." They climbed out of the car and scanned the courtyard. It looked like they were the first ones here, as best Hazel could tell. The fate of a baker.

"So we're keeping an eye out for any newcomers, no?" Charlie asked.

Hazel pondered that. "In theory, anyone is a suspect at this point. But I would think we're looking for somebody that's been around for a while. I mean, Bart could be a suspect. He's almost as old as the farm itself."

"Or somebody that keeps coming back to the farm again and again, right?"

She flinched. Again it occurred to her what that could potentially mean, but she didn't want to think of it. Her father had been here thirty-four years ago, and by all accounts, he was nearby once again.

"The farm does have a way of attracting the magical sort," Hazel acknowledged.

Charlie scowled in concentration. "We'll figure it out. But speaking of attracting strange folk, we've got about fifteen minutes until Mrs. Prim and Proper shows up."

"Why not just refuse to let her in?" Hazel asked.

Charlie gave her a look. "Have you forgotten? This lady is persistent. The first two days, she knocked for the entire fifteen minutes until I let her in. It's a miracle she didn't have bloody knuckles."

"All that for a cup of Earl Grey."

They were about to climb the steps to the café when somebody shouted across the courtyard. "Hey, Charlie! Mrs. Bennett!"

A young woman stood outside one of the corner towers that had, to Hazel's knowledge, stood empty even with the transformation of the East Barn into a community hub. Until now that was. Clearly, somebody had moved in during Hazel's absence.

Charlie waved enthusiastically with both arms. "Hey, neighbor!"

"Mrs. Bennett, if you've got a few minutes," called the woman, "I've got an update on that special request you made."

Hazel didn't know what to say so she just waved again and called, "Thanks!"

That seemed to satisfy the woman, who opened the door to the corner tower and disappeared into the warm glow of an orange light within.

"Who was that?" Hazel asked.

Charlie replied. "Just moved in a few weeks ago. She runs Herb Your Enthusiasm. It's an herbalist, tea, apothecary shop . . . type thing. Her name's Sarah Carner."

Hazel snapped to attention. Sarah?

"How does she spell that?" Hazel asked.

Charlie looked at her strangely. "You've got business with her, Mrs. Bennett. Why don't you go find out?"

"What? I can't do that!"

Charlie rolled her eyes. "You really know how to waste a perfectly good disguise."

"What's that supposed to mean?"

"What good is pretending to be somebody else if you're not going to use it to your advantage? I would have thought a world-famous actress would have learned that lesson."

"This is different, Charlie. That was a job."

"And a murder investigation is less important than playing make-believe for a living?"

Hazel opened her mouth to protest but stopped herself. She had to admit Charlie had a point there. "I was just hoping to not get arrested today," she said.

"I'm just saying, if you're looking to figure out the lay of the land on the Farm, that's the lady you want to talk to."

Hazel was insulted at the insinuation that somebody else—especially a newcomer—might know Bennett Farms better than she did. She must have worn the look her on her face because Charlie added, "Relax. I mean in terms of strange activity. Sarah is the queen of foraging. She's been scouring the farm for late-fall edibles and medicinals—the woman has a keen eye for king boletes that are to die for."

"Charlie."

"She spends a lot of time foraging. Maybe she's seen some weird activity while she's been poking around the farm. It could help us in tracking those poltergeists down."

Hazel nodded. She didn't want to mention that there might be another reason worth talking to this Sarah Carner.

"Here," said Charlie. "I'll take Clancy up to the café."

I have feelings, you know.

"I've got a whole-wheat honey muffin in the day-olds with your name on it."

I'll accept your muffin, but I cannot be bought.

Hazel headed across the courtyard. A quaint, hand-painted sign hung over the door. *Herb Your Enthusiasm.* Hazel chuckled. This Sarah—or was it *Sera?*—certainly had the East Barn naming aesthetic down. A pair of waders stood beside the door to the shop, a fresh coat of mud still drying on them.

Hazel knocked.

"It's open!" shouted Sarah from within.

Stepping inside was like stepping into a little slice of fairytale. Bushels of herbs hung from the ceiling, shelving with handwoven basketfuls of nuts, crabapples, a variety of mushrooms, and jars filled with dried herbs and flowers. Hazel could see why her mother, whose hippie tendencies had refused to fade even later in life, would be more than happy to patronize this place.

Sarah was busy at a long wooden worktable, working a mortar and pestle as she ground some herb that Hazel didn't recognize. She was young, obviously a no-fuss, no-muss kind of person, dressed in a muted Fair Isle sweater and a pair of worn corduroys, her brown hair pulled back in a ponytail.

A sign hanging on the front of the worktable caught Hazel's eye: Sarah Carner. Ah ha, not Sera. Well, that was a dead-end theory.

"Good morning, Mrs. Bennett," said Sarah, smiling. "I'm surprised to see you back on your feet so soon. Are you feeling better?"

Had her mother been unwell? Hazel tried to hide her worry, but she could feel it play out across her face. "Yes, feeling right as rain." Hazel cringed. Right as rain? Is that something her mother would even say?

Hazel had a million questions that she would normally ask of a new artisan in the East Barn—where was she from or how she came to run such an interesting business—but Hazel had to play this like she was her own mother . . . like she already knew this Sarah.

"You're up early . . ." Hazel said.

Sarah smiled and glanced toward the door, perhaps checking to see that it was still closed. "I'm not typically an early riser," she said. "But I've been coming in early a few mornings recently . . ." She said it conspiratorially, like Hazel should know what she was talking about.

"There's a moratorium on being out on the farm until we investigate these rumors about rabid animals," Hazel gently reminded her.

Sarah blushed. "I know," she said. "But there was no better time to fulfill that *special order* you made."

Special order? Hazel assumed it was some obscure Eastern medicine root or fungus that promised youthful energy and improved bowel movements. That sounded like the sort of special order her mother might place with an herbalist, but something in Sarah's eye— the almost frantic glimmer of excitement—made Hazel think twice.

"Oh," said Hazel. "The *special order*. Of course. And how did that go?"

"Good news," said Sarah, setting the pestle aside. "I found those berries you were looking for. I have to be honest, I don't know what to charge you for them."

"What would you normally charge?" asked Hazel.

Sarah laughed as if she'd just heard the punchline of the funniest joke, but when she saw Hazel wasn't laughing, she stopped abruptly. She went to a wooden cabinet behind the worktable, pulled open one of its countless drawers, and took out a small basket covered with a flap of rawhide. She set it on the counter and looked up at Hazel expectantly.

"I haven't said mum about it to anyone," said Sarah in a hushed voice. "Just like you asked."

Hazel smiled. "Discretion is key."

Sarah started to unwrap the rawhide but stopped. "Mrs. Bennett," she said slowly. "I've spent my life studying botany, collecting the bounty of Mother Nature. I could walk into any Vermont forest and name everything growing there from the mycena leiana on a rotting log to wild asparagus"—she took a deep breath—"but I've never seen anything like these."

She pulled back the rawhide, revealing a handful of berries. To say they were unusual fruits would have been an understatement. Each fruit was small and misshapen and looked vaguely like habanero peppers in size and shape, but that's where the similarities ended. Everything else about the berries was all wrong. For starters, they glowed a dull pink, like somebody had spilled the contents of a glowstick all over them. They gave off an overpowering fragrance that wafted up to Hazel almost as soon as Sarah had unwrapped the bundle, something sickly sweet, almost nauseating.

"I've never seen anything like them. I almost couldn't bring myself to collect them," Sarah said. "But then I figured it must be an invasive species. Or there must be something wrong with them. Maybe they're contaminated with chemicals? Radioactive?" She laughed a nervous high-pitched laugh. "But that made no sense."

No, no, it didn't. What *were* these? Another interloper from the Postern, this time in plant form? Regardless, her mother had known about them and had specifically asked for help in seeking them out. What for?

"Where did you find them?" Hazel asked. "In the Tanglewood?"

Sarah screwed up her face in confusion. "No, of course not. I stayed away from there, just like you requested when I signed on. Though, between you and me, I think I could collect some amazing edibles from the Tanglewood if the family ever reconsiders that policy." She noticed the queer look Hazel was giving and she added, "I get it, I get it. Old-growth forest, trying to keep it pristine and untouched by the literal and figurative footprint of man. It's noble. Just saying . . ." She winked. "But these," she waved a hand over the berries, "I found right where you said I would: in the Folly."

Cassius's Folly. The marshland was about as far away from the Postern one could get without leaving the farm itself. What were berries that were so clearly infused with magic doing growing there? Interlopers were known to come through the Postern and wander freely across the farm until captured, but all strange and magical flora had always been contained to the Tanglewood.

"Sarah," said Hazel, again choosing her words carefully, "did you run into any . . . problems in retrieving them?"

Sarah looked around uneasily. "A woman's imagination can play tricks on her in the dark," she said definitively, as if that was all the answer she needed to give.

"The farm has a way of playing more tricks than most places," Hazel explained. "I grew up here. I should know. What kind of trick are we talking about?"

Sarah laughed nervously. "Oh, it was nothing. You know how sometimes when you're alone, you think you hear voices?"

"I hear voices all the time," said Hazel, smirking. Rooster voices, no less. "Is that what you heard in the swamp? Voices?"

"Crying," Sarah said softly, shivering once. Then she looked up suddenly, laughing nervously and fiddling with the handle of the basket. "But I got these and got out of there." She shook her head. "Silly."

"The power of the imagination," Hazel said, smiling politely.

Sarah seemed eager to change the subject. "I'm not in the habit of selling materials whose safety I cannot guarantee. Are you sure you know what you're doing with these?"

Hazel smiled. "I did ask you to collect them for me. So let me give it the Bennett guarantee." Whatever that meant.

"Are you planning on ingesting these?" Sarah asked. "I'd have to advise against it. I know a botanist up at Green Mountain College that would be happy to run an analysis on these in her lab. I mean if this is a new species then—"

"No lab!" Hazel blurted more forcefully than she had intended. "And, no, I'm not going to ingest them. They're for dyeing wool."

"Of course," said Sarah. "I didn't mean to pry. It's just that if you're looking for a homeopathic migraine remedy, I have plenty of belladonna on hand . . ."

"Of course you do. Thanks for looking out for me, Sarah. I'm so glad you found your way to the farm. I'll just take the berries for today."

With that, she grabbed the basket and hurried from the shop. Perhaps she could hand-deliver them to the *real* Amy Bennett soon enough—and finally get answers to the growing list of questions in the process.

CHAPTER EIGHTEEN

Hazel closed the door to the Cup and Crumb—perhaps a bit louder than was advisable. Clancy squawked from somewhere in the back hall, and Charlie, who stood behind the counter getting the espresso machine going, jumped up in terror.

Hazel hurried to her side. "Charlie, you aren't going to believe this but Sarah found—"

Charlie cut her off, shoving a tray loaded with a buttered toast and a cup of tea into her hands. "HERE, HAZEL," Charlie blurted a little too loudly. "Would you be so kind as to bring this to *our guest's* table?" Charlie motioned not so subtly with a jerk of her head.

Mrs. Prim and Proper was already seated by the window, hands folded in her lap. She was facing forward, but her eyes were fixed directly on Hazel, an amused curl at the corner of her mouth.

Smooth, came Clancy's caustic barb, drifting up to them from the back room.

"Zip it, rooster," muttered Charlie.

"Thank you," mouthed Hazel. She hardly wanted to go shouting all of Bennett Farms' deepest secrets for the world to hear, even if those secrets were threatening to burst her at the seams.

Hazel took the plate and saucer to the table and set them down gently in front of the woman. She gave no indication of whether she found the offerings acceptable, only stating curtly, "That does *not* belong to you," she fumed. "You look ridiculous. Take it off."

Hazel's breath caught in her throat.

"Yes," the woman said. "I can see through it. I don't know how you got your hands on Transcendent magic, but you're sullying it."

"I would take it off if I could," Hazel said.

The woman looked at her, her nose wrinkled in disgust. "I would prefer that this not become a habit," she said, "*you* serving me."

Hazel's jaw dropped. "I'll have you know I have two years of waitressing experience and—"

The woman cut her off. "You abominations with your emphasis on *time*." She waved her hand dismissively. "As if it *matters*. I would prefer the *oracle* serve me."

Hazel's jaw dropped even farther, as impossible as that seemed.

"I've never been fond of witches," said the woman, picking up her tea and cautiously sipping. "You Bennetts are particularly . . . *odious*."

"Hey now," said Charlie, stepping in. "Nobody talks to *anybody* like that in *my* café."

"Your café, dear?" she asked. "You're merely a placeholder. You are dismissed," the woman said, waving Hazel and Charlie away.

"How about tomorrow you find a different door to knock on?" asked Charlie.

"Gladly," said the woman, waving them off like flies as she took a delicate bite from her toast. "Tell Clancy I said hello."

Charlie walked briskly back to the counter, but Hazel grabbed her by the wrist and detoured her to the back hall.

What just happened out there? asked Clancy as he pecked at a loaf of bread Charlie had set on the floor for him.

Charlie tried to respond but only managed to sputter like a boiling kettle.

"She *knows*," Hazel said.

"Knows what?"

"Everything! That I'm a witch, that Charlie is an oracle, that *you* exist!"

Can't say I recognize her, said Clancy.

"And that's part of the problem!" Hazel said. "There are so many confusing things happening right now and you are the missing link. Except that you can't remember a single useful thing."

Clancy was silent.

"For all I know you *are* a murderer and we have no way to fact-check it."

I'll do it, Clancy said.

"What?"

I'll submit to the memory dredge.

Charlie stared at them blankly until it dawned on her what they were suggesting. "What? Me? No, no, no. Not again. I already did you one solid on this adventure. I need to refresh and recharge."

"Charlie . . ."

"Like a spa day," she said. "How about we head up to Burlington and book a day at the Mirage Spa. I could read your past present and future from a jacuzzi!"

"Charlie, there's a life on the line here. We can't rest until we locate the killer."

"As the lead surgeon, do I get a say in this?" Charlie asked. "Does the Book of Bennett have a how-to guide? Exactly how does one dredge up memories?"

"I stayed up most of the night scouring the book for clues," Hazel said. "Unfortunately, I came up empty."

"Dang," said Charlie. "First things first, we need to get to the barn-raising."

"So what do we do about the customer?" Hazel asked.

"We can't just let her kick us around like that on our own turf," said Charlie.

"Right. I'll go," said Hazel.

"Nuh-uh. We'll go together."

Charlie held out her hand for Hazel's.

"You don't think holding hands will make us look a little weak?"

"This is why you're Sherlock and I'm Holmes," said Charlie as they walked over to the table.

"Listen," said Charlie. "I don't know who you think you are. And I don't care if you're the biggest tipper to ever walk through that door, but if you've got dirt on us, let's have out with it."

The woman didn't take her eyes from her teacup as she carefully picked it up and delicately sipped. Only once she had returned the teacup to its saucer, did she finally look up, amused. "Dirt?"

"Secrets," replied Hazel.

"I know more about your lives than you do presently," she said coolly.

"No idea what you're talking about, lady," said Charlie. It was a tried-and-true Charlie Campbell defense that had gotten the two of them out of trouble on numerous occasions.

"Oh please," she said. "I don't have time for this nonsense."

"Who are you, and how do you know so much?" Hazel asked.

"You Bennetts have become sloppy. Imagine having a teashop and bakery being operated in a place of such importance. Despicable. Dangerous. Why has nobody put a stop to this yet?"

"What do you mean?" queried Charlie.

"My dear, who is the guardian witch of this Conjunction?" she asked.

"Conjunction?" asked Hazel.

"The farm, dear," she said, rolling her eyes in exasperation. The woman paused long enough to look Hazel up and down, a smirk passing over her lips. "They just don't make them like they used to."

Charlie huffed. "I'll have you know they make them *better* than they used to, thank you very much!" Charlie produced the receipt from her apron and slapped it on the table.

"I'll see myself out," said the woman as she grabbed the receipt and glanced at it. She placed a twenty-dollar bill next to it and scribbled out something as Charlie and Hazel looked on in dismay.

"Don't let the door hit you . . ." Charlie muttered as the woman rose to leave.

Hazel watched her go, then turned toward her bestie.

"Charlie," Hazel said. "Can I see that receipt?"

Charlie pocketed the twenty-dollar bill and held up the receipt so they could both see it.

There was a short note written in perfect cursive.

Thanks for the entertainment
Tell Asa I said hello
-Sera

Hazel bolted from the café and barreled down the stairs. She scanned the courtyard, but it was too late. Sera was already gone.

"This is stupid," muttered Hazel, adjusting the scarf so that it clung more tightly to her face. "I feel like I'm dressing up as Cordelia Strange for Halloween."

"Maybe you'd rather have to explain to everyone at the barn raising why there are *two* Amy Bennetts in attendance," said Charlie.

"Does it look any less strange to dress me like an assassin?"

Charlie shrugged. " 'Tis the season."

I think it's a marked improvement. Maybe covering your face can be your new thing.

"Quiet back there or I'm going to put rooster tenders on the menu," said Charlie, adjusting her rearview mirror so she could see Clancy in the back seat.

The barn raising was going to be well-attended. Hazel felt nervous as they approached the site and saw the number of cars parked in the Skylark Meadow. It looked like half the town was here to participate. Though Hazel shouldn't have been surprised. Juniper's move to turn Bennett Farms into a strength for the community had endeared her to everyone. Hazel had never been prouder of her big sister.

Charlie parked her VW and started unloading goodies. "You go ahead. I'll worry about the baked goods."

People were standing around conversing, laughing, high-fiving newcomers. Hazel did her best to slip into the crowd unnoticed, though she wanted nothing more than to tear off her scarf and greet Linda Wilkins, owner of the Larkhaven General Store. Hazel watched her tell a joke with such deafening force that it had appeared to stun her audience into silence.

Hazel searched the crowd for her mother but didn't see her there. Part of Hazel was relieved. Perhaps hiding her face the whole time would be unnecessary. But she couldn't deny the growing worry. Was her mother unwell?

Hazel continued to scan the crowd.

She sucked air through her teeth.

"What?" asked Charlie, appearing at her side. "What is it?"

"Didn't you have food to unload?"

"What? Oh, I put Tommy Wilkins and his goons to it."

"Trouble, six o'clock."

Charlie followed her gaze to the man dressed like a farmhand in canvas pants and a flannel-lined button-up. "Is that the guy Juniper hired at the beginning of the summer to help Ronnie?" Charlie asked.

"One and the same," Hazel replied.

Alex had been undercover at the time, working for the Council to investigate claims of a dark wizard operating on this side of the Postern. Despite the straightlaced, clean-cut figure he presented, Alex had played the part of salt-of-the-earth, hard-working type to the T.

"Coming back here after making a not-so-grand exit? That's either brave or stupid," said Charlie.

Charlie had it all wrong. Nobody would remember Alex—after all, he had been cleared of all suspicions in the murder of Eric Moore and, she suspected, quickly faded from memory. What they had to worry about right now was that Alex would recognize them. Or Hazel more specifically. The mask had passed the sniff test for a number of mundanes so far, but would the illusion pass the scrutiny of a skilled wizard?

Ready or not, Hazel was about to find out.

Just then a familiar pickup truck rolled across Skylark Meadow and parked at the end of the line of vehicles. She'd never been so happy to see the Yota in all her life. A moment later, the door opened and Tyler slid gingerly from the cab. He looked like he'd just gone on an all-night bender—with his chunky sunglasses and his cap pulled low. He joined the edge of the crowd as discreetly as possible, clearly trying to avoid being noticed.

"Looks like the walk of shame to me," said Charlie, not a hint of mercy in her tone.

"I'll catch up with you later," Hazel said, slipping off through the crowd. She let her scarf drop to her neck as she sidled up beside Tyler. "You look a little bleary-eyed," she muttered. "Party too hard last night?"

He startled. "Oh, hi, Mrs. Bennett," he said. "I wish. I spent the evening taking care of that problem."

"I know," she said, lowering her voice. "I was there."

He looked at her strangely, his eyebrow cocked.

"It's me," she whispered. "Hazel. I put Baker's mask on. Voila, instant Halloween costume."

Tyler was dumbstruck. His eyes searched Hazel's face—or her mother's—frantically.

"What happened to you last night?" she asked.

He looked around uneasily. "One of the zombies made a break for it," he said. "There was no time to explain in the heat of the moment. I just went after it. I'm sorry." She tried to envision one of the shuffling undead moving fast enough that anyone would need to "make a break" to catch it. Something about this story sounded fishy to her. "By the time I returned, you were gone. I spent the rest of the night playing Graveyard Santa Clause, delivering corpses to all the good little graves and coffins."

"Do me a favor and never write children's books," she said.

"I thought I had a winning premise there," he said, grinning.

"Speaking of your writing," Hazel said, "what's that stack of papers on your desk . . ."

He stopped and looked up suddenly. "How do you know about that?"

"You forget that I'm turning into a world-class detective," she said. "Plus I saw it on your desk when I went looking for you the other night. Is that the book you've been working on since I got back?" She had caught him from time to time furiously scrawling something in his notebook but whenever she got close, he would cover the page. That he refused to share was only mildly irksome, but he insisted it was just how he worked. He didn't talk about or show his work to anyone until he'd finished the first draft. "I've learned to keep it close," he had once explained to her. "The more I talk about it, the less I write about it. If I spill the beans, it's not long before I lose interest in the writing part. Sorry." But apologies were not needed. Who was she to question his creative process? She'd certainly seen stranger artistic proclivities during her stint in Hollywood. So she waited. But what she had seen on his desk had certainly looked like a finished draft of something.

"If this is going to work," she said, "you're going to need to learn to trust me."

"I do trust you," he said, an irritable edge to his voice. "You can read it whenever you want."

"One of these days, you're going to have to let me—wait, what?" She was so used to his stalwart refusals to share his writing that his response caught her off guard.

"It's just sitting on my desk, driving me mad," he said.

"Is this why you've been so on edge since I got back?"

He looked at her nervously. "I haven't been on edge," he said a little too defensively.

Their conversation was interrupted abruptly as Juniper jumped onto a pile of lumber. "Thanks for gathering here on the eve of my birthday!" Juniper called over the crowd.

Hazel groaned. How had she forgotten it was Juni's birthday? Her sister, the Halloween baby.

"I knew my friends and family wouldn't miss the chance to watch me slip over the hill and begin the long, gradual descent to the grave." The crowd erupted in cheers and mock jeers.

"Honey, if you're over the hill, then I'm six feet under it!" bellowed Linda from the back of the crowd, setting off a chorus of laughter and hoots.

"We've had a few setbacks on this project to say the least," Juniper continued. "But we're going to find the silver lining here by building me the biggest birthday cake imaginable."

Another cheer went up from the crowd. Hazel basked in the glow that emanated from her sister. She'd never seen Juniper in front of a crowd before; her sister possessed an ease and poise that would have played well on a stage or a screen. But it was more than that. Juniper had an ethereal glow to her this morning—as if her skin caught the golden light of that fall morning and embellished it—improved on what nature had to offer. Had she always been so radiant?

"You'll be split into teams with very specific jobs. To get your assignment, come see this handsome gentleman over here." She gestured grandly at David, who stood nearby, absently scratching his beard. "My man with the plan, the yin to my yang, and the guy who is definitely going to give me a foot rub before the day is over, my husband, David!"

Tyler and Hazel eventually made their way up through the ranks to where David waited for them. Link, Hazel's nephew, sat dutifully by his side at least trying to look interested.

"Put us to work, good sir," said Tyler, bowing dramatically.

David grinned until he saw Hazel. "Mrs. Bennett?" David asked, his brow knitted in confusion. "Are you feeling better?"

"Gammy!" crowed Link.

So her mother was unwell. Perhaps it was just the latest battle in her mother's war with migraines. They were something she had struggled with as long as Hazel had known her. According to family lore, it was something all Bennetts—especially the women—had to look forward to when they reached their middle age.

She smiled. "Much," said Hazel, trying to speak as little as possible. "Now put me to work."

David faltered, gave her one last incredulous look, and then nodded, "Right." He scanned his clipboard. "Most of the groups are full at the moment. Tyler, I've got you in the hoisting crew, which is gathering right over yonder. Mrs. B, you could just take it easy and watch the show if you want. Here, take my chair."

"I can walk Gammy back home," Link offered. "She doesn't look so good."

"You're not getting out of this," David said pointedly.

"David, just give me a job," said Hazel curtly.

David looked panicked for a moment and scanned the list again. The wise actions of a man that knew enough to fear his mother-in-law. "I've got room in the gofer group." He pointed toward one of the groups now convening at the corner of the barn foundation.

"That's a good boy, David," said Hazel, patting him on the shoulder and perhaps relishing too much the chance to mess with her brother-in-law.

Hazel and Tyler parted ways, and Hazel went over to her group, which waited near the refreshments table. Already this was turning out to be a positive experience. She was delighted to see that Harper had been put into this group as well, though from what Hazel could see, her niece wasn't nearly so excited to be sidelined. While Harper was hardly the tomboy her mother had been growing up, preferring books and moody fashion statements to mucking stalls and driving tractors, she was not a girl that liked to sit around waiting. Heck, she was hardly a girl anymore. Somehow in the month that Hazel had been gone, Harper had grown up. She looked less the teenager and more a young woman. The streak of Kool-Aid dyed hair was gone, leaving only dark locks the same shade as Amy's. She had traded her dark clothes for something a little more seasonal—a knitted tunic, which she had stuffed her hands into.

"Gammy!" Harper sang out as Hazel approached. "You made it!"

Hazel grinned. "Just try and keep me away," she said, embracing her niece. As soon as they touched, Hazel's skin prickled, and she felt the hairs on the back of her neck stand up. She pulled back and looked at her niece.

"Are you okay?" Harper asked.

Hazel smiled. "Yeah, fine. I refuse to be counted out when we're about to have a good ol'-fashioned barn raising."

Harper smiled, clearly unconvinced, but ultimately let the matter drop.

The work on the barn began in short order, and Hazel was amazed at the speed in which the pile of lumber and assembled frames were lifted, hammered, and fashioned into a building. The work progressed without fanfare, and Hazel's group spent their time retrieving tools for workers and filling empty cups with cider and coffee. Hazel welcomed the role. It allowed her to keep her eyes open and be on the lookout. She kept a particularly close watch on her clan—Juniper, Harper, Link, David, and Tyler. They seemed the most likely targets. Granted, they still had one day until Halloween, but she wasn't taking any chances.

She thought of her mother, alone at the manor right now, and scowled.

Hazel heard a gentle snicker somewhere nearby. For a moment, a cloud passed over the sun, dimming her surroundings, and she spotted what she was looking for. A ghostly head and pair of hands floating amidst the workers as they hoisted and pushed the next section of the barn into place with poles. A critical moment to be sure. Wait, what was that? A second disembodied head and hands, identical to the first, stood a few feet away inspecting another individual pushing up a pole.

Twins.

Hazel's heart skipped a beat. Another set of victims here in broad daylight. They'd been invisible in direct sunlight, but under cloud cover they were barely perceptible—like sketches on tracing paper.

A cry of alarm went up from the workers as poles were torn from their grasps and sent hurtling through the air like javelins. The twins cackled and set off, tearing through the crowd like windstorms, whipping up dust and leaves before cackling in delight and rising into the air and disappearing like dandelion fluff on the wind.

Hazel sprang into action, running toward the faltering crew, as they strained to hold up the teetering frame with the few poles that remained to them.

"Mrs. Bennett, stay back!" David shouted, but Hazel ignored him. She was underneath the tottering section of wall before anyone could stop her.

For a moment, it seemed like the workers might complete the push—that they might get the wall in position and save the operation from disaster, but then the poles bowed and bent suddenly. A loud, dry snap echoed through the field as they splintered in two. A collective cry went up from the crowd. The workers threw their arms up over their heads. Hazel threw her arms up too—fingers splayed and her palms screaming in agony as she pushed every ounce of pent-up energy outward. She didn't think about what to do—she merely reacted.

A surge of pink light erupted from her palms, meeting the frame with a sudden but silent wall of force. The falling frame stopped just short of crushing her and the workers.

The effort of it made Hazel tremble. For a moment, she thought she might lose control of it, that it would collapse on top of her, but without warning the frame started to rise, tilting upward.

Hazel was acutely aware that she was not alone in her effort. She was flanked on either side, but she didn't have time to consider it. She poured all of her focus into pushing the frame upright. As soon as it was, the workers jumped into action and secured it in place.

It was only then that Hazel let down her guard and she looked to her helpers. On one side of her stood Harper. Her niece's hands glowed with a whitish light that flared around the edges like flames. A second later, they crackled like weak fireworks and the light fizzled out. On her other side stood Alestranos Rosewood, his wand drawn and still pointed toward the frame, his jaw set squarely and his chest rising and falling.

It took a few minutes for the fervor to die down, but when it did, Hazel realized that everyone was looking at her, jaws agape. She locked eyes with Alex, his cobalt-blue eyes returned the staring at her knowingly.

"Oh crap," she muttered to herself.

CHAPTER NINETEEN

Charlie was next to her suddenly, slapping car keys into Hazel's hand and pushing her toward the VW. "You need to get out of here," said Charlie. "Now. Take Harper and drive."

Hazel didn't need to be told twice. She grabbed Harper by the hand and took off running, pulling her niece with her. The crowd parted for them and they reached the Beetle without incident. Hazel hopped into the car and started it up, waiting just long enough for her niece to jump into the passenger's seat. She gunned the pedal, kicking up clods of dirt in the rearview and punishing the Beetle's suspension as she sped for the road. Not until she pulled onto the solid dirt surface of the North Track did Hazel spare her niece a glance. Harper looked downright terrified.

"You have your Knack," said Hazel, who had she not been so terrified, would have been weeping with joy.

"I-I-I kept meaning to tell you, Gammy," Harper stammered.

Hazel looked upon her niece with admiration. "You have your Knack," she repeated, her voice heavy with emotion. She couldn't hold back the tears anymore.

"Oh, Gammy," Harper said, frowning. "Not the tears."

"Sorry, sorry. I can't help it," Hazel replied. "I just didn't expect this to happen so soon. You're so much younger than I was when I got my—" Hazel stopped abruptly. Maybe Harper hadn't noticed the slip or would write it off. But based on the way that Harper was scrutinizing her like one of those Magic Eye puzzles . . .

"Auntie Hazel?!" Harper whispered hoarsely. "Is that you?"

Hazel couldn't contain her grin. She should have known that her niece would have been clever enough to see through her disguise.

"It's me, kid," she whispered back.

Harper burst into a peal of joyous laughter. "Why do you look like Gammy?"

"It's almost Halloween, isn't it?" Hazel asked cheekily. She reached out and took Harper's hand in her own. "You have no idea how much I want to stop the car and hug you right now. But we're probably being followed." She checked her mirrors again but didn't see anyone behind her.

Harper's joy quickly fell away, replaced with a look of deep concern. "Followed?"

Hazel scanned the sky and checked her mirrors. She saw nobody, but she was certain Alex wouldn't be far behind. And if he was close, then so was Ryker.

"What's happening, Auntie Hazel?"

"We magicked in front of people," said Hazel.

Harper's face screwed up in concern. "I magicked," Harper corrected.

"For all the right reasons," Hazel assured her. "You saved lives. And what good is having a gift if you don't use it to help others? To hell with the consequences."

"It's those stupid ghosts," Harper scowled. "I should have known they would show up."

"You've seen them before?"

"They've been running amok at the manor from sunset to sundown. It's been rough sleeping at the manor. Dad is thinking of setting up temporary living quarters at the East Barn until we can get an exorcist in there or something."

Hazel shook her head. "What exactly is going on around here? The dead don't just rise from their graves for no reason."

"It was me," said Harper slowly. "It's my fault."

"How is that possible?"

"I used the phone booth."

Hazel's jaw dropped.

Harper stammered. "I . . . I needed to make sure you weren't . . . I thought I knew what I was doing . . ."

Hazel shook her head. "It's not your fault," she said. "I never told you how to use the booth. I . . . thought I would have time." She cursed again. She had vowed to be a better teacher than she had been a student. When Hazel had been a teenager, her Gammy had tried explicit instruction with Hazel, to prepare her for her Knack. But Hazel's head had been filled with dreams of running off to the big city to become an actress. Now, as the eldest Bennett-family witch, she had a much easier task ahead of her. She could hardly ask for a better student than Harper, who seemed to have no limitations—she was bookish and brave and far more clever than Hazel had been. And yet, Hazel had still blown it. "When we solve this," she said. "You and I are training side by side. We're just going to have to make room in the homeschool schedule for Spellcraft one-oh-one, even if Gammy complains." She faltered. "Gammy. Is Gammy okay?"

Harper nodded and then shrugged. "She's been holed up in her room for a few days. It's her migraines. Really bad this time."

"Has she seen a doctor?" Hazel asked.

Harper scoffed. "Gammy go to a doctor? Maybe a medicine man. She ran out of that foul headache tea she takes."

Hazel knew the concoction well, the foul-smelling concoction that her mother used to take whenever her migraines came knocking.

"Come back to the manor," said Harper. "We'll hide you there. You can see Gammy."

Hazel shook her head. "I want to, but I can't risk it. I can't risk you, the rest of the family. They'll be watching."

"You're in disguise!" Harper pointed out. "You look just like Gammy!"

Hazel shook her head again. "This is only a temporary solution. I can't live with a mask. I spent too many years doing that. I want to come home, but it should be safe." But she couldn't deny her path would likely lead her to Bennett Manor before that time. If what Harper was saying was true—that those two poltergeists were victims in her investigation—then she would have to find a way in.

"Besides, this cover is blown now too," she said. "They're going to be looking for me, they're going to be looking for Gammy. They might be looking for you."

"I need to get inside Bennett Manor," said Hazel.

"So let's go," said Harper. "We could talk to Gammy. She'll know what to do."

"It's not that simple, kid," Hazel said. "That guy back there? He's trying to arrest me. There are two others just like him who'd like to do the same."

Harper pondered what Hazel had said, her worry playing out on her face. "Is that why I've seen people creeping around the manor?" she asked. "I tried to tell somebody but everyone has been so . . . distracted. Auntie Hazel, everything fell apart once you disappeared."

Hazel drew her mouth tight and bit into her lower lip. "I'm so sorry, Harper. It wasn't my choice to leave, but I'm doing everything in my power to make sure that doesn't happen again. Which is why we can't just go waltzing in the front door of Bennett Manor just now." Then she arched an eyebrow. "But a discrete way into the manor? Now you're talking."

"If only we could find Hisolda's passage," said Harper.

"Whose whatnow?"

"Hisolda Roisin Bennett," said Harper. "The original matriarch of Bennett Farms and the first of the Bennett witches." Hazel knew full well who Hisolda was, but she let her niece continue. "During the Revolutionary War, Hisolda aided the rebels by providing them with a place to stash munitions and supplies," she said. "According to family lore, there was a secret natural tunnel which emptied into the lake. A subaquatic tunnel. Under the lake's surface."

"I could kiss you right now," Hazel exclaimed. "You're going to be a hell of a witch, you know."

Harper beamed. "I hope I can be as good as you someday."

Hazel laughed heartily. "Kid, you're probably going to be as good as me by Christmas."

Hazel checked her side mirror again and spotted something in the sky behind them, dodging in and out of the mirror's field of view. No doubt a Wand on a broom. She swore under her breath.

They rounded a bend in the North Track, bringing the covered bridge that crossed Skinned Knee Creek into view. "Get ready," Hazel said as she steered the VW onto the bridge. When she reached the middle of the bridge, she slammed on the brakes.

"What are you doing?" Harper asked.

"You're getting out here," Hazel answered.

"What? Why?"

"Because we're being followed and I need somebody to go check on Gammy to make sure she's okay," said Harper, leaning over Harper and opening the passenger door. "Get out and climb into the rafters. Wait twenty minutes and then go back to the manor."

"Auntie Hazel—"

"If there's trouble, call Tyler's cellphone. He'll come running. Now go."

Harper stepped back, looking at her aunt helplessly.

"Don't worry," said Hazel. "I'll come to the manor tonight and take care of those poltergeists."

With that, she took off, leaving Harper on the bridge, and sped up the North Track, taking the corner into the harbor hard enough to make the little Beetle slide on the loose stones scattered on the road. It was enough to inspire a squawk from the back seat.

"I'd almost forgotten you were back there," she said.

I was having the most disturbing dream about defending a coop from predators. Mind explaining what's happening? came Clancy's unamused voice from the back seat.

"We've been made," she said. "Alex is following us like the Wicked Witch of the West with a vengeance."

With a flutter of wings, Clancy sailed awkwardly into the passenger's seat. *What's the plan?*

"I dunno. Hold hands and drive into the Grand Canyon?"

I'm not quite sure what that means, but I'm going to pass.

"In that case, we're just going to drive for now," she said.

They swept past the driveway that climbed up to Bennett Manor, and Hazel stared up with longing at the peaked roofs bristling with chimneys. So close, but so far. In a moment, they were past and speeding along the edge of the harbor. She looked toward the water and was pleased to see a young woman sunbathing on a rock, flicking a fishy tail in the air. Nerissa. I'll see you later, she thought.

She swung hard left again as the road turned back into the farm. She sped past the caretaker's cottage and zipped into the tunnel of trees that marked the start of the South Way.

"Maybe we can lose them in the trees," Hazel said.

Great idea. Perhaps you have a car-sized mask so we can emerge in a horse-drawn wagon.

She was cruising smoothly down the South Way, obscured in the trees when Alex dropped into the road. She considered gunning it and calling his bluff but she had enough proverbial blood on her hands. She didn't need to splash on any of the real variety.

He stood still in the road, broom in one hand, the wand in the other, pointing it directly at the Beetle. She put the car in park and slowly got out, her hands raised like this was the culmination of a real police chase.

"Alex," she called out. "You don't want to do this."

"Oftentimes, duty has little to do with want."

"Or is this a justification so you can sleep at night?" she asked.

He frowned. "Hazel, don't make this any harder than it has to be."

"I'm only making it as hard as it needs to be," she retorted. "You know I'm innocent. You know this is a setup and Circe is pulling the strings."

His jaw tensed and he stared down at the ground.

"Or is it Ryker that's calling the shots?" she pressed.

His eyes snapped back to her at the mention of his partner's name.

"No," he fumed. "Ryker is a Wand, just like me. I know he seems gruff sometimes—"

"Gruff?" she scoffed. "Vermont farmers are gruff. Sailors are gruff. Ryker is, at best, a psychopath with authority."

Alex shook his head. "He is loyal to the law. Sometimes to a fault. He doesn't know you. He just knows the story that Circe has spread."

"But you know a different story."

He ground his jaw but remained silent.

"If I'm so guilty, why haven't you arrested me yet?"

He was silent again, and when he finally spoke, it wasn't to answer her question. "They've built a really strong case against you. If you go back there, you will not leave an innocent woman." He sputtered. "You will not leave. Period. Full stop."

"Then I guess I shouldn't go back," she said pointedly.

"You'll never be safe here unless we clear your name," he said.

"We?"

"You need to go," Alex said suddenly. "Ryker will be here soon."

She grabbed her satchel from the car, tucked Clancy under one arm, and took off into the Tanglewood.

CHAPTER TWENTY

The moon's reflection ribboned across the gentle bobbing surface of the lake as Hazel crept to the shore and knelt beside the water. She'd spent the day creeping through the Tanglewood. She worried about the fallout of her public display of magic and tried to keep her mind off it by scouring the Book of Bennett once again for clues, but she couldn't focus. Instead, she spent hours trying to get Baker's pen to perform its same ghostly act, but it remained inert. When night had finally fallen, she'd snuck into Tyler's backyard, stashed Clancy in the coop despite his wildest protests, and crept to the harbor.

Now she knelt down and dipped her fingers into the frigid water. How was this even supposed to work? Should she slap the surface of the water in morse code? Maybe just stick her head in and scream?

Hazel was still pondering that thought when a head poked from the water a few yards offshore. Just the mermaid she'd been looking for!

"Hazel Bennett!" exclaimed a familiar voice. "You haven't been arrested!"

Hazel motioned for her to keep it down. "If we keep talking like this, I still might be," she whispered.

Nerissa came closer, pulling her body into the shallows. "Right. Sorry about that," she whispered. "What are you doing here on so grim a night as this?"

"Remember that tour of Bennett Manor we talked about?" Hazel asked.

Nerissa perked up. "Are we doing that already?"

"Not quite," said Hazel Bennett. "You said you knew all the ins-and-outs of the underwater world around the farm."

Nerissa smiled and nodded.

"Have you ever heard of a secret underwater passage that leads into Bennett Manor?"

"I think so," said Nerissa. "I mean, I've only ever seen to the point where the water ends. I have yet to drag myself across the floor and explore any further. It's murder on my scales."

Hazel gulped. She knew exactly where that tunnel went—the only place in Bennett Manor she avoided on principle: the cellars. As a rule, basements and cellars were reserved for all manner of horrors that populated her imagination—your flesh-eating monsters, your serial-killer dumping grounds.

"I need you to take me there," said Hazel.

"You've got it," said Nerissa. "All aboard!"

Hazel winced. "I'm still being hunted . . ."

"Got it," Nerissa whispered, adding a barely vocalized, "Choo!"

Hazel slipped into the water, reflexively hyperventilating at the shock of it. There was no getting used to that. What she wouldn't give for a wetsuit right about now.

"Should I go back through the Watergate and grab a vamprey for you?" Merissa asked.

"No!" Hazel retorted a bit too loudly, then again, softer this time, "No. That won't be necessary. I'll just . . . I'll just hold my breath."

Nerissa looked at her doubtfully. "That sounds like a horrible idea, but this is your adventure."

Nerissa guided her across the mouth of the harbor, swimming along the surface and pulling Hazel effortlessly. If it weren't for the life-sucking temperature of the water, it might have been a fun, dare Hazel say pleasant, experience. Finally, they reached the other side and passed along the bottom of the cliffs below the mansion. Hazel had been down here a few times as a kid, playing on the rocks and jumping in the water. She shivered now, not because of the cold, but at the knowledge that there had been some sort of gaping tunnel beneath them.

"Ready?" Nerissa asked.

Hazel snapped a ball of light into existence. "Ready."

"Might want to take a big breath."

Hazel sucked in a lungful of air and nodded. Nerissa dove fast down the edge of the cliff, dragging Hazel with her. Hazel tried to keep her eyes open for what it was worth— but even with the light, everything was just a messy blur. They didn't have to go far to find it—a jagged hole burrowing into the cliffside. Nerissa swam into it. The tunnel sloped downward and seemed to stretch for ages. Just when Hazel thought she couldn't hold her breath any longer, they emerged from the water, bursting into a cavern floor.

Hazel hoisted herself up and collapsed, lying there until she had caught her breath.

"I wish I could take you farther," said Nerissa. "But I stop where the water does."

"Maybe someday we can figure a workaround," said Hazel.

Nerissa grinned. "I would love that! For now, I have to get going before anyone notices I'm missing. They get all up in arms if I'm over here at night. Not that it's ever stopped me." She started to dive back under when she stopped for a moment. "You be careful in there," she added. Then with a splash and a flick of her tail, Nerissa was gone.

Hazel smiled. "It's my home," she said. "What is there for me to fear?"

But despite her years of acting lessons, she wasn't convincing herself. Bennett Manor had always been filled with potential danger and she knew it. It was stuffed with magical artifacts—one of which, she reminded herself, had landed them in this mess to start with. From time to time, tinier varieties of interlopers had been known to take up in the disused portions of the house. One summer, when she'd been ten, she'd helped Ronnie and Gammy clear a nest of kobolds from the eaves of the building's South Wing.

Hazel climbed to her feet and inspected the cavern. The cavern sloped upward and away from the water, finally leveling out at its far end. At its peak were stacked countless barrels and crates. Hazel approached a crate and gave it a light kick. The wood gave way under her foot. Rotten. Inside lay a musket.

These crates contained the munitions Harper had been talking about. She moved on. Somehow she didn't think a waterlogged musket would help her in this fight.

A rough-hewn passage burrowed into the wall at the far end of the cavern. Hazel wondered how far beneath the manor she was.

The air nearby shimmered and Hazel had her hands at the ready before Theo materialized, still dressed in his Minute Man fatigues, but this time bearing a musket.

"Next time, give a girl a little warning," Hazel glowered.

"My apologies, Lady Bennett," he said, bowing his head.

"Theo," she said. "Why did you bring a gun?"

"I thought it best to be prepared. The twins are not particularly agreeable."

"I've noticed. Can you even shoot a ghost?"

Theo stopped and seemed only now for the first time to be considering the question. "Perhaps a spectral bullet is the only thing that can?"

"What a time to test it," she said.

Theo looked at the ancient stockpile. "Well I'll say," he said. "So that's where Hisolda kept all the munitions."

"You didn't know about this?"

"Hisolda and I were married a mere five years before the war for sovereignty—and a mere seven before my untimely demise at the hands of a British soldier. I regret that I did not have a chance to plumb the depths of Bennett Farms' secrets."

Hazel considered the spoiled munitions one more time. "Let's get going," she said.

They entered a high chamber that made Hazel think of a European cathedral—it's ceiling a perfectly constructed dome complete with an expansive fresco. But the painting had seen better days. Whole sections of the plaster had fallen away into sodden-mold-infested piles on the floor. What remained commanded Hazel's attention.

"What is this?" she marveled. She tossed her light gently toward the ceiling, sending it sailing upward until it settled near the peak of the dome, illuminating the painting. The painting depicted the farm in all of its glory. There was the Tanglewood with the Postern furtively peeking above the trees. There was the manor. In the background stood the hedge maze. A multitude of magical creatures crept from all of the hidden nooks and crannies of the farm—goblins and fae and unicorns and more than she could count. But it was the figures in the foreground that commanded Hazel's attention.

A young woman in petticoats, her dark hair flowing wildly around her head, stood opposite a man with a pair of gossamer butterfly wings sprouting from his back. A fae. He reached out for the woman's hand, and their fingertips brushed.

Behind them stood an old man that looked like a caricature of a wizard—the voluminous purple robe and pointy hat, the flowing white beard, his face stern and heavy with wisdom. Merlin, perhaps? Next to him stood a young man with a crop of blond hair and a mischievous grin.

"Who are these people?" Hazel asked.

"I can't say as I've ever been down here," Theo said. "But that is, without doubt, my fair Hisolda."

"I hate to ask an indelicate question, but who's the fae she's cozying up to?" Hazel asked.

"You must remember that I married into the family, Lady Bennett," he said. "I was originally a Windham. The Bennetts had their secrets long before my life intersected with them. In fact, I wasn't even Hisolda's first husband." He added that last fact a little sheepishly. "The first one just up and left one day, never to return."

"Bennett women have a knack for falling in love with runners." She thought of her father, and she was wondering if he was ever going to make an appearance in this whole sordid adventure. She was also curious about his connection with Sera. She'd contemplated her note about a million times that day but was unable to make heads nor tails of it.

"We should keep moving," she said.

She gave the fresco one last look. She noticed two figures off to the side that she'd almost passed over. One was dressed in flowing white robes and sprouting white-feathered wings, the other in black robes with leathery black wings. At first she thought the fresco had sustained damage because their faces had blurred—smudged by years of water damage—but upon closer inspection, she realized the blurs were an intentional part of the original painting.

"Transcendents," she said. It was a depiction of the two ways in which Transcendent behavior had been characterized by humans. Angel and demon.

Hazel didn't know what to make of that—or any of the fresco's content, to be honest. Was it just a fanciful depiction of the Bennetts' close connection to the magical world? Something told her it was more than that.

"We should keep moving, Lady Bennett," Theo said.

"Of course," she murmured, considering all the passages branching off from this room. "But which way?"

A devilish snickering came in reply.

"Did you hear that, Lady Bennett?" Theo asked nervously.

It seemed to be drifting from one of the passages. Hazel approached and listened. There it was again, a haunting fit of laughter up ahead.

"This way, Theo," Hazel said.

"Are . . . are we sure we want to follow that sound?"

"We're here to hunt ghosts."

He flinched.

"Other ghosts," she clarified.

Theo cleared his throat. "I do not think your Baker will leave before he has all of the escaped spirits back in his basket. And I fear that includes me."

She stopped and considered Theo. "Why don't you want to cross over, Theo?"

He drew himself up, puffing his chest and squaring his musket against his shoulder. "My love is not there," he said. "I will not go quietly to an eternity without her."

Hazel's heart melted. "That's touching, Theo. But why is Hisolda not in the . . . thereafter?"

"None of the HRBs are there," Theo said. He had once told Hazel that the Bennett women did not leave ghosts. Now it turned out they didn't cross into the afterlife? Exactly what sort of fate awaited her? She gulped down her fear.

Another fit of laughter drifted down the passage, followed by a second and distinctly separate peel of laughter. Twins, she thought. She hurried forward, summoning another ball of light to guide her, Theo hurrying to catch up. The passage twisted and turned, dipped and climbed, intersecting with other passages and narrow staircases that dropped into darkness. At every juncture, she stopped and listened for the impish laughter to guide her in the right direction. At last the network deposited her into the cellars, that long cascade of vaulted chambers that, even now, made her shiver, and not just because she was wet and cold.

Hazel moved, creeping through the cellars and shuddering every time she walked through a spiderweb—which was often—and jumping every time something scurried—which was constantly. The laughter that had led her here had vanished, and she couldn't help but wonder if she was being baited. No matter. Up ahead, she saw the archway that led into the wine cellars, and she knew she would find a safe way up into the house from there.

She entered, stepping quietly between the racks of dusty bottles and casks. Without warning, a few bottles suddenly launched from the racks, rocketing across the room and shattering against a stone column.

"I fear those vile hooligans are on to us," said Theo.

"Remember, Theo, they're part of the Bennett family tree."

"Some branches demand pruning," he observed.

"That hurts our feelings," pined a disembodied voice.

A moment later, two heads materialized. Based on their behavior, she had pegged both for teenagers, but now that they materialized clearly, she saw they were both fully grown men, albeit with a few disturbing differences—the sunken eyes and the ghoulish grins that stretched from ear to ear like jack-o'-lanterns. A pair of hands soon followed for each head, but that's where the solidification stopped.

"You must be Horace and Alistair," she said. "You're my great-uncles."

"You've got the great part right, lady," said one of the twins, "but I'm nobody's uncle."

"You're definitely a monkey's uncle, Horace," said the other ghost, grinning wickedly.

The first twin, Horace, turned his attention back to Hazel, "And that would make you . . . Helena's granddaughter?"

Hazel smiled. "That's me."

"Huh, how is sis doing these days?" Horace asked.

"She's passed . . ."

The poltergeists' grins faded for a moment, but only a moment. A second later, another wine bottle torpedoed across the room and exploded.

"Can we just focus for a minute?" Hazel asked.

"Hey," said Horace in mock offense. "I don't like your tone!"

"Yeah, where are your manners?" said Alistair. "Doesn't the Bennett code of conduct and decorum mean anything to you?"

"Does it mean anything to us?" asked Horace, raising his hand like a dutiful student.

"Probably not, but that's not the point," said Alistair, sending Horace into a fit of belly laughter.

Before Hazel could stop them, they were off and running. Well, not so much running as they were whisking through the air.

"Wait!" Hazel shouted, but a moment later they'd floated upward and disappeared through the ceiling.

"To think that the Bennett family produced those monsters. If it hadn't gone on to produce you, I would think the entire line had gone to ruin."

"There's still time for that if we don't find our killer," Hazel said. She went to the creaky set of steps and ascended to the kitchen. Her heart quickened, though she didn't know whether it was because she was coming home again or because each step brought her family closer to danger.

CHAPTER TWENTY-ONE

The manor was quiet and dark, save for the distant ticking of clocks and creaking of the house shifting its bones. She hardly took that as a good sign. She doubted the twins were done with her yet, and she wondered where they might be lying in wait. Before she went searching for them, she went to the cupboard where her mother kept her special stash of headache tea. Hazel had always thought headache tea was a code word for some of her hippie tobacco, but all this time, there might have been more to her mom's home-scavenged and home-brewed tea.

Hazel rifled through the cabinet until she came up with the metal tin marked with a Mr. Yuck sticker. She popped it open. Only a single dried berry rattled around inside the container. So her mother had run out of her tea. No wonder she was holed up inside her room. It was a good thing she had picked up those berries from Sarah.

"Ah-ha, dipping into the ol' transgressor repressor," said one of the twins as his head emerged from the counter like a grisly whack-a-mole.

"What is that supposed to mean?" Hazel asked.

The other twin descended from the ceiling. "The mother smother."

"Do you two ever speak sensibly?" Theo snapped.

Hazel pinched the bridge of her nose and took a deep breath. Maybe she would get nowhere with these two. Another dead end. She reached into her pocket and wrapped her hand around Baker's pen. She pulled out the pen and raised it over her head.

"Oh no!" squealed one of them. "She's going to make us do homework. Run, Horace!"

"The nerve!" Alistair cried.

The poltergeists zipped away on a wave of laughter, leaving her standing with the pen in one hand and the empty tin in the other.

"Should we, uh, pursue them?" Theo asked.

Hazel shook her head. "That's what they want. The last thing we need to do is play their games and get them riled up. They'll wake up the whole house and draw every Wand within earshot."

Forget the twins, she had a more important mission.

She crept from the kitchen and mounted the stairs, artfully stepping in all of the spots that didn't creak. The upper hall was dark and filled with niches. She hung a left and headed toward her mother's room—what had once been an attending servant's quarters. Her mother preferred the modesty of a small room. She always liked to say she couldn't help what household she had been born into, but at least she could still pick her room.

She found the door locked.

Hazel's heart quickened. Her mother spent a lot of time locking doors in Bennett Manor—mostly to keep children away from danger—but when it came to the bedrooms off the second-story hallway, she didn't believe in locked doors. Closed doors for privacy? Sure. But not locked ones.

Hazel jabbed her pinkie finger toward the lock and cast the same spell that had granted her access to the chapel. With a gentle click, the lock gave way.

"You're a quick study, Lady Bennett!" Theo remarked.

Hazel smiled. "I come from good stock."

Hazel turned the knob slowly, silently. Before she even had the door open, she'd decided she would just check on her mother and then leave. Just to make sure she was well enough. Just being here in her room would surely put her in danger if one of the Wands caught wind of her presence.

Hazel slowly opened the door and listened for the sound of her mother's breathing.

"Mom?" she whispered. "Are you here? I brought your special order from Sarah . . ."

No answer.

Hazel dared a little light, coaxing it into existence in the palm of her hand.

The room was in disarray. The covers and sheets had been torn from the bed, the nightstand lamp shattered on the floor. "No, no, no," said Hazel.

Again the twins appeared. "Oopsie," said Horace, materializing in the corner.

"Did you do this?" Hazel demanded.

"Us?" asked Alistair, appearing from the floor as if riding a spectral elevator. "Oh no. This is strictly a domestic affair."

"Where is she?" she demanded.

"Hey, don't ask us," said one. "We're just here for the entertainment. Right, Alistair?"

Alistair's disembodied head nodded.

She collapsed on the bed. "Don't you care about your family? She's your niece and she could be in danger."

For the second time that evening, their smiles faltered.

"I just want to ask you a few questions," Hazel said.

"There's a sad sack in Cassius's Folly that would probably beg to answer questions," Horace said.

The Folly? Hadn't Sarah said something about seeing strange things in the Folly when she'd collected those berries?

"You were murdered, both of you," she said. "Don't either of you care?"

"We were?! Do you hear her, Horace?" asked Alistair. "Our great-niece here says we were done in."

"Oh yeah?" Horace asked. "By who?"

"That's what I'm trying to figure out! Stop playing games!" she snapped. "I'm trying to help you."

Horace stopped and considered her. "You're one to be talking, what with hiding your true self."

"It's this mask," she said, futilely poking around the edges of her face to find a seam.

"Tsk, tsk," said Horace. "That's what you get for playing with Transcendent magic. They have it out for us, you know."

Hazel stopped picking at her jawline. "Wait, what? The Transcendents don't like the Bennetts?"

"That's putting it mildly," said Horace.

"I'd say they downright hate us with a rage hotter than the fire of a thousand suns," Alistair explained.

"A thousand and one," Horace clarified.

"Two," Alistair added, not to be outdone.

Suddenly that one tidbit of information solidified somebody's place on her suspect list. "Baker," Hazel said.

"Butcher and candlestick maker?" asked Alistair.

She ignored the twins. If Baker was the murderer, then why had he assisted Hazel in interviewing and capturing his victims? Was he using her to cover his trail? Was he simply toying with her? Perhaps keeping her busy while he conducted other plans and another murder? If that were true, that meant that at best she had been duped again, and at worst, she had been made an accomplice by unwittingly cleaning up the evidence.

"Son of a . . ." she muttered.

"A maiden?" asked Alister.

"A very respectable lady?" asked Horace.

If the killer were Baker, Hazel would need to be certain . . . and be prepared. She didn't know the depths of a Transcendent's powers, but she suspected it would take all of her skills and wits to come out on top.

"Do you remember what happened to you?" Hazel asked the twins. "Any details about the night you were murdered?"

"We were out conducting our usual Halloween rituals," said Alistair.

"Trick-or-treating?" Hazel asked.

"Mostly just tricking," Horace replied. "We started close to home."

"By throwing eggs," Alistair added.

"You egged your own house?" Hazel asked, unamused.

"Not our house," he said. "The house of Robert Ames." That name was vaguely familiar to Hazel. She thought Gammy had mentioned it once or twice as the farm's caretaker when she'd been a young girl. "If anyone needed a good egging," continued the twin, "it was that guy."

"Your father would be ashamed of such behavior," Theo chided.

"Father?" Horace scoffed. "What father?"

Hazel winced. Another Bennett without a father figure. Hazel felt for them. "I'm sorry," she said. "Nobody deserves to grow up fatherless."

"Don't be sorry," said Alistair. "We never cried over it. Why should you?"

"Anyway, back to the good stuff," Horace said. "We had just egged ol' Robert's house and we were on our way to the East Barn to see if there was a truck or a car we could borrow."

"Anything with wheels, really. It's a long way into town," explained Alistair. "Especially when you're carrying a thirty-pound bag of rotten produce."

Horace's disembodied head nodded in agreement. "Anyway, we found a truck with the keys tucked up in the visor. But that blasted cat was sleeping in the driver's seat and refused to move."

"What cat?" Hazel asked. Bennett Farms was practically crawling with cats. The family crest featured the snow-white felines that prowled the grounds.

"The creepy one with too many parts," said Horace.

Clancy. Yet again her familiar intersected with the scene of the crime.

"Everything gets kind of fuzzy after that," Alistair added.

Horace nodded. "Yeah, like when I try to focus on it, all I see is a blur . . ."

"Gammy?" came a voice from the doorway. Hazel looked up to see Link standing in the hall, squinting and rubbing his eyes. "Who are you talking to?"

"It's nothing, Link," said Hazel. "Go back to bed."

But Link had already spotted the twins bobbing in the air. His eyes grew wide and his skin paled. This was like chumming the water as far as the twins were concerned. Their grins grew wide, again slicing from ear to ear.

"Oh look," said Horace. "Somebody wants to play!"

"Horace, Alistair," Hazel warned. "Don't do it."

They paid her no mind. The game was on and they were going to play it. They whipped around the room, kicking up a racket as they pulled the debris scattered around the room into a cyclone.

"Stop that this instant!" chided Theo, breaking his silence and suddenly finding his courage.

His demand was answered with a projectile—a lamp that hurtled through his ghostly form and shattered against the wall.

Hazel used the distraction to her advantage. She pulled Baker's pen from her pocket and whipped it at the twins. The chain erupted in flame as it lashed out, wrapping around the twins and dragging them toward her.

"We've been double-crossed, Alistair!" Horace screeched.

"The humanity! We're too young to re-die!"

Their wails were cut short as the pen siphoned their spirits. The whirlwind died and the debris clattered to the floor.

When Hazel looked up, the entire family had gathered outside the door and Theo had disappeared.

"Mom?" Juniper asked. "What the hell is going on?"

"Are you okay, Mrs. B?" David added.

Hazel laughed airily. "I—I think I saw a rat."

Juniper eyed the destruction in the room. "How big of a rat are we talking?"

"Okay, okay," David interjected. "Everyone back to bed." He ushered Link down the hallway, sparing the room one last wary glance.

"You too," said Juniper, turning to Harper. Harper looked to Hazel knowingly before she begrudgingly trudged off.

Juniper was the last to leave. "We still need to talk about what happened today," she said.

"Is the barn finished? Is everyone okay?"

"It's done," Juniper replied. "I don't even know what's going on. I don't even know how to explain what happened to myself, never mind to the entire community that witnessed a very public display of magic."

"It was the only way," Hazel said. "People were in danger."

"So, suddenly you have the Knack?" Juniper asked incredulously.

Hazel crossed the room and put a hand on Juniper's shoulder. "It's me, Juni," she said. "It's Hazel."

Juniper snapped to attention and stared her in the eye. "How did David and I first meet?"

"Which version would you like to hear? The real story or the story you told mom?" Hazel laughed.

Juniper smirked. "Real."

"You two met at some dive bar in Burlington when you were just eighteen. You used a fake ID and your assumed name was Holly Bush. David was tending bar and he chuckled when he saw your ID. Incidentally, his real last name was Bush. After some time he joked that if you ever got married, you wouldn't have to change your last name. Initially, you were horrified because you knew if you ever did get married, your name would be Juniper Bush."

Juniper laughed, tears forming in the corners of her eyes as she pulled Hazel into a bear hug. "What the hell happened to you? This is too much. You disappear for a month and you return looking like mom."

"It's a disguise," Hazel explained.

"Take it off, please."

"Wish I could," she said. "I can't find the zipper on this thing."

"Wait a minute," said Juniper, pulling away from the hug and looking around the room. "Where is mom?"

"I was about to ask you the same question."

Before they could explore the matter, Harper burst into the room. "I thought I told you to get back to bed," said Juniper.

"Auntie Hazel!" Harper shouted, perilously ignoring her mother, "somebody is banging on the front door. You need to hide!"

Hazel rushed to Harper and hugged her.

"What's going on?" Juniper demanded.

"I'll explain," said Harper.

"You'd better," Juniper said, though her voice had lost its stern edge. She looked to Hazel with concern. "Whatever's happening, go. Figure it out. We'll get rid of our guest."

CHAPTER TWENTY-TWO

Are you sure you want to be left here?" Nerissa asked.

"I need to find a safe place and nobody is going to come looking for me here," said Hazel. It was true that the entire harbor was crawling with Wands, and she needed to get away, but that wasn't the only reason she'd had Nerissa deliver her here. What was it the twins had said about Cassius's Folly? That there was a sad sack waiting there to answer questions. And hadn't Sarah mentioned hearing noises here while harvesting the berries?

"If you say so . . ." said Nerissa, swimming between the dead trees that marked the edge of Cassius's Folly. "Do you want me to just stick you on a log or something?"

"Over here is fine," said Hazel, pointing to a tuft of dry, grassy earth. Nerissa deposited her on the spot and Hazel dragged herself from the water, shivering. If she didn't end up with pneumonia by the time this was all done, it would be a miracle.

"I owe you," said Hazel. She really did. Hazel had fled Bennett Manor and escaped into the Cliffside Garden, and, from there, worked her way down the craggy rockface to the stone shore. It turned out Nerissa hadn't gone too far, and she'd been more than willing to taxi Hazel around the shore until they'd come to the Folly.

"Just give me that tour when the time comes and we're even," said Nerissa, flicking her fin above the surface of the water.

"Deal."

With that, Nerissa flicked her tail and disappeared beneath the water.

Hazel sat, listening to the peepers and the frogs still singing in defiance of the coming winter. She listened for some time before she picked up on something else, a keening that didn't belong in the natural order. She cupped her hands behind her ears and turned them like sonar as she honed in on the sound.

Somebody was crying.

No, sobbing.

Was it another spirit? She had interviewed and wrangled every ghost in the dossier except for Judith. She started plodding her way deeper into the swamp, jumping from tuft to tuft and balancing across fallen trees. She stopped from time to time, listening again, and slowly triangulated her way toward the source.

She'd never ventured into Cassius's Folly before—nobody had as far as she knew, since Cassius's untimely demise—and she quickly saw how it had earned its name. The swamp was nothing more than a ravenous mouth toothed with dead trees.

Finally, Hazel reached a dryish tuft—a patch of grass so thick it held her aloft from the muddy waters. The crying was close now. She called out gently into the gloomy dark.

"Hello?" she called. "Is there anybody there?"

The crying stopped.

"Hello?" she called again.

The reply came so weakly that she almost mistook it for some more nighttime chatter, but when a nearby rotting stump suddenly shifted, she cried out in alarm.

Her hands were already up, crackling with pink energy before she realized the stump was in fact a man who had become so hopelessly stuck in the morass that only his shoulders and head remained above the mud. "Has somebody finally heard me?" he asked in a tremulous voice.

The figure looked up, its waxen face glowing in the moonlight. Hazel gasped. It couldn't be.

"Wilhelm?"

Sure enough, it was Wilhelm, the undead coroner from Quark who had busted her out of prison. What was he doing here? Had Wilhelm wandered through the Postern to find her and gotten lost? It flitted through her mind that he looked less withered, though decidedly no less dead than the Wilhelm she had met on the other side of the Postern.

"What are you doing here, Wilhelm?" she asked.

His chin started to quiver. "Nobody calls me by my middle name," he said, his face swimming with confusion. "Just Cassius."

"Cassius?" she parroted.

"Cassius Wilhelm Bennett," he said.

The answer punched her like a closed fist, and she had to reach out to a nearby stump to steady herself. "Bennett?" she repeated.

"I . . . I got lost . . .and the swamp tried to eat me—but my foot found a stone beneath the mud and I was able to push my way back up." He blinked and looked around as if dumbfounded by his own circumstances. "Who are you?"

"Hazel," she said. "Hazel Roisin Bennett."

He stiffened at the name. "A fellow Bennett," he said. "Is Hippolyta well?" he asked, desperation in his voice. "I . . . I have to find the berries."

Hippolyta. Hazel recognized the name as one of her ancestors, and the berries—did he mean the same berries that Sarah had foraged from the Folly?

"She . . . she needs the berries," Wilhelm continued. "The midwife says Hippolyta needs to have her tea before it's too late."

"What are you talking about, Wilhelm?"

"It's too dangerous! Midwife Goodblood said an expression of her hidden side during labor could . . . overwhelm her." He became suddenly exasperated. "As a young Bennett woman, you must know what I'm talking about!" He started struggling in earnest now, straining against the ooze that imprisoned him.

Hazel was beginning to put the pieces together. The Wilhelm in Quark was merely the Wilhelm of the future, an undead creature who had survived the ages, lived through the Bloom, and because of that traumatic magical conflagration, had no recollection of his past. How many years had he spent struggling in the swamp? She realized that he wasn't just another escaped spirit running amok on the farm. The legends of a ghostly wail emanating from the farm went back generations. Hazel wished she had an ironclad memory like her niece. Surely Harper would be able to tell her exactly what year it was when Cassius had stumbled into the folly that now bore his name.

"Wilhelm . . ." she said slowly. "What year is it?"

Wilhelm looked horrified. "That you would ask such a question while I struggle for my life!"

"Wilhelm, I will help you . . . but I need you to answer the question."

"It is the year of our Lord eighteen hundred and eighty-three!"

Hazel sucked in her breath as another epiphany struck her. Four files, four different Halloweens. A murder every thirty-four years, with one gap in 1883.

Except Wilhelm had never crossed over to the afterlife and subsequently never escaped with the others. This explained why his name had been missing from the file and why there was seemingly a gap in the murders.

"I'll get you out, Wilhelm . . . Cassius."

She moved forward, stepping off the dry tuft and sinking again up to her knees in the swamp. Let's just hope they don't rename this Cassius and Hazel's Folly, she thought as she took another step and sank to her thigh. "This isn't working," she said. "I need to try something else." She retreated to the tuft and looked around for something that might aid her, a branch she could fish him out with, but she saw nothing.

Perhaps she would just have to employ good old reliable magic. She thought of the digging spell she had cast at the barn, but she was absent any digging implements to use as a focus. "Come on, Hazel," she muttered to herself. "If you can do prop work, you can do pantomime."

She took a deep breath and channeled her powers into her hands until they felt near to bursting. Then she cupped her palms as if she were to scoop a bug out of a pool. Once she had settled on that imagery, she latched onto it. With one fluid motion, she reached toward Wilhelm and lifted upward. The water and mud around him rose into the air as if he were carried upward by giants and hung there. Hazel separated her palms slightly to create a funnel. The mass of earth and water responded, siphoning off and pouring downward back into the swamp.

Wilhelm was at last free from the quagmire, oozing thick layers of mud like some sort of swamp monster. He tried to take a step forward and stumbled, splashing in the swamp water. He climbed to his feet again, the remaining mud sloughing off from his body. As he stepped into the moonlight, something on his back caught the pale glow and scattered it, like crystal. For a moment, Hazel thought something from the swamp was still stuck to his back, glued on with the muck, but as the mud continued to fall away, she realized what she was looking at.

Wings.

A pair of tattered wings, crumpled and broken like pieces of paper, clung to his back.

She felt light-headed and suddenly her legs gave out. She fell into the muck, her elbows deepened into the cold swamp ooze, but she barely noticed it.

Wilhelm was at her side, pulling her to her feet.

"You . . . you . . ." Hazel stammered, "you have wings."

"Of course, I have wings," Wilhelm said. "All fae do.

CHAPTER TWENTY-THREE

Hazel stumbled into the chapel yard, practically dead on her feet but fueled by a burning need to keep moving. If she was still, she would have to think, and if she had to think, she might consider what it meant that Cassius W. Bennett was fae.

Despite her panic, she couldn't seem to move fast enough. A volley of memories and details still pelted her. The fresco under Bennett Manor, where Hisolda Bennett was brushing fingertips with an unnamed fae. The Bennett family's penchant for fathering children with men that didn't stick around. Of her own father, Asarum Moonwake. Asarum Moonwake?! His name could have only been more obvious if he'd been named Faey McFae-erson. The Bennetts unusual ability to cast spells without wands.

A strange detail popped into her head. She'd had a butterfly-milk cappuccino during her first visit to Quark—a concoction presented to her at the Brewhaha Café. Butterfly milk was, it turned out, a consumer-friendly term for powdered fae chrysalis. Cordelia had sipped it without so much as batting an eye, but for Hazel the reaction had been severe and violent—profuse sweating and a searing pain as if somebody had slashed her across her shoulder blades. She glanced warily back at Wilhelm. Yes, exactly where his wings were attached.

Wilhelm followed. "Why are we coming here?" he asked. "My Hippolyta needs me."

"The berries," she lied. "There's a patch of them that grows here." She might have felt guilty lying to him if the entire Bennett family hadn't been spoon-feeding her a lie her whole life.

"And my mother!" she shouted to nobody in particular, stopping midstep as the realization hit her. "We'll talk about my father, indeed!" She picked up a nearby rock and chucked it at a tree as she grunted primally, but the rock went wide and sailed into the forest. God, she had a horrible throwing arm.

"Are . . . are you okay, Hazel?" Wilhelm asked.

"I'm fine! I look fine, don't I?" She gestured to herself frantically. "Completely fine and completely human! Nothing unfine or unhuman to see here!"

Wilhelm drew his lips tight, a brief look of man-in-trouble terror flashing across his face. "Of course," he said quickly.

"We're walking again," she snapped as she continued to storm across the cemetery, scowling at every Bennett headstone she passed. Liars, she thought, the whole lot of them.

Wisely, Wilhelm followed silently. Hazel noticed that the disturbed graves had been mended, the earth on each freshly leveled and seeded with grass. She felt pity for a moment for all the gruesome work Tyler must have done to return the shambling dead to their proper burial sites. She would have to apologize to him later. Now there was a real man, one who didn't have wings and didn't run or fly away when the going got tough.

Hazel stopped midstep again as something else struck her. It was she who had run out on Tyler. Had that been the fae in her that had sent her running from the farm all those years ago? "Damn it!" she howled as she picked up a chunk of discarded masonry from the chapel restoration. With a feral scream, she hoisted it above her body like a raging cyclops and heaved it with all her strength. It flew a mere yard and a half before plummeting into the soft earth. That only made her angrier.

"Moving!" she shouted. She rounded the edge of the chapel and made a beeline for the mausoleum, a squat stone structure at the back of the yard. She passed a tombstone that read Cassius W. Bennett. "That's you," she said, continuing at her breakneck pace.

"Wait, what?" Wilhelm asked.

"I said we're moving!" she snapped.

She finally reached the mausoleum, and she pulled the doors open.

"Oh come now," Wilhelm protested, finally finding his voice. "There can't be any berries in there."

She whirled around to face him. "I lied about the berries! There are none here, but I need you to get inside asap or we're going to have problems."

"Please don't throw me," he said, raising his hands in defense.

She conjured up a ball of light and marched inside, Wilhelm close at her heels.

In summer, the cool of the mausoleum had felt welcoming, but now as she was still damp from the swamp, it was bone-chillingly cold. Her boots tapped against the mosaic floor, the tiling black throughout except for at the floor's center where the tiles rendered the secret Bennett-family crest—the one reserved for the family witches. A roundel with a black two-tailed, two-earred cat inside, encircled with a wreath of rose vines and the phrase fascino non fortuna. By magic, not by fortune. This was the mausoleum reserved for all who lived their life by that crest. All of the HRBs.

The solemnity of the place suddenly made her feel calmer.

She walked the edges of the vault, running her fingers across the marble facades of the closed niches, feeling the names that were engraved there. She paused at the one that read Helena Roisin Bennett—her Gammy—and murmured a quiet hello before moving on.

When she located the niche she'd been looking for, she knelt before it. Hippolyta Roisin Bennett. She waited for Wilhelm to catch up.

"Why are we here?" he demanded.

She set the ball of light in front of the niche so that it floated there, and she pointed. He scowled but followed her lead. Instantly his scowl fell away. "Hippolyta?" he asked, confused. He looked to Hazel, searching her face for some kind of answer. "Why is Hippolyta's name here?"

"You know the answer to that."

"No," he said softly at first, and then again, louder. "No! She's at the house—soon our child will be born!" It was his turn to rage against an inconvenient truth. He turned and started storming from the vault.

"You won't find her at the manor," Hazel called after him.

He stopped in the door, his shoulders slumped, his tattered wings turning over the silver beams of moonlight like pools of mercury. She wondered what those wings had looked like when Wilhelm had been alive and his wings had been undamaged.

"How long has it been?" he asked, all joy wrung from his voice.

"It's twenty nineteen."

"I never made it back from the swamp, did I?"

"No," she said.

His shoulders shook soundlessly. The sight of it twisted Hazel's heart. She felt horrible for the callous way she had led him to his truth. "Cassius . . . I'm sorry," she said. "I should have done this more gently—but I was shocked, angry. And there's another Bennett life still on the line here. A Bennett that can still be saved."

"What of Hippolyta?" he asked. "The midwife said if she didn't have the berries, she might not survive the labor."

Hazel pointed to the niche. In small letters beneath her name were engraved the dates that encompassed her life: 1861–1923.

"She lived," he whispered. "She survived the labor. And the child?" he added tremulously.

"My great-grandmother, Henley Roisin Bennett," said Hazel, running her hand on the niche next to Hippolyta's.

"A girl," he breathed, and he broke down sobbing again.

Hazel gasped for breath. She had pegged these fae wrong. Unfairly. Wilhelm shook with the sobs of a husband who loved his wife, a father who loved his unborn daughter. Hazel bit hard on the inside of her cheek; it was all she could do to keep from breaking down on the spot.

When he spoke again, his voice was filled with a sweet sorrow. "What can I do to help?" he asked.

"I need you to think," Hazel said. "You went to the swamp looking for berries. What's so special about them?"

"In half-bloods, fae phenotypes—if present—don't manifest until later in life," he said. "The berries can suppress those transformations."

Hazel glowered. Migraine medicine indeed, she thought to herself.

"Hippolyta was in labor and the midwife was well-trained in these matters. She thought the stress of birthing a child and manifesting her fae traits—"

"Fae traits?"

"Her wings."

"Oh . . ."

"The midwife thought it would be too much. That we might lose her. She had already lost so much blood. So I raced to the swamp. I was wandering its edge frantically searching. I couldn't find them. I was desperate. And then . . . somebody was there. He offered me help."

He now? Hadn't the others said it was a lady who had done them in? "Who?" she asked, leaning in.

"I . . . I don't know. When I think of his face . . . it's hard to picture."

She thought of the fresco beneath the manor—the angelic and demonic characters with smudged faces, just like Baker's visage when he had removed his mask. "Like it's a smudge?" she asked.

"Yes!" he exclaimed. "Like a charcoal drawing that somebody has rubbed their thumb over."

"Like a Transcendent," she said, more to herself than to Wilhelm. She knew it. Baker. It wasn't just that the other victims couldn't remember their murderer. When Baker had removed his mask, the face underneath had appeared as nothing more than a vibrating blur.

Wilhelm scoffed. "Transcendents? Children's tales. Every fae grows up hearing the same warnings—to stay close and listen to their parents or else the Transcendents will get them."

Hazel considered this. All cautionary tales had a hint of truth to them, some more than others. There was more to these stories than Wilhelm realized and Hazel knew it. The only question she had was why Transcendents held so much loathing for fae? And was it enough to cause one to commit murder?

"I need to go," she said. "I'll come back for you."

But Wilhelm wasn't listening anymore. He had crumpled to the floor in front of Hippolyta's and Henley's niches, his forehead pressed to the marble façade of one, his hand to the other.

Hazel turned and quietly hurried from the vault, closing the mausoleum door behind her.

CHAPTER TWENTY-FOUR

Hazel snuck across the farm under cover of night, narrowly avoiding the Wands as they patrolled the skies searching for her. She searched every nook and cranny of the farm that she could think of, from the dairy barn to the secret laboratory beneath Split Tree Hill, to the sugar house, where she found the small horde of undead that Tyler had corralled there—and which she quickly dispatched of with Baker's pen.

She even dared to sneak to Tyler's cottage. It was clear she could not cover all the ground she needed to by herself, but when she slipped through the kitchen door and into the house, she found it empty. No Tyler. No note. Where had he gone off to? A missing mother, a missing boyfriend.

She changed into a fresh set of his clothes, turning up the hem of the pant legs, and stole a bite to eat from his kitchen. She penned another note, this one saying just: It's Baker. Have to find mom. Search the farm.

She slipped into the backyard again and crossed the lawn. Midway to the coop, she stumbled over something. She didn't dare conjure a ball of light, but she knelt down and located what had tripped her up. A boot. She searched more and found another, and, nearby, a pair of jeans and a shirt. All of them Tyler's.

Why had Tyler disrobed in the backyard? What had been so imminent that he felt the need to switch outfits? None of this made any sense. She made a note to question him about it later and proceeded towards the coop.

"Are you there, Clancy?" she asked.

Only because you imprisoned me.

She opened the door and scooped up Clancy. "Sorry about that," she said. "I didn't think you wanted to spend the night snorkeling in the lake."

If I ever come back as a trout, I'll join you. I'm more upset that you're waking me up in the middle of the night.

"We can sleep when we're dead," she said as she set out down the South Way.

If we've learned nothing else from all of this, it's how patently false that statement is.

Somewhere in the distance, something—a coydog?—howled at the moon. She tucked Clancy under her arm, grateful to have the company.

"You'll be happy to know we don't need to dredge your memory. Yet."

I'm ready for it, you know. If it will help.

She shook her head. "We'll get there. Another adventure, another time. Right now we just need to save mom."

Amy is in trouble? An authentic concern gripped Clancy's voice.

"She's missing and I am worried that she is the next victim," replied Hazel.

Why does this murderer have it out for Bennetts?

"I don't know. We can ask Baker when we find him."

Baker? I wish somebody could have warned you about how duplicitous he was . . .

"Fine, you were right the whole time," said Hazel.

And to think you floated the idea that I had done the deed. Do you know how hard it would be to murder a human when you haven't even had thumbs for two hundred years?

"You could talk them to death. Let's try to keep it down. I'm still being hunted, remember?"

Hazel managed to sneak into the East Barn well enough in advance of sunrise and to keep Clancy quiet until she'd been able to cast a spell to open the door.

Now what?

"Now we wait for Charlie to arrive so we can make a plan," she said, settling into a comfy armchair in the back hall. "There has to be a way to lure Baker out into the open."

Maybe you can threaten to take away his vacation days.

She chuckled. "If there were a way to pull that off, I might try it."

Hazel must have fallen asleep at some point because she awoke to the sounds of screaming and laughter and the slamming of a door.

She vaulted to her feet, panting hard, magically charged hands at the ready. Suddenly the light in the café flipped on, and the sound of Charlie stringing together long chains of swears drifted back to Hazel.

"Rooster!" Charlie shouted. "What is a rooster doing in my stash of day-olds?!"

Hazel stumbled into the front of the café and found Charlie, dressed as a black-robed, pointy-hatted witch, gently using a twig broom to bat Clancy off of a massacred muffin.

"It's Clancy, Charlie," Hazel called out.

Charlie nearly jumped out of her skin and whirled on Hazel, the broom raised and ready to strike. "Criminy, girl," Charlie said. "I nearly took your head off."

"Sorry," Hazel apologized. "I guess I fell asleep waiting for you to show up."

And the only way I could keep myself from crowing was to keeping filling my beak with baked goods.

Hazel stretched and looked toward the front windows where the sound of screams—which she now realized were screams of delight—persisted. It was already full-on day. "Wait, what time is it?"

"Four thirty," Charlie said, "and I need to get cracking. Your sister is going to kill me if I'm not open and doling out candy and coffee in about three seconds."

"What?!" Hazel exclaimed. "Four thirty?! In the afternoon?!" She'd slept away the entire day yet again? "Why are you here so late?"

"Well, normally I'm closed on Thursdays," Charlie grumbled. "But today is the Trick-or-Bleat Extravaganza."

"Trick-or . . . bleat?"

Charlie rolled her eyes. "Because of the sheep barn," she said. "Anyway, the courtyard is chockablock full of costumed sugar-high kiddies right now. And I thought ghosts were unsettling. Yeesh. All of the shops are supposed to act as trick-or-treating stations. I, of course, am not used to getting my butt into gear on a Thursday and I'm so far behind schedule I can't even see it anymore."

"Need any help?" Hazel asked.

"I need *all* the help, mon amie, but you've got more important fish to fry," she said. "It's Halloween. You need to get out there and work your magic. Literally and figuratively."

"Charlie, mom is missing," Hazel said.

"Missing?"

"I went to the house last night and she was gone."

Charlie's brows knitted together in worry. "I don't like the sounds of that."

"We need to find her," said Hazel.

"Where do we start looking?"

Hazel had no idea. She shot Charlie a helpless look.

Somebody knocked on the café door, and Hazel's heart skipped a beat. Had Sera come for a midafternoon piece of toast and cup of tea? Instead, she found Tyler waiting at the door, her note in hand. She let him in and relocked the door.

"I'd hoped you'd be here," Tyler said. "I found your message."

"I don't know where to start," she said, so she just dove in, recounting the details of her evening with one minor omission—the part where she had discovered the missing half of her heritage.

"So Baker is the culprit?" Charlie asked.

I warned you all, but nobody paid any attention to the rooster.

"I thought you weren't a rooster."

Now's not the time for a semantic argument.

"So what now?" Tyler asked.

"We need to spread out," Hazel replied.

Tyler slipped off his backpack and produced a set of walkie-talkies. "Seeing you're currently without a phone . . ."

"You're amazing," Hazel said, kissing him on the cheek.

"Guilty," he said.

"Speaking of. Remind me to ask you later about the mess I found in the backyard," she said.

Tyler stiffened and his face went slack.

"Relax," she said. "If you're some sort of closet nudist, we can probably come to an understanding."

Charlie frowned. "Ew, guys."

Tyler welcomed the change of subject. "Let's start here at the barn," he said. "I'll search the empty towers."

"I'll check with the other shop owners," said Charlie.

"Char, don't you need to operate the café?" Hazel asked.

"With Mama Bennett in danger?" Charlie retorted. "I'd rather take the heat from your sister for abandoning my post. Besides, the last thing these little rug rats need is another piece of candy."

"Thank you, Charlie," said Hazel. "And in that case, I'm leaving my bag here." She slipped her satchel off and ran it to the back hall. "Okay, good to go," she said, returning to the café.

"Wait, you two can't go out there without costumes," said Charlie.

"Charlie, is *this* not enough?" Hazel asked, gesturing to her face.

"You don't think going out as your mother might be problematic?"

"I consider myself bait," Hazel retorted.

"Okay, morbid," said Charlie, turning her eyes on Tyler. "And you?"

"I'm going as a werewolf in human form," he said flatly.

"Buncha Halloween Scrooges over here," Charlie grumbled as they stepped outside.

Under different circumstances, Hazel would have welcomed the sight of families and children dressed in costume and trick-or-treating at the shops around the courtyard. But considering the farm was growing more undead than vegetables these days, she couldn't believe that Juniper had decided to go forward with the event.

The trio quickly separated and went off to their individual tasks. Hazel worked her way through the courtyard, responding as kindly as she could to all friendly faces and greetings. Hazel spotted more than a few people that had been at the barn raising the day before. They exchanged peculiar glances as she walked by.

Hazel passed stations where kids fished for apples—a much more hygienic alternative to bobbing. Others were having their faces painted. Groups of children hurried from shop to shop, trick-or-treating at each station. Hazel spied Sarah Carner in front of Herb Your Enthusiasm and smiled and waved. Sarah waved back.

Hold on, said Clancy. *Did you see that?*

"See what?"

I think I just saw a ghost.

"Was it Judith?" Hazel asked. She craned her neck, trying to catch a glimpse of something truly ghostly, but all she spotted was a sea of Captain Marvels, ninjas, princesses, and the like.

No. It looked just like . . . never mind . . . I think I'm seeing things . . .

Hazel found Juniper on the far side of the crowd, dressed as Rosie the Riveter and overseeing a pumpkin-painting.

"What, no pumpkin *carving*?" Hazel asked.

"Too much liability when knives are involved."

"I thought Bennett Farms dealt almost exclusively in liability."

Juniper looked at her wryly. "Who am I talking to?" Juniper asked.

"Your favorite Bennett," Hazel responded.

"Hi, Hazey," Juniper said quietly.

"How can we be doing this right now?" Hazel asked, waving at the festivities around her.

"The farm has to keep running," said Juniper. "You know that. It's still in its first year as a public entity and a proper business. Everything still rests on a knife's edge."

"Juniper, there's so much more going on here! What about public safety? What about *mom*? We need to *stop* another murder."

It was already starting to get dark, and the families with younger children would soon give way to older kids, middle and high schoolers, and then to the adults that had come to spend their Thirsty Thursday at a proper Halloween bash. Hazel knew her mother's odds of survival dropped as each minute ticked away.

Juniper hung her head and pinched the bridge of her nose. There was a weariness in her face that was uncharacteristic of her sister, who was the tireless workhorse type.

"This could ruin the farm," Hazel said. "This could ruin a life."

Juniper was silent for a moment. "Hazel, you know what happens if the farm goes under. There are a thousand and one land developers that would love to snatch this place up and fill it with condominiums and McMansions."

Hazel's radio crackled and Tyler's voice came through. "Are you there, Hazel?"

She gave Juniper one last look as she pulled her radio from her pocket. "Yeah, I'm here."

"Just checked the last tower," he said. "I've got nothing so far."

Juniper gave her a curious look and Hazel shrugged.

"We'll keep looking," she said. "Meet me in the courtyard and we'll come up with a plan." She tucked her radio away.

"Duty calls," Hazel says. "I need to keep looking for mom. It's getting dark."

"Hazel," said Juniper. "She'll be okay."

Hazel looked Juniper in the eye. She wondered how much her sister knew about their fae roots, if she even knew anything at all. That was a conversation for another time, perhaps a family meeting . . . once the family was all accounted for.

"We're running out of time here," Hazel said.

A sound came to her then through the crowd. A steady, low-pitched whine. Hazel scanned the crowd for its source and finally her eyes settled upon it.

Judith.

The ghost shuffled through the crowd, pulling her burden of hospital machines behind her. Festivity-goers gave her a wide berth, parents cast uneasy glances at her and pulled their children a little closer. Hazel started after her, shouting her name, but the spirit either failed to hear her or paid her no mind. Either way, she was headed for the archway and out of the East Barn, and before Hazel could close the distance, she slipped out into the night.

Charlie appeared at that moment. "Charlie, hold this for me," she said, passing Clancy to her.

Hey! If you think it's a joy being your unwilling passenger all day, you're mistaken!

"Tell Tyler to keep looking for mom," Hazel yelled to Charlie, then she took off running toward the archway.

CHAPTER TWENTY-FIVE

The sheep barn was flashing with colored lights and thumping with the bass of some inane Halloween dance track as Hazel crossed Larkhaven Meadow and wove her way through the rows of cars parked there. The barn doors stood wide open, and Hazel could see that, inside, the party was already in full swing.

But it wasn't the hoopla that held her attention. She spotted a gently glowing figure shuffling around the edge of the barn, away from the action. Hazel followed, rounding the corner just in time to see Judith disappear into the barn's basement level.

"Judith?" she called out as she stepped inside. Last time she'd come through this entrance, she had needed to crawl through the splintered ruins of the old sheep barn. Now, she found easy passage. The bottom level was where the sheep would live when they were moved into their new home, but for now the stalls were empty, save for the beds of fresh straw that had been laid down in preparation. No doubt Juniper was holding off until the party was over before showing the new tenants in. A small mercy, considering how loud the bass was thumping overhead.

Hazel found Judith where she had expected: in the corner of the basement, the place where her bones had been hidden beneath the earth. She stood, limped-shouldered, one of her machines droning a steady flatline.

"Judith," Hazel said.

The woman looked up.

"It's me," Hazel continued. "Hazel Bennett."

The woman looked again. "Of course," she said. "You're in disguise."

Hazel touched the edge of her jaw. " 'Tis the season."

Judith smiled. "Have you solved it yet? Have you found my killer?"

"Not yet," she said. "But I know who it is. Would you like to know?"

"It is the only thing I came here to find out," she said.

"His name is Ignatius Baker. He's a Transcendent. It's a—"

"I know what a Transcendent is, young lady."

"Oh," said Hazel, taken aback. "I just thought you would have questions."

"*You* followed me here," said Judith, a quizzical look on her face. "I assumed you were the one with questions."

Only one came to mind. Hazel fished into her bag and pulled out the little plastic baggie. "Just one," she said. "I found this in your medical bag. What is it?"

"Feathers," Judith replied. "From your sister. Human children are often born with a layer of downy hair on them. *Lanugo* it's called. Fae are born dusted with *pluma*, a colorless down. Your mother let me take some—for my records and my studies."

"I suppose I do have another question," said Hazel.

"You've got my attention."

"If we're fae, why don't we have wings?"

"Technically, you're half-fae, but who's counting," Judith began. "And it turns out wings are a recessive trait. Sometimes it expresses, sometimes it doesn't. And when it does, it doesn't seem to happen until later in life. A little post menopause surprise."

"That makes no sense," said Hazel. "Humans reach maturity when—"

"Young lady," said Judith, "I was a midwife. Don't lecture me on human physiology."

"Sorry," said Hazel, blushing.

"It's hard to figure out the rules of half-fae physiology when the sample size is so small," Judith said.

Hazel laughed nervously. "I don't understand."

Judith looked at her, the corner of her mouth turned up in a pleasant half-smile. "You don't know how special you are, do you, dear?" she asked. "Fae and human cannot produce offspring," she said. "It is an established fact. With one exception."

"The Bennetts?"

Judith smiled. "The Goodbloods have kept that Bennett-family secret for generations. To be a part of that secret—it was an honor. And it was the only thing that would make me trek all the way to the Postern."

"You're from *Quark*?"

"Of course, dear," she said. "How do you think I know so much about fae and Transcendents? You don't think a mundane midwife would be up to the task of delivering a baby covered with *pluma*, do you?"

Hazel smiled. "I suppose not." She paused and pondered the weight of everything Judith had just divulged. "You died for that secret," Hazel said. "Your killer was a Transcendent. Somehow he knew the secret too."

Judith nodded gravely. "Transcendents would. They can smell fae blood and fae magic. The enmity between fae and Transcendent runs deep."

"Why?" Hazel demanded.

"Fae magic is rooted in the earth, and Transcendent magic is rooted in the cosmos. I've always thought it's as simple as that. Two worlds forever divided, unable or unwilling to understand the other. Doesn't seem all that different from hate in the human world, does it?"

"But why kill you?" Hazel asked. "It was so senseless!"

"Your killer saw me as complicit in this ultimate crime," she said. "Aiding fae in creating what Transcendents would most likely see as an abomination." She saw the look on Hazel's face. "I do not think you're an abomination, young lady. You are a miracle of life." She hobbled closer now, dragging her machines with her. "Though, between you and me, I never held a baby that wasn't a miracle."

Hazel smiled and fought back the swell of emotion that rose up inside her. This woman and her family tree were entangled with Hazel's own. Hazel had initially thought her abrasive, but she saw now this was just a woman who was willing to fight for what she believed in.

"It won't be necessary to *capture* me," Judith said. "I think I'm ready to go now. All I wanted was justice, and I can see you have the matter well in hand."

"I haven't caught him yet," Hazel said.

Judith smiled. "You will get the right man," she said. "And I'm suddenly feeling very tired. Holding vengeance in your heart for so long—it wears a spirit down."

The flat tone in the machine hiccupped, and then it broke into a steady rhythm of beeps, the monitor tracing the regular peaks and valleys of a heartbeat. "Thank you, Hazel Bennett," Judith said as she faded from view, leaving only the steady rhythm of the monitor lingering for a few moments longer.

Hazel was hardly in the mood for partying when she stepped into the main space of the sheep barn, yet somehow she knew a party scene would likely draw Baker out. It was hard to see somebody who preferred Hawaiian shirts and Bermuda shorts saying no to a place with a cash bar and a buffet. And, as she scanned the crowd, she saw that her instincts had been dead on.

Baker stood at the buffet table, piling jumbo shrimp onto a plate that already balanced a teetering stack of Halloween cookies. He was still dressed in the same absurd tropical regalia but had added a rubber demon mask to top it off.

Hazel pulled her walkie-talkie from her pocket. "Tyler, are you there?"

The walkie-talkie spat back a wad of static and emitted a strange howl before Tyler finally answered. "Yeah, I'm here." He sounded out of breath.

"I've got him," she said. "Baker. He's here at the sheep barn. Get over here right away. I'll try to keep him busy."

"Hazel," Tyler said. A long pause followed. "Don't do . . . anything . . . rash."

"Are you okay, Tyler?"

Static.

"Tyler?"

She waited another minute, but no response came. Hazel ignored the horrible knot twisting in her guts. She would worry about Tyler later. Baker had already moved away from the buffet table, balancing two plastic cups sloshing with beer and his plate of cookies as he made his way across the barn floor.

Hazel hurried to intersect his path. Rash was all she had time for.

"Baker!" she shouted.

Baker stopped and turned, sloshing a bit of beer onto his hand, which he licked clean. He perked up when he saw her. "Hey!" he shouted. "It's my new partner! I see the mask has worked well for you! Good for you."

"A little too well," she said. "I can't take it off."

"Oh," he said nonchalantly. "It's a little sticky."

He shoved his drinks at a passerby. "Don't you dare drink that," he commanded. Then he reached out for Hazel. She pulled away.

"Just trying to help," he said, defensively. "Keep it a few more hours for all I care."

She nodded, and he reached forward again. She took note that as he came close, he turned his face away and wrinkled his nose like he was smelling something abhorrent. Granted, she hadn't taken a proper shower in a few days, but she thought it might have had to do more with what Judith had told her—that Transcendents could *smell* fae.

He pressed his thumbs gently into her temples and pulled on her face. There was a popping sound, like pulling a suction cup off a window, and then a rush of cool air tickled her face.

"I was starting to miss the ol' face case anyway," he said. He pulled off his rubber mask and tossed it to the floor, for a moment revealing a blur where his face should have been.

Hazel quickly stooped to pick it up. She realized she'd been missing for a month and making her return here and now might not be the best idea. Besides, a girl never knew when a wand was lurking. She slipped the rubber devil mask over her head, sighing in relief when it turned out to be just your standard rubber mask that made zero attempts to latch onto her face.

Baker popped the wooden mask into place. The features morphed and twisted until, at last, a face had formed. It was close, but the face was wider, more chiseled, the chin decidedly bigger.

"That's not what you looked like before," Hazel observed.

"Oh yeah," he said. "It's nice like that, you can change faces. I pretty much just do variations on the same one. Makes it easier to get dressed in the morning. Where were we? Oh yeah, I was just getting going. Good luck with all that spirit wrangling."

"I'm finished," Hazel said. "So you're right, you should get going." She pulled the pen from her pocket and slid it into the front pocket of his Hawaiian shirt.

"I'm not going anywhere yet—it's All Hallow's Eve and I've got a good six hours left on my vacation!" he exclaimed. "I'm going to party it up like I'm not going to live forever."

"We need to talk," she said.

"Unless it's about margaritas, I don't want to hear it," he said. "If you don't mind me, I've spied a fetching young lady that I'd like to get back to wooing." Hazel followed his gaze and saw Linda Wilkins waving to them and waggling her eyebrows lustily.

He grinned. "Well, good luck to you. I have to be honest, this place is a lot more interesting than the last time I was here." He turned to leave, but she grabbed his wrist and pulled him back.

"Easy there!" Baker complained. "These beers were not cheap!"

"So you admit you've been here before," she said.

Baker laughed. "Of course I've been here before. We rotate stations all the time. It's supposed to be a way to stave off complacency, keep the job fresh—and us honest. Blarblarblar. Eventually, we rotate back around."

"How often?" she asked.

"I haven't the foggiest. Keeping track of that stuff just sucks the marrow out of existence, if you know what I mean."

"Could it be every thirty-four years?"

"Could be," he said. "Could also be twelve or fifty-two or a hundred and six. What are you getting at?"

She had no more time to be coy, to hide behind masks. Her mother's fate hinged on it. "It was you," she blurted. "You're the murderer."

He stared at her long and hard, searching her face, and then he burst out laughing. "Oh that is rich," he said. "I'm glad you're better at wrangling ghosts than you are at solving crimes. Seriously though, this beer is going to get warm. I have to jet before that goddess gets away."

He again turned to go and again Hazel grabbed his wrist. When he turned back, the goofy grin was gone from his face. His eyes flared red.

"You're wearing on my patience," he snarled.

"And you're wearing on mine," she spat back. "Where's my mother?"

The question seemed to catch him off guard. He looked perplexed, then amused. "Your mother? You humans are always so cryptic."

"You've taken her," she said. "The latest in your sick tableau of killing fae." She refrained from saying *half-fae*, given what Judith had told her. She was certain Baker was aware, but she was wary of being overheard on that point quite yet.

"Oh ho ho. Let's hold on a minute," Baker protested. "I might be a little lazy, and perhaps I've been known to party a little too hard from time to time, but I don't buy into that whole hate-the-fae ideology that goes around the office. To be honest, I'm not even sure what we're talking about, but I do know this beer is getting warmer and my chances are getting colder by the minute, so if you'll excuse me."

He stopped for a minute and fished into his pocket, coming up with a wad of bills. "Listen, have a drink on me," he said. "You look like you could use it." When she didn't take the money, he reached out and stuffed it into her coat pocket.

He retrieved his beers, sauntered across the room toward Linda, and handed her one of the drinks. Was he telling the truth? Was he just here to kick back and relax? It couldn't be. Because that meant she'd had it all wrong this whole time and that she was fresh out of leads.

She pulled out her radio. "Tyler," she spat into the radio. "Are you there, Tyler? It's not *him*. It's not Baker! I . . . I was wrong again . . ."

"Sometimes you just need to know when to quit," said a gravelly voice next to her. Before she could turn to face him, he had grabbed her wrist and clapped something over it. An ornate handful of dark metal that was all too familiar now girded her wrist.

A dampener.

She looked up into the grinning, scarred face of Ryker Flint.

CHAPTER TWENTY–SIX

I f you want to make this easier on yourself, just come along quietly," said Ryker. "But either way, your flight is over. Let's go." He yanked on the lead that trailed from the dampener, pulling her with him.

Instinctively, she raised her hand and tried to clobber him with a magical blast, but her hands didn't even produce so much as a wisp of smoke.

"Nice try," Ryker said, without looking back over his shoulder. He pulled on the lead again until she was walking side-by-side with him.

They passed out of the barn, leaving behind the revelers and the music.

"You don't understand," she said. "My mother has been abducted. I need to save her."

Her pleas fell on deaf ears. Ryker just smiled with grim satisfaction and kept marching her through the Skylark Meadow.

They walked wide of the East Barn, clearly to keep from being seen, and it was obvious to Hazel where they were going. He was heading to the Tanglewood and en route to the Postern. If she was going to get free, now was her chance. She turned to him, driving her knee up hard between his legs.

The action brought them almost face-to-face, but he registered no pain in his features. He merely stared back at her for a moment, his nose wrinkled in disgust, before headbutting her so hard that stars flashed across her vision.

When her sight had returned, she found she was sitting on the ground, Ryker standing over her. "Are you quite done?" he asked. Without waiting for a reply, he yanked Hazel to her feet.

She stumbled on, still trying to regain her senses. Before she knew it, they had passed into the tunnel of trees that marked the east end of the South Way, blotting out the moonlight except in dappled flashes.

"There is only one person guilty of this crime," Hazel said. "And she's sitting in a mundane prison right now, receiving a fair trial. Shouldn't I at least get the same courtesy as a real murderer?"

"Shut up," said Ryker.

Hazel again tried to break away, throwing all of her weight into the leash in hopes of wrenching it from his grasp, but he held it tightly, keeping her firmly in place without moving so much as an inch.

"This isn't the way to the Postern," she said.

"We're not going to the Postern," Ryker replied.

A chill ran down her spine. "Where are you taking me?" she asked.

Ryker pushed her toward the side of the road, away from the Tanglewood and toward the farm again. They passed through the tree line and stepped into a moon-washed field. Up ahead, she saw the swell of Split Tree Hill cutting against the night sky.

"Won't this upset Circe?" Hazel asked. "If you rob her of the chance to get her revenge?"

"I don't care a wit about this Circe Strange you keep speaking about," he spat.

They passed into the trees at the other side of the hill, at the base of Split Tree Hill. He stopped when they reached the skeletal remains of a hedge—a remnant of the maze that had once stood there.

"This seems like an appropriate place," Ryker said.

"For what?"

"For you to die," he said.

"Too bad you don't have your wand," said Hazel, smirking at the thought of his wand sitting inside her satchel.

Ryker seemed undeterred. He raised his hands, palms up, and a brilliant golden light burst from the ground beneath him, illuminating him like the teller of some campfire ghost story. How was that possible? Unless he were fae or . . .

Ryker reached up and placed his fingers on his temples, and in one fluid motion, his features transformed. His beard melted away, his features mollifying until a moment later, Mrs. Prim and Proper herself stood there. Sera.

"You're a Transcendent?" Of course. The fresco beneath Bennett Manor had shown two figures with blurred faces off in the wings—an angel and a demon. Hazel had thought it represented the dual nature of the Transcendent, but it had been more literal than that. Two Transcendents worked each rotation.

"Nothing gets by you," Sera said. "I can't imagine how you failed to solve this case. I even gave you a printed packet of information. I enjoyed the game at first, but I've grown bored."

"You?" Hazel asked, failing to grasp what Sera was saying. "My father sent those packets."

"No he didn't," Sera said, sighing in exasperation.

"You know my father?" Hazel asked.

"I know *of* him," Sera responded. "I can't say I'm well acquainted with him. He's mostly been a thorn in my side as he is the only person to con on to what I've been doing. Anyway, I knew enough to send you a convincing letter."

"You sent the folder?" Hazel asked again.

Sera rolled her eyes clearly annoyed at Hazel. "And broke you out of jail."

"Why would Wilhelm and Lev help you?" Hazel asked.

"I told Wilhelm that if he didn't do as I asked, I'd find him here on the farm and obliterate him and effectively kill him twice. He would cease to exist here, and never arrive in the future. Though I fully intend on doing so anyway."

"Why are you doing this?" Hazel asked.

"You're an abomination," she said. "Your entire family is a blight on existence. An affront to the laws of nature. Fae and Transcendents are supposed to be the only true magical entities in the world. All other magic is just borrowed power. So it had to be. Your mere existence flaunts the natural order of things. A witch who wields fae magic. It had to be you. Every thirty-four years I rotate back to this station and I do my part to make the universe a better place."

"A better place! You make it better by killing people? Where is my mother?" Hazel demanded.

Sera sniggered. "Your *mother*? What would I care?

"You have her!"

"I tire of this talk," Sera said. "Let us be done. My time in this place is almost over. If we hurry this up, maybe I can squeeze in another Bennett before the night is over."

Sera raised her hand and unleashed a burst of power that slammed into Hazel and knocked her to the ground. Something jabbed her in the side—a pointed object in her pocket. Hazel slipped her free hand into the coat. The pen! Baker's pen, chain and all. He must have slipped it back into her pocket when they were talking in the barn. But why? It didn't matter. It was here. She just needed a moment where Sera let her guard down. It had to be soon, she was already feeling woozy; she didn't think she could take another hit like that and maintain consciousness.

Hazel heard a distant howl, and in a moment of punch-drunk lunacy, she joined in. Why not? One last call to the wild before her life was snuffed out. She put her head back and howled.

"What are you doing?" Sera asked, perturbed. "You humans make no sense."

The howl repeated but much closer this time, followed by the sound of branches snapping and dried leaves crunching underfoot as something sprinted through the forest.

Sera stopped and listened.

"What is—"

Her words were cut short as something massive burst from the darkness and slammed into Sera, knocking her to the ground in a mass of fur and snarls. Hazel didn't stop to consider it. This was the opportunity she had been waiting for. She didn't bother trying to remove the dampener. She'd spent enough time in one to know that, without a key, her efforts would be futile. She'd have to do this one without spells.

Running seemed like the best option at the moment. She started to bolt back toward the open field. If she could get back to the East Barn, maybe she would be safe. And also lead a killer and feral beast to a crowd of innocent people?

She stopped in her tracks. She couldn't run. She needed to stay and ensure that justice was done. *Real* justice. Not justice at the hands of some furred savior. She forced herself to turn back around.

The creature was standing above Sera now, its back to Hazel, its body illuminated in the golden light that still seeped from the forest floor. It was massive, taller and more muscled than any man, and covered in a thick shag of fur. It sensed that Hazel was watching it and it turned its head to the side, revealing a canine muzzle.

"What are you?" Hazel asked, trying to sound braver than she felt.

The beast replied with a guttural growl and took a step toward her.

"Easy now," she cooed, stepping back slowly. She slipped her hand into her pocket and closed it around the pen. She had no idea what effect, if any, it might have. The creature advanced, quicker now, and soon it was looming over her, chest heaving and tongue lolling.

Hazel pulled the pen from her pocket and whipped it over her head. The chain ignited in a flash of flames, and the creature cringed as the flames lit up its grim muzzle. Ranks of slashes crossed one side of its face, stopping just short of its eye and the corner of its muzzle.

"No, it can't be," she gasped. "Tyler?"

But it explained so much about the last few days. His disappearances at night—during a full moon no less. The tale that Charlie had told her about his attempt to cross through the Postern and brave the Dimwood to find Hazel. He had disappeared for several days, and when he'd returned, he'd been battered and bruised. By what, it was now clear.

Hazel let the pen drop to her side, and the flame extinguished. The beast snarled and raised its hand, claws bared and ready to strike. Hazel winced and turned her head. The blow never came. When she opened her eyes, the beast was shuddering.

"We'll figure this out," she said. "Together."

The beast threw back its head and howled, a long, mournful lament that sent shivers down her spine. When it had finished, it dropped to all fours and loped away.

"Tyler!" she shouted, but the beast kept going until it had disappeared into the darkness. She listened to the snapping of branches receding until there was, again, silence.

She turned her attention back to Sera, who was just now getting back to her feet.

Hazel was done with this. She was going to put an end to it one way or another. She whipped the chain back to life and approached Sera.

"I see Baker is freely handing out his toys," Sera said. "I'll have to report that indiscretion to management." She stepped forward, holding out her hand. "But that doesn't belong to you so hand it over."

Hazel held the pen aloft, ready to whip the chain back to life if needed. Without warning, the pen shook and tore itself from her hand, rising into the air as if guided by an invisible hand. A blue ribbon poured from the tip of the pen, a ghostly jet of ink that whipped and cavorted through the forest, encircling Sera. Hazel could just make out the myriad of faces in the swirling ring.

Sera looked amused by the display. "This is cute," she said. "What is this, some sort of revenge?"

"Consider it justice," said a ghostly voice from within the ring.

"Or just a good time," said another, which Hazel recognized as one of the twins.

"Round and round we go," added the other.

The ring of spirits collapsed, tightening around Sera like a tourniquet. "What are you doing?" she shrieked. She pawed at the spirits in a futile effort to pull them off, tearing at both her clothes and her face. In the tumult, her mask popped off and fell to the forest floor, revealing a smudge where her face should have been.

A deafening crack split the air and knocked Hazel to the ground. When she looked up, Sera and the spirits had disappeared and the golden light had faded, leaving Hazel in darkness.

In the distance, an anguished howl drifted through the night.

"Tyler," she whispered.

The headlights of a car came bobbing across the nearby field and stopped just short of the tree line. Car doors slammed. "Hazel!" somebody shouted. Was that Juniper? A moment later, Juniper and David were at her side, helping her to her feet. "What happened?" Juniper asked. "Where are they?"

"How did you find me?" Hazel asked.

"We had a little help," said Juniper.

Hazel looked up to see more people coming into the forest—Charlie with Clancy tucked under her arm. "I looked into a fishing-for-apples bucket and I saw you," said Charlie. "I told you it always works when I need it most. What happened?!"

"It's over," Hazel said. "It was Sera. She was a Transcendent."

"Mrs. Prim and Proper?"

Hazel nodded. "She was Ryker too," said Hazel. "I'm not sure if she had been him the whole time . . . or she just assumed his identity."

"I think I can answer that," said somebody behind Charlie. Alex approached, and just behind him, a thin shimmering shape that Hazel recognized as another spirit. At first, she thought it might be Theo, but when the apparition drew near, she saw it was an older gentleman with a sharp goatee and a gnarled mustache. There was wisdom and serenity in his face. He made Hazel think of a mountaintop hermit, a sage whose advice was sought by all in the land. Hazel had the distinct impression she had seen him *somewhere* before.

Clancy anticipated her thoughts. *It's Silas*, he said. *Silas MacGregor.*

Of course. The man that had tried to help Cordelia Strange break her curse, only to be repaid with an untimely death.

"What . . . what are you doing here?" Hazel asked.

"Say, who is this gorgeous young creature!" Silas crooned.

Easy, Silas.

"I'm Hazel Bennett," she said.

Silas bowed deeply, throwing aside his stoic demeanor and trying to take and kiss her hand like some lovestruck bachelor from the days of yore.

"And I'm starting to see how you got suckered by Cordelia Strange."

"What?" said Silas. "What's wrong with a man who knows how to treat a lady?"

Silas, this is the woman I was telling you about. The one that solved your murder.

"Beauty *and* brains!" cooed Silas.

"Though I'm not one to talk," said Hazel. "Cordelia duped me too."

Silas became serious for a moment. "So Clancy has told me. I'm sorry you got yourself into a bit of legal trouble on my account. I intend to clear it up. I figure I'll make a fairly good firsthand witness to my own demise."

"Finally, a ghost worth befriending," quipped Charlie.

CHAPTER TWENTY–SEVEN

Hazel stood before the Postern in quiet contemplation, holding her breath, waiting for Alex to speak.

Alex sat on the ragged strip of stone wall nearby, his hands folded in front of him like he was giving a sermon. "All charges have been dropped."

"All of them?" Hazel asked, not quite believing what she was hearing.

"Everything," he said, nodding. "Silas testified before the Council and they ruled that your behavior, given the context of being falsely arrested and charged with murder, was forgivable."

"And Circe?" asked Hazel.

The corners of his mouth twitching. It was the closest she'd ever seen him come to smiling. "In true Circe fashion, she promptly flew into a fit of rage."

"Please tell me there will be consequences for her."

Alex's almost-smile vanished. "The Council has already issued a formal statement essentially exonerating itself . . . and Circe. Not everyone signed it, but enough to make it a majority. It will get swept under the rug."

Silence hung in the air for a moment as Hazel considered the implication of this.

"They found Ryker finally," Alex said. "He was tucked into a tree hollow. It looks like we can add one more murder to Sera's tally."

"When did she do it?"

Alex shook his head. "We don't know. Sometime after he came to the farm to track you." He shook his head. "He was Circe's lapdog, but he didn't deserve that."

"No, he didn't," Hazel agreed.

"But that's that," said Alex. "It's over."

He stood up and brushed the seat of his pants.

"Thank you," Hazel said.

"For what?"

"For believing in me. You had the chance to bring me in but you didn't."

He shifted uncomfortably. "It didn't feel right. There was something fishy about the whole thing."

Where is Silas now? Clancy asked, finally breaking into the conversation.

Alex chuckled. "He's reclaimed the deed on his property. He plans to reopen Once Upawn a Time as soon as he gets everything in order."

Only Silas would spend his eternity hocking useless trinkets, said Clancy, fondness in his voice. *We'll have to pay him a visit sometime soon.*

"Quark will always welcome you," Alex said. "Though you should step warily. Circe does not forget, and she certainly does not forgive."

"Noted," said Hazel. "I'll be sure not to expect a Christmas card this year."

Alex flashed another almost-smile. "Duty calls," he said. He nodded to Hazel, his gaze lingering for a moment, and stepped back through the Postern. A cartoonish pop filled the air and he disappeared.

Free at last, Clancy said.

Hazel sighed. She wished she could savor the moment, but she'd come home to a farm and a life that had irrevocably changed.

Hazel started back through the Tanglewood. Harper and Link would be finishing their morning chores soon and she had magic lessons with Harper before lunch. The kids had taken a few days off from their regular homeschooling duties. Their teacher was still missing and it felt wrong to continue the Amy Bennett School of Above Average (But Secretly Fae) Children without Amy Bennett. Besides, everyone's free time had been spent coordinating with Detective Gibbens for another search effort.

Tyler was gone too. She had seen no sign of him since he had saved her from becoming Sera's next victim. Hazel had gone to his cottage that night and found it a mess. The suitcase she'd left under the bed was gone, his drawers asunder as if he'd packed in a hurry, and the manuscript on his desk—she'd finally found that in the firepit in his backyard. He'd left a note on the counter: *I almost hurt you. I can't take the risk.*

For now, Hazel laid low. As far as the world knew, she was still missing. Perhaps she would keep it that way. Maybe fewer people would come knocking on the farm's proverbial door if they thought she wasn't home. She'd busied herself on the farm as best she could, thrown herself into her magic so she could become a successor of whom Gammy would be proud and a better teacher for her niece. She spent time helping Wilhelm adjust to his new reality and setting up a comfortable apartment in the Bennett Manor cellar—the only place that didn't remind him of Hippolyta.

And for now, Hazel kept the secret of the Bennett lineage to herself. There would be a time to call a family meeting and share it, but this wasn't then.

She could feel the weight of it pressing down on her, but for the first time in her life, she thought she could withstand it. What choice did she have? There were so many people depending on her. Being weak, fickle, uncertain—these were insecurities she could no longer hide behind.

Hazel hadn't walked very far through the Tanglewood when something caught her attention. She'd missed it on the walk in, with the sun filtering through the trees and shining in her eyes, but now, with the sun at her back, she noticed it. A faint pink glow through the trees.

Haven't we had enough adventure for a while? Clancy asked.

"Shush."

Hazel crept forward slowly and as she came around the corner of a cluster of boulders, she gasped. A giant pod hung from the branches of a gnarled ancient wolf tree. It looked vaguely like a butterfly chrysalis. For a moment, Hazel panicked. Her mind returned to the giant time-bending moth that had run amok on the farm in August.

"What in the . . ."

Is it too late to keep moving? Clancy asked. *I don't like where this is headed one bit.*

Hazel ignored him, cautiously approaching the tree and gingerly reaching out with her free hand.

The chrysalis shifted suddenly and Hazel yelped, leaping back. Clancy squawked. Whatever was inside was attempting to get out. The shell stretched and distended, as its contents wriggled and bent inside.

Let's go. I've seen how this horror movie ends.

Hazel had no intention of leaving. She could see now as the thin diaphanous membrane of the pod stretched and rippled that the *something* inside was actually *someone*.

"There's a *person* in there, Clancy," she gasped.

With a gentle ripping sound, like old Velcro separating, the entire pod split from top to bottom, dumping its contents onto the ground.

Hazel could hardly believe it as the shape moved, stretched, and rose to its knees. To *her* knees. Amy Bennett, knelt before them dressed only in tattered rags. Hazel ran toward her only to stop short as she noticed the pair of massive and magnificent monarch butterfly wings that unfurled from her mother's back. They flexed slowly and gently as they began to dry in the open air, flashing orange and black and white.

Hazel stood transfixed, struck mute by the sight.

We're going to have a hard time getting her through the manor door . . .

Her mother, at last, opened her eyes and looked up. Seeing Hazel, she grinned. "You're home!" she exclaimed.

Hazel just stammered a string of unintelligible phrases.

"I think it's time you and I finally had that talk. I have something to tell you about your father," her mother said, taking Hazel gently by the shoulders. "And your grandfather . . ."

ACKNOWLEDGMENTS

There are fewer thanks to go around for this book because it turns out life in quarantine with kids in the house makes it difficult for people to beta read. And to do just about everything else. Who knew? That also means that the thank-yous are bigger this time around because fewer people had to shoulder the load.

First off, ever and always, thank you to my wife for putting my outlines through the wringer, for listening to me despair (repeatedly) when things weren't going well, and for serving as my first line of editorial defense.

Thank you to my tireless mother for being my closer and catching my many senseless errors—all with a blistering turnaround time. If any mistakes remain, it's because I can never stop fiddling after the fact. It's a curse.

Another thank-you goes out to Ileana Munoz-Renfroe, for giving me some invaluable feedback on early chapters, for running an amazing Facebook group for cozy authors and readers (seriously, go check out the Cozy Mystery Village on Facebook), and for trusting me with her first book. I can't for the world to read it!

Last but not least, thank you to my readers, who give me a reason to keep revisiting Bennett Farms and spinning new mysteries for Hazel and crew.

CONNECT WITH E.L.

Subscribe to the E.L. Wilder newsletter at www.elwilder.com in order to receive updates, get bonus content, and read free episodes of the **Homespun Psychic Cozy Mystery** series.

Find E.L. on Facebook at www.facebook.com/elwilderauthor.

ABOUT THE AUTHOR

E.L. Wilder here! I'm a Vermont author and the misguided creator of the Farm to Fable Paranormal Cozy Mysteries and the Homespun Psychic Cozy Mysteries. Vermont is a contradiction of nature and culture, tradition and progress, practicality and whim, maple syrup and Ben and Jerry's. And I am nothing if not a product of my environment. Especially the Ben & Jerry's. Fortunately, when I'm not writing or editing, I stay fit by tending to a flock of children and chickens. To be clear, those are two separate flocks (and I try not to confuse them, despite their striking similarities).

MORE FROM E.L. WILDER

Farm to Fable Paranormal Cozy Mysteries
Down on the Charm (Book 1)
A Familiar Sense of Dead (Book 2)
Scrying Over Spelled Milk (Book 3)
Reap with One Eye Open (Book 4)
Killed and Raised in a Barn (Book 5)
Hexed of Kin (Book 6)—Coming 2021
A Carol of Spells (Book 7)—Coming 2021

Witches of the Misty Keys Cozy Mysteries
Christmas Spells Are Ringing (Book 1)
Love at Cursed Sight (Book 2)—Coming 2021

Homespun Psychic Cozy Mysteries
(this series is exclusive for subscribers to E.L. Wilder's newsletter)
Poisoned Alpacas and Psychic Stitches (Novella 1)
Shanked Sheep & Haunted Spinning Wheels (Novella 2)